Tallahatchie Lies

a work of fiction

Cyan Brodie

for Karen always

Text Copyright © Cyan Brodie

Cyan Brodie has asserted his right to be identified as the author of this work in accordance with the Copyright, Designs and Patents Act, 1988.

All rights reserved. No part of this publication may be reproduced, stored in a retrieval system or transmitted in any form, or by any means, electronic, mechanical, photocopying or otherwise without the written permission of the author.

First published in December 2018

ISBN-13: 978-1727589313

ISBN-10: 1727589319

'Tallahatchie Lies' began life as a short story of just over 5,000 words called 'Ode to Gospel Fry'. Inspired by Bobbie Gentry's 1967 song 'Ode to Billie Joe' it soon became clear there was more to tell.

This novel is a work of fiction, and although many locations and institutions do exist, the descriptions and events portrayed in this story are for the most part fictionalised. The same goes for the characters, including those historical figures who are featured.

Tallahatchie Lies

Contents

ODE TO ANGEL DRAGO — *Where it began*

ODE TO BERTHA SWAN HARDY — *When it began*

ODE TO MINT DRAGO — *How it began*

ODE TO GOSPEL FRY — *Where it changed*

ODE TO DONNA MAE COBHAM — *When it changed*

ODE TO BO DEAN MACARTHY — *How it changed*

ODE TO TRUMAN HARDY — *Where it ended*

ODE TO PARKER LEE HARDY — *When it ended*

ODE TO KATIE JO COBHAM — *How it ended*

ODE TO ANGEL DRAGO

- 1 -

1923 - 1932

Where it began.

I reckon this story could have begun in any one of those nameless places my folks passed through along the highway between South Bend and Davenport as they headed west beneath the stubbed toe of Lake Michigan. Pa was a travelling showman and Momma was his Cherokee bride - though her exotic appearance owed more to greasepaint and 'Aureole' hair dye than any Red Indian ancestry.

I was born plain Lucille Trenton - Tuesday, June 5th, 1923 - as pale as if I'd been dipped in buttermilk.

Pa could swallow fire and juggle live doves. Momma was

the lady he sawed in two. And occasionally he'd put her inside a coffin and drive sharpened staves through the lid to the delighted screams of the paying audience. I can't imagine what tortures he had planned for me once I became old enough to stand on my own two feet. An albino child would surely bring in the crowds. But once we reached the outskirts of Chicago, it seems he found a replacement for Momma - a new victim to slice in half and skewer.

We woke one Sunday morning to find him gone. He'd taken the covered wagon and both horses, along with Momma's finest sequined dresses. All he'd left behind was an empty bed in a cheap hotel room and an outstanding account for $13.

This much I know to be true.

When you grow up tethered to a mother who changes the men in her life more often than her bed sheets, it becomes a case of relying less on specific memories and more on feelings - the good and the bad. In my experience, there were days when it was impossible to tell either apart.

I remember spending time with my cardboard dollies and their cut-out dresses - only to find them hours later screwed up on the kitchen floor. Or struggling to please Momma as she tried to teach me my letters and numbers - only to have her scold me for being such a muttonhead. The fact is, my interests didn't take me there. I spent most of my formative years exploring the confines of the communal staircase with Milton who lived across the hall. He was a year younger than me - freckle-faced and with a mass of red ringlets that his momma never once thought to cut. I saved her the trouble.

I showed Momma the handful of curls I'd stolen and asked her if I could have hair like Milton and chocolate specks on my face to match. She told me my tiny white eyelashes and flawless skin were already perfect. She wanted me no different than I was. As for my hair, she never once ceased to marvel at the way it shone, as fine as spun starlight.

"Don't ever cut off your beautiful hair, Miss Lucille Trenton. Promise me that."

"I promise, Momma."

A promise made to be broken.

Life was seldom easy. Momma stayed out late at night and often came home with fresh bruises, grazed knuckles and the liquor reek of cuss words on her lips. Then there was the time, she turned up with a grey-haired man who wore fancy leather gloves and carried a black walking stick.

"He's gonna be staying with us a while," she whispered. "And if you're a good girl for Momma, he might be your new papa."

But the night he took one drink too many and sat me on his knee a little too eagerly, she turned her bread knife on him and made damn sure he didn't show his face here again.

"Go to Hell, you bastard whore," his parting shot.

"As long as you lead the way and pay at the gate."

Once we heard the street door slam shut, Momma wiped away her tears and picked out one of her magazines to flick through. There were ladies in fancy crinolines, and white veils like the kind I got to wear when the sun was too bright for my eyes.

"Pretty dresses?"

She let me colour in the pictures.

Less than a week later the grey-haired man returned with papers instructing us to quit the apartment, and we ended up inside a rooming house on Hohman Avenue in Hammond. Too far from the lake to smell the fresh tide, but close enough to taste the sulfur tainting the air and watch the gas flares weave their dance above each smokestack.

There must have been a time in my imaginary past when I was pure and unsullied; soothed by the smells of caramel candy and fresh shampoo. But now, whenever I smell scented soap, the only thing I can recall is Momma's anguish after I was stolen for a short while.

What do I remember about those hours in the woods?

The gaslights in our apartment had been flickering for days, and Momma had spoken to Mr Hickson about it. So when I heard him whistling on the staircase then tapping on our door, I let him in. Momma warned me not to open the door whenever she was out, but this was different. This was our janitor who fixed the faucet when it dripped and took out the trash from the stairwell every Tuesday morning.

He asked me to go with him down into the street. "I need me a number eight wrench, and I need a little girl with bright blue eyes to help me find one."

We headed off towards Broken Corner. Then when we reached one of the alleyways he pulled me into the shadows and said Momma had told him how I'd been a bad girl. She'd said I needed to be taught a lesson. It was already late and the streets were empty. I began to holler, but he picked me up like a sack of flour and headed for Harrison Park.

Once we crossed the footbridge, he stood me against a tree with his left hand against my throat then the other hand found its way inside my clothing; fingers running back and forth along the crest of my hip bone as he tested the skin. He pulled my vest over my head and my gaze became fixed upon his lips - lips stained with tobacco juice, as if he'd been sucking at berries.

He peeled off the rest of my underwear. Left it lying there on the fallen leaves. I was ashamed of how threadbare it looked. Pink roses faded through too much laundering. A bouquet of winter flowers left to die in the frost.

When he knelt alongside me, he began to whisper names I heard Mint use years later. Bathsheba. Delilah. Jezebel. Blasphemies spilling out of his mouth like twisted prayers before he staggered to his feet and waded into the undergrowth. Gasping for air.

When they brought me home, I swear Momma would have allowed me back inside her womb if she possibly could. Clamped me to a new umbilical cord and nourished me and sheltered me until I was ready to be born again.

She lathered my anaemic corpse and held me to her breast until her shift was soaked through, her sobs skewering my heart with their intensity.

"I'm sorry I was a bad girl, Momma."

Yet she forgave me. I'd survived when she thought me

already lost, so I couldn't make sense of her tears. Couldn't make out what it was that pained her so much. Maybe that's the reason I stopped growing for a time. Almost five years as I recall. I was still an innocent child. Still seven years old, but except for my fingernails and hair I was as good as dead.

Two years after I got taken they broadcast a news story on the radio about a baby boy who was stolen from some rich people in New Jersey. Momma showed me his pictures in the newspaper. He had a mass of curls like Milton and looked ever so cute with his chubby cheeks and his one-piece play suit. That baby got murdered without a second thought, and shortly afterwards Momma quit working nights in the creep joint down in the Loop. She told me she'd rather work the streets near home so she could keep one eye on the apartment.

- 2 -

1938

Times were hard and winters in Chicago took their toll. The January blizzard of 1938 finally caught up with us - hurricane wind and heavy snowfall keeping everyone indoors until Momma got past caring what she had to do to earn a buck or two. She brought men in off the street. Two bucks for a warm bed and a warm body. There were bums who smelled dirty and whose worn-down shoes left grey-brown crusts of dirty ice on the carpet. There were also well-dressed men who brought in the scent of hair oil and cigars. But no matter who they were, the stinging smell of winter always followed on their heels each time the street door swung open.

My tiny cot was stuck in the corner behind a blue velvet curtain that had once served as a bed-spread. A dressing table stood at its foot with hinged mirrors. As soon as we finished tea and the radio was turned down, Momma would tell me it was time for bed. She could watch me in the mirror if she had a mind to, but my orders were to stay quiet as a mouse under my sheets until she was done.

None of our callers ever seemed to give a damn that I was in the same room. I'd hear one or two whisper an occasional endearment, but then I'd catch a glimpse of their reflections and I'd hear strained voices as they swore and called Momma a heap of bad names. That's why she said never to trust what comes out of a man's mouth. A promise or a curse, it made no difference.

By the time the winter sun tried to make amends, icicles cold enough to bite guarded the window lintel next to my cot. I'd usually end up crawling into Momma's bed each morning to get warm. There was something elemental about the smell left over from the night. It made my skin grow clammy inside my nightshirt, and sometimes I'd find the taint of ammonia deeper inside the cave of her bed - the same scent the janitor had left on my fingers. His scuffed prints in the wet grass the only sign he was man rather than beast.

Momma would lie half-asleep next to me and allow me to play at being mother for a while. I'd soothe her with meaningless whispers and stroke her stiff hair and kiss the tears on her wind-burned face until there were none left. But as the day wore on, my left arm would become numb from where I'd slipped it underneath her waist. And I'd often have to ask Momma when she planned on fixing us some breakfast.

One day she rolled over onto her side and squeezed me so tight I got scared she meant to hurt me. "I don't know how we're gonna manage this month," she moaned. "By the time I pay my bills there won't be enough left to get us properly fed, honey."

I pulled free and sat up beside her. "It's okay, Momma.

Now the snow's stopped I can work too."

She laughed. "Honey. You're barely fourteen years old and as delicate as a china doll. You're my precious little snowdrop. I ain't sending you out on the streets. I'd rather die first."

"I don't mean go out on the streets. You can bring in more gentlemen and I can work right here next to you."

Sometimes we spin lies to patch up our damaged lives. But there comes a time when these lies replace reality because the truth is too painful to bear. Truth or lie, what followed could have happened any number of ways.

In the first version of events, Momma wipes fresh tears from her face and pulls me closer to her breast.

"You know, Lucille? I swear I can remember the exact moment you were conceived, honey. And your pa was so proud when you were born. If he found out I'd let things come to this, he'd hunt us both down and he'd kill me for sure."

In the second I reassure her, wise beyond my years. "I won't let on."

I'd watched them couple night after night. Heard their breath catch as one, and seen the glow spread across Momma's face. That's the only time I ever saw her happy. All I wanted was for Momma to be happy again.

That's when she holds me in her arms and tells me she will never let such a thing happen. I am too fragile and innocent - her precious child. "I don't want you ending up like me, honey. Promise me you won't."

Another promise made to be broken.

And in the third version she ends up cursing me, slapping my head hard enough to make the room spin before I feel myself falling.

But the reality is, next morning Momma went out for a loaf of bread and she never came back.

- 3 -

1938

It was hunger that finally made me follow her into the cruel cold. I'd been frightened to go even as far as the grocery store in case Momma came home while I was out and thought I'd been taken once more. But in the end, I found the courage to cross the street and walk in on Charlie.

"Hey, honey bee. What you doing out here without your scarf and gloves? You're gonna freeze your butt off."

My teeth were almost chattering too much to speak. "You seen my momma?"

"Not this afternoon, honey. Why, you expecting to meet up with her in here?"

I shook my head.

"She ain't been near for a week or more. The weather's keeping everyone indoors. It's like they brought back Prohibition." He swept his arm as if to emphasise the space surrounding the bar. The room was empty except for two workmen stood at the far end draining their glasses and a middle-aged man with a grey newsboy cap, lounging in a window seat and reading a folded up newspaper.

He glanced in my direction as my gaze pulled everything I could see closer and closer like it was hauling in a fishing line. The meagre stump of a chicken leg sat on his plate.

"Something you want, kid?"

I shook my head clear of the temptation.

"Leave her be, Mint. If Mona finds out you been associatin' with her daughter, she's likely to claw your eyes out."

Mint raised his hands in surrender and returned to his newspaper, but I couldn't help myself. I dashed close enough to snatch the chewed-down bone and ran for the door.

Charlie was quicker. "Whoa, there. Just you hold on." He grabbed me by the arm and steered me back towards the table.

Mint laid down his newspaper. "For Christ's sake, kid. When's the last time you ate?"

By then I'd torn off a strip of cold chicken skin, but it turned to glue in my mouth. I couldn't speak. And as soon as they sat me down, I gagged and spat it back onto his plate. Then I placed the bone beside it and wiped my snivelling nose with my sleeve. I wanted my momma.

"Hey, now. There's no need for that. Charlie's gonna dish you up something hot. Right?" Mint tilted his head in Charlie's direction. "And you, Missy. You sit right there and don't move a muscle."

I lowered my head and played dumb until Charlie brought

back a plate piled high with fried chicken and French fried potatoes.

"Now you dig in." Mint sat and watched me eat. He didn't say another word 'til I was nearly done. "You needing some soda to help that go down?"

He settled the bill at the bar then came back and stood beside me. "Maybe I should take this princess home and see if her ma's turned up. Unless you know of any other family she might have in the neighbourhood."

Charlie shook his head. "No. There's just Mona and the kid."

Mint pulled down the peak of his cap. "In that case, unless she shows up, it looks like I've found myself a whole new heap of trouble."

I'd left the door unlatched. Momma had never gotten round to letting me have a key of my own. Inside the apartment, it was somehow even chillier than when I'd left. The debris of our miserable life was laid out for all to see; the sour smell of abandonment like a reprimand. The rooms were still as empty as when I'd gone off in search of her.

I'd started shaking even before we reached the top of our staircase. And it wasn't just from the cold. I didn't want this stranger inside our home. Didn't want him anywhere near us. Looking at Momma's silk underwear draped everywhere. Dirty bedding - stained and ripe with body odour. Dishes in the kitchen, caked with the clotted residue of our last proper meal together.

He cursed as a roach scuttled across the linoleum, then

stamped at another two as they emerged from under the skirting board.

"You got no heating on in all this cold?"

I shook my head, mute with shame.

He turned on the kitchen tap. Our pipes had dried up the morning after Momma left. I'd forgotten to keep the cold tap running through the night. "If your pipes are frozen, you're gonna have more trouble on your hands once they thaw out."

I looked up in bewilderment.

"Let's see what else we got."

Part of me was already dreading what he might do once it became clear Momma wasn't coming back. It was all my fault, except he never once said that.

"How long's your ma been gone, you say?"

"She went for bread."

"And you been here all by yourself."

I shook my head and smiled.

"So who do you stay with when she's not home?"

I led him into the bedroom. My cardboard dollies were lined up on the dressing table. But he paid no heed as he wrinkled his nose and headed for the window.

"Christ, I know it's cold enough to freeze the tits off the Statue of Liberty out there, honey. But you need to freshen up this room." He tried to open the window but it was stuck fast. "Goddamn it. Look at the state of this bedding. How can your ma turn a blind eye to all this?"

He began to haul the sheets from Momma's mattress. Beneath the dusting of cheap talcum powder, they were stained brown, as if she'd left them on her bed to mark the outline of every man who had ever lain down with her. "She keep any clean linen?"

I shook my head. They were her winter sheets. Summer sheets were in one of the dressing table drawers.

The mattress underneath was just as dirty, smeared black and sagging at the centre. "Look there. You got bed bugs." He lifted the mattress and stood it on end. The floor beneath the frame was grey with drifts of dust and cobwebs. "D'you sleep in the same bed as your momma? 'Cause if you do, you're gonna need someone to give you a good washing down."

"I'm not a damn kid." I pulled back the curtain and showed him my cot. It was barely large enough for a body to lie along, let alone sleep in. He tugged the top sheet away, dislodging my pillow, and something heavy tumbled into the tight gap between both beds.

Mint reached down and picked it up. "This your ma's?"

I nodded, burning with guilt as he thumbed through the contents.

"There's four dollar bills in here and a heap of loose change. How's your ma intending buying bread without her pocketbook?"

Fresh tears trickled down my cheeks, and I tried to wipe away my snivelling nose. "I took it without her knowing."

- 4 -

1938

The night I stole Momma's pocketbook, I remember being woken by the sound of the latch on the bedroom door. I snuggled back down under my blanket, but I could hear someone rummaging in the drawers of her bedside cabinet. I folded down the edge of the sheet so I could watch his mottled reflection in the mirror.

This was no hobo, but he had the famished look I'd learned to recognise only too well. He held up the necklace Momma sometimes wore when she went out to the bar to meet a special friend. I didn't like the way he dismissed it with a smirk before slipping it inside his trouser pocket.

"You're still dressed? Jesus, we ain't got all night." Momma had appeared in the doorway in her silk gown. Then she crossed over to the bedside light, and I could make out that all she wore underneath were her stockings.

"I'm payin' so what's the rush?" he said. "You ain't exactly got them queueing up out in the street."

"Just sayin'. It's fucking freezing in that corridor."

I sensed he was still sizing up the room, even though his attention had suddenly switched to what Momma had on offer. "I thought you'd gone to get me a fresh towel?" His voice had a foreign edge to it. But so many of Momma's callers were immigrants passing through on their way to California. That's the excuse they always gave when she asked if they'd like to call again sometime.

"I can go get you as many towels as you want once we're done, honey. I'd call for room service, but this ain't exactly the Ritz. And I need payin' up front, in case you've forgotten."

The look of hunger never once left his eyes as Momma reached for her bag and took out her pocketbook. Then I watched him hand over a couple of dollar bills before getting ready to climb on top of her.

"Let me help you with that, loverboy," she said.

Momma always kept her bag right underneath the frame of the bed next to my cot. I could picture him reaching for it once they were finished and stealing all her money when her back was turned. He might even hurt Momma, if she caught him in the act.

She'd told me often enough what to do. "Scream! If any man ever tries to hurt you, sugar, you scream and scream until someone comes runnin'." Except this was Momma's bedroom. We were meant to be safe here. And besides, there had been occasions when Momma cried out, yet no one had ever come running.

I could hear the springs in her bed creaking in rhythm with their breathing. "That's my boy. Keep it up." Momma groaning in between his gasps.

29

I crawled under the sheet until my head was at the foot of my cot then reached out a hand into the darkness. Hair pins. Crumpled tissues. Some loose matches, an empty cigarette pack and a compact with a broken lid. And a padded pocketbook. I snatched it free and slithered back to the top of the bed before hiding my treasure under the pillow.

I almost laughed as I heard him searching later then snapping the catch of her bag closed and dropping it back onto the floor just before the bedroom door opened again.

"There you go, honey. A clean towel and no extra charge." Momma fussed over him as he cleaned himself up and got dressed. She helped him put on his shirt and fasten his flashy red silk necktie. Then she gave him a long drawn-out kiss, and I heard him promise to meet up with her later for drinks before she muttered something about the bake shop and I heard the outside door slam closed. I was too tired to pay her any attention.

It was only when I woke up properly that I felt the bulge beneath my pillow and pictured her choosing a fresh, plump loaf, sprinkled with flour and poppy seeds, still steaming from the oven. Reaching into her bag and a queue of customers pushing past her as she searched and searched before letting out a gasp of anguish.

She couldn't return home empty-handed, without a buck to her name, let alone a nickel to buy a crust. He hadn't even left her a couple of cents.

Oh. She'd figure out what happened. She'd curse her stupidity for leaving him alone in her bedroom while she fetched and carried for him. Treating her latest caller as if he was somebody special just because he acted like a gentleman to her face. Flattering Momma with his silken red tongue and fancy cufflinks. Promising to meet up with her later that evening for drinks. Momma drooling at the very thought - acting like they were already on honeymoon.

And now here she was, alone and destitute, same as all the other poor souls forced to wander the empty streets looking to earn a dime. Already I could imagine the chill gusts off the railroad gnawing at her battered spirit. She might have followed the line of tracks heading further away from Broken Corner. Looking for other wretches who harboured no shame while they battled to survive, before falling to her knees and cursing every man who ever drew breath.

- 5 -

1938

Mint and I had sat up all night going over and over what would happen if I stayed in the apartment on my own. There was no money to pay the rent, and the frozen pipes would flood the entire building by Spring.

"Momma says you can't take a rag off a bare ass, so nobody can make us settle what we owe," I said.

"But if your momma don't come back, the landlord ain't gonna let you stay here, toots."

I could take my chances at the Orphan Asylum or die on the streets. But neither seemed part of the magical life story I had planned out for myself. The only other option was that I tag along with Mint Drago and see where that took me.

"All I'm askin' is that you trust me. We'll leave a note with Charlie in case your momma turns up. Let her know you're safe."

I was too tired to argue. My bones ached and my heart grieved for Momma, but feeling sorry for myself was unlikely to get me out of this fix.

He kept going through my lines with me all the way to the Lavender Garden hotel. "Anybody asks, you're my niece. You got that?"

"Mhmm."

"Lucille Drago."

"Yeah. Okay. I got it."

"Now make sure you behave."

A sickly smell of rose water and cigar smoke greeted me when we entered the lobby.

"Hey. Mr Drago. You're kinda previous, ain't ya? Got an early morning hard-on in need of attention?"

The guy at the desk changed his tone when he caught the look on Mint's face and spotted me lingering like a guilty shadow on his tail, unwashed and unclaimed, with a pillowcase stuffed full of my life's belongings trailing at my ankles.

"I'm sorry. I guess you ain't here on business."

"Just go find Miss Lily," Mint said. "I need to see her. Pronto."

"Mint, honey." A blue satin figure emerged from a corridor down to our left. "And who's this angel?"

"My niece."

"Cat got your tongue, hon?"

"I'm Angel. Angel Drago." I extended my hand the way I'd watched Momma do. I liked my new name. It seemed kind of fitting.

Mint arranged a bed for me until he returned from his business trip east. He planned on driving his truck to Buffalo to collect some auto parts. "Five hunnerd miles each way. Two weeks if the weather allows it, then I'll be back. I promise. So be good for Miss Lily."

Another promise to break. I'd already prepared for the worst. I was getting used to being abandoned, despising every new lie that came spilling out of anyone's mouth.

He turned to Miss Lily. "I'm putting her in your care. Don't let me come back here and find her gone."

I could tell she wasn't accustomed to being spoken to this way. "What do you think I'm runnin' here, Mint? Some kinda charity home?"

He peeled some greenbacks from his wallet and fed them her as he made it clear he knew exactly what she was running here. "I know it ain't the Everleigh, that's for sure. Just make sure she's cleaned up, fed and watered and given a warm bed to sleep in. And find her something more fitting to wear while you're at it; maybe get one of the young girls to keep her company."

She nodded as she wrapped her fingers around the notes, but he held onto them a moment longer.

"And I promise you, if I find you've harmed one hair on her head, or any place else for that matter, I'll burn this cathouse down. We clear on that?"

Dinah was a couple of years older than me, I reckon. But she carried an innocence that belied her age as effectively as I hid mine. On the surface, she was a slip of a kid, tiny like a bird and with eyes that looked a size or two too big for her skull. But under her chocolate brown skin, I imagined a framework tough as steel and a temperament to go with it.

"You gotta take a bath because Miss Lily says so."

"And who's gonna make me?"

The thought of stripping off in front of this girl wasn't such a big deal. But the mirrors all around us were unnerving. I could see that my hair had become a rat's nest at the back where I couldn't reach to brush. It had been two months or more since Momma had last washed and combed it out. And the scent of fancy soaps and perfume weren't enough to cover my shame. I knew how bad my body smelled. I hadn't bathed in weeks.

Yet I was reluctant to scrub myself clean to the bone. It seemed deceitful - one more way of forsaking my momma. With every trace of her touch washed away, I'd end up a nobody. A nothing. All I'd have left would be threadbare memories and a new set of lies.

"Nobody gonna make you. But Ma says if you don't get cleaned up, there's no way you're planting that scrawny white ass of yours anywhere near my clean bed. You gonna be sleeping in the yard with the dogs."

The thought of sharing a bed with this girl made me flinch. "I don't intend sharin' a cot with some dirty nigger girl anyways."

She cowered as if I'd taken a whip to her before recovering her dignity. "You ungrateful li'l bitch. You've no cause to speak that way."

I knew I'd done wrong. Momma would have put me straight with a smack in the mouth even before I'd get the chance to apologise. "I'm jus' sayin'. I don't want your charity. I get to do what I want - not what you say."

"Well you'll get a damn sight more than our charity unless you learn to bite that tongue of yours. Ma'll be soaping it for you - bath or no bath."

The tub had fancy brass taps the likes of which I had only seen in Momma's magazines. And it was already three-quarters filled, with bubbles floating on its surface like sugar candy. The steam and the scent of hot, soapy water were enough to turn my head in the end.

"Okay. I guess I owe you an apology. But I'll manage on my own, thank you very much."

I turned my back on her and stripped off. Then I dipped one foot into the broth before climbing right in. It wasn't the heat that made me gasp; it was the gentle caress of liquid velvet enveloping my naked flesh.

"I been told to take these dirty rags away. Miss Lily likely as not burn them. Just you make sure you scrub yourself all over."

She picked up my clothes as if they had been stripped from a disease-ridden corpse. I wriggled my toes then lay full stretch until the water came up to my chin. It was bliss.

Dinah eventually came back with some towels and offered to shampoo my hair.

"I never seen hair as fine as yours," I heard her mutter.

A crown of luxuriant black ringlets came down to just below her shoulders. I reached out a hand to take a sprig in my fingers. "You don't have to say that. Your hair's tolerable enough, I guess."

"Hmm."

"Momma always says my hair is real pretty," I continued. "But there were times I asked her to colour it for me."

"That so?"

"Mhmm. She always said no." I could feel her fingers massaging the soap into my scalp. "But it would be nice to have hair like yours, all the same."

Dinah laughed. "You don't know a blessed thing, do you, chile?"

I was given a pair of heavy cotton dresses to choose from, a warm vest that almost came down to my knees, two pairs of baggy grey bloomers and some rumpled woollen stockings.

"It's all we got that'll fit your scrawny ass. I swear, you look like you ain't eaten a square meal for a month or more."

Someone brought us scrambled eggs and bacon, and there were triangles of toast and real butter in a dish.

"You do mighty fine here, don't you?" I said.

Dinah nodded as she stuffed more bacon into her mouth. "It wasn't always like this. I got born on Bed Bug Row and lived there 'til my grandma passed away. We ain't been here much more than four years."

I was almost too tired to keep my eyes open. "You and your ma?"

"Yeah."

Another yawn.

"You look like you're all done in, sister. I left you a clean night-shirt on the bed. Get yourself tucked in. I'll join you when I'm good an' ready. If you don't want to share a bed then you'll probably have to sleep with Lester the mop-up boy."

I was too tired to argue.

"And if you get caught short in the night, there's a pot underneath the bed. Promise me you ain't a bed wetter."

"What d'you take me for?"

"I'm only sayin'. That's all."

The sheets were heavy and snug and the pillows were soft as the finest down. Everything smelled of perfume and clean linen. I had space to stretch out, and it wasn't long before I went under. Something warm cuddled up close to me sometime during the night, but it didn't cause enough of a stir to drag me out of my sleep. I was so lost to the world, I didn't even dream of Momma. And when I woke up, there were already beams of bright winter sun striping the bed cover.

I could feel a warm body laid out next to me, small and slight as a child. Then I took in the details of the room and remembered where I was.

As my eyes adjusted to the light, I reaised it wasn't Dinah sharing my bed. I saw an ear and a head attached to a slender neck that disappeared inside a flowery, flannelette night-shirt the same as I was wearing. But this creature wasn't my friend. I let my fingers trace the veins beneath the skin and mould their touch to the roundness of the skull.

I shook her shoulder gently and she stirred; turning onto her back as she rubbed her eyes awake.

"What's up with you now, chile?" Dinah said.

"Why d'you cut off all your hair?"

She turned to face me and stared at me as if I was an imbecile. "You not so smart as you think. For your information, I ain't got a single hair on my entire body."

"No hair at all?"

"That's the gospel truth. I got knocked down by a tram on Dearborn when I was nine year old and all my hair fell out. Miss Lily took one look an' said to get me a wig. But I only wear it when I'm in the parlour servin' drinks 'cause it makes my head itch something awful."

I laughed at the image, but I could tell she was serious.

"Everythin' else stopped growin' for a time," she continued.

"Everything?"

She ran her fingers over her small breasts and down to her flat belly. "Yeah. Ma took me to Doc Wilson who keeps the girls clean, and he said it must be shock. Said to give it time and I'd get to have hormones like everybody else. But my hair ain't ever grown back."

I reached for her hand and held it gently. "Same thing happened to me one time. When I was seven I got taken by a bad man an' things kinda stood still for a while."

Dinah stared at me as if searching for the lie, but the look that grew in her eyes showed she believed my every word.

"But then you got better. Right?" she said, pulling a stray hair from my eyes. "I keep wishin' I had real hair, even though Ma says I'm cute enough to eat without any French dressing on top, thank you very much."

"Where's your ma now?"

"She'll be asleep." Dinah nodded to the adjacent room. "She sleeps most of the day on account that she works all night."

I nodded. The life I knew was no different.

"Ma's a ten buck girl. Says I can get to be the same if I pass my grades. You know what I mean by that, right?" she sniggered.

"Course I do." Another lie that would never come to light.

"Lester done it to me about six months ago."

"Done it?"

"Ma says it only hurts the first time. Though if you ask me, it hurts a damn sight more times than just the once."

I was picturing all sorts of suffering.

"Miss Lily says I can be a two buck girl any time I want. But Ma says I'm better than that. If I keep doing the exercises like she showed me I can be a ten buck girl by the time I'm sixteen."

"Exercises?"

She whispered in my ear. Then she pulled me under the bed sheets and showed me what she meant.

- 6 -

1938

Lester had the kind of crooked smile that could melt your insides and frighten you half to death both at the same time. According to Dinah, his face got lop-sided from getting hit on the head by a spade when he was three years old, but I didn't believe any such thing could happen to a child.

"You asked him yet?"

Dinah began sniggering and her gaze flickered like a shameful secret too wicked for sharing in polite company. "Only if you're sure 'bout this. 'Cause once it's done, it ain't ever gonna grow back the same."

As if I believed such nonsense.

We chose a quiet Sunday afternoon when an air of lethargy had settled over the entire house. There were banks of iced-over snow on the sidewalk, but even though a thaw had set in overnight there was hardly any street traffic. We could hear tinkling in one of the adjacent rooms. Cherise in just a pink silk slip sat at the piano in the Parisienne Room picking at the notes like a chicken pecking for grubs. And close by someone kept calling for Ida. A red-haired woman padded about in just brassiere and panties, looking to borrow a set of curling tongs. But most of the girls were in their bedrooms asleep or preparing for callers.

"You be sure to keep still, honey." Dinah sat at my side and gazed spellbound as Lester took hold of my shoulders.

Then once the worst was done and he lathered my head to shave the remaining stubble down to bare skin, she gathered up my hair and stuffed it inside an old stocking. Lester knew of a doctor on Sibley Street who would pay good money for hair as fine as mine.

"How much he gonna pay, d'you reckon?"

Lester rubbed his chin. "I dunno, sistah. Why? You not trustin' me to gedda fair price?"

Dinah laughed. "I don't trust you not to keep most of it back for yourself."

"Leave him be, Di. He done a real good job."

I couldn't stop running my hands over my bare scalp. The skin felt as clean and smooth as hers now.

"You think so? You need to take a good look at yourself in the mirror, sugar. You look like you just climbed up out of somebody's grave."

I was too scared to peek too closely. Scared to discover the irreversible reality of what had been done. Wary of what Dinah's momma would have to say when she saw what we'd been up to. Or Miss Lily. Or Mint for that matter, if he ever returned.

As soon as she caught sight of my head, Dinah's ma

whipped Dinah's ass and threatened to throw us both on the street.

But Miss Lily never failed to see an opportunity to raise a buck or two. "What about that dandy photographer from New York? Him with the bow tie? Or that French artist guy?"

The novelty of having two pubescent girls as hairless as the day they were born was not lost on her. One completely white, the other coffee brown, and both posed together on the same bed. There were men more than ready to pay ten bucks a call, just to capture the image of us lying naked side by side staring into each other's eyes, close enough to touch, yet untouchable.

Men were willing to pay entry into our bedroom, merely to watch us get undressed and have our pictures taken. Two young girls laid out upon Miss Lily's finest silk sheets. Legs twined around each other until we became one impossible creature that even my pa's magic wouldn't be able to separate.

The first thing Mint did was curse us all to Kingdom Come. "You're all crazy as a bunch of alley cats. I should tear this place apart."

The second thing he did was go out and buy me a bonnet.

"If you think I'm driving half the way across America with a baldy headed freak sitting in the cab for all to see, then you've got another think coming. I ain't ever been eighty-sixed my whole life, and I ain't planning on getting so the next time I walk into a bar with you on my arm."

In fact, it wasn't until we stopped to gas up in Kansas that he allowed me outside in daylight with my head uncovered. Dinah had been wrong, as I suspected. My hair had grown back as fair as ever. But still Mint continued to cuss everyone involved. For the hair cutting and everything that followed. I didn't have the nerve to tell him most of it had been my idea.

There was a rage in Mint's eyes as I told him how Dinah and I would become famous throughout America. The exquisite combination of black and white flesh captured in absolute harmony. Our photographs were to be printed in fancy magazines as far away as Boston and San Francisco and maybe even Paris. The kind of magazines Momma always used to love thumbing through in the afternoon.

"You think your pictures are gonna end up in '*Vogue*' magazine or maybe on the front cover of '*Pep Stories*'? Miss Lily was jiving you, toots. Didn't your momma ever teach you any sense?"

She had indeed. Those nights when I couldn't sleep. The storm of lust raging behind the blue curtain keeping me on edge. The sounds of shared pain and ecstasy, anger and relief reaching a peak and my own stomach clenching and unclenching. Nights when I watched the top sheet slide down to expose skin gleaming with the sheen of sweat. Flesh steaming and muscles writhing as Momma's fingers clawed at their backs. Her bare feet, grimy and calloused, raised high above the mattress while prayers and curses spilled from her lips.

That's why I'd gotten Lester to carry out another task while Dinah ran me a hot bath for later. She said it would help.

"Momma?"

"Your momma ain't here, chile."

Dinah continued soaping my shoulders and whispering promises sweet enough to give the comfort I craved. I swear I saw the glisten of tears on her cheeks as my sobbing eased, even though my insides continued to throb. My legs had only convulsed the once. But that had been enough to kick me free of Lester's grasp.

"Jus' let the water soak your insides, honey."

She told me the pain would never be so bad again.

"That's not what you said before."

"You ain't gonna be here long enough to find out. So there ain't no cause for you to put yourself through any more sufferin' on my account."

"But I wanted him to do it like you said so I can get to work here with you."

"Listen, sister. There ain't no place for you here. For all your smart talk, you got no more moxie than a newborn kitten."

"But you can teach me."

Dinah wrapped her arm around my bare shoulder. "I don't want you gettin' hurt anymore than you already have. Is that what your ma would want for you? All that pain an' degradation for two bucks a trick?"

- 7 -

1938

Mint had been hired to collect a truck-load of bibles en route to a backwater town all the way down in Mississippi. He carried with him a list of addresses and a letter of introduction from the pastor at the First Baptist Church of Hammond. It allowed easy access to various churches along our route, from Illinois through St Louis and Kansas City; Springfield, Missouri, to Tulsa; to Lubbock and Abilene, before backtracking east across Louisiana to Jackson, Mississippi.

"This here's my niece, Angel Drago."

That never once failed to get us a welcoming smile and a warm invitation to take tea with the local ladies of the congregation. I often wondered whether introducing me as his wife would produce the same reaction. One or two times, when he waltzed me into a roadside bar and tapped me on the rear, it felt like we were as good as married.

He'd taken me from the Lavender Garden with barely a word of where we were headed. All I knew is that he couldn't leave Chicago quickly enough - as if there was someone on his tail. "This new mayor, there ain't a single damn cop you can trust in this city."

For the first week he drove most all day and his endless talk wore away the miles. We'd only stop to answer the call of nature or to grab a mess of food from a roadside store while fuelling up the truck. Mint bunked up in the cab at night and had set up a heap of blankets in the back for me to sleep on. But I'd still lie awake listening to the wind snatch at the tarpaulin. And most mornings I'd be up and dressed long before the truck's engine started up and we hit the road.

It wasn't until after we left Missouri that Mint stopped cursing the city. I'd heard about the crates he'd been transporting from Buffalo, filled with Chicago typewriters.

"The paperwork was for auto parts, but someone in City Hall tipped a word to the authorities. If I'd been caught, I'd be locked up in Joliet for gun-running faster than you can say 'Chattanooga'. I wouldn't be driving this truck load of bibles, that's for sure. And my guess is your sweet ass would be resting in someone else's lap."

He began to tell me tales from the bibles he was toting. Moses in the bulrushes and King David and Goliath, and Joseph's coat of many colours. I took to wondering if we'd both be transformed into pillars of salt as the flat prairie lands stretched on either side of us. It seemed that Mint couldn't help looking over his shoulder for trouble, and I flinched with each mile as the tug of longing pulled tighter and tighter until I felt I would tear in two. My heart still yearned for the forbidden scents of Miss Lily's house and the taste and texture of Dinah's skin.

These were the things I never told Mint. Not even when I

crept under his blanket the night we parked up alongside the Kaw River less than spitting distance from the Topeka road. My tears that night were genuine enough, but the display of helpless innocence just one more lie.

We spent a week parked beside that creek - a mile or so outside Topeka. For a time it felt like we were indeed husband and wife as I reveled in the warmth and shelter of Mint's bear-like body. He had no real schedule in mind. His intentions were to make Greenwood, Mississippi, sometime late summer where the bibles were being delivered for rebinding. Then once they were offloaded and he got paid he would continue south in order to reach the delta before winter.

But there were other times when I felt as if I was no more a part of his life than his beaten-up truck. Those were the nights he took to drinking the same way a landlocked fish might take to the open sea.

I'd be left sitting at a table on my own sipping a soda, forced to listen to him laugh and joke with the other men at the bar. Sharing tales of how once he'd been in cahoots with John Dillinger and how the Chicago cops didn't have the smarts to wipe their own butts without an instruction book.

And when his voice became more slurred and their attention wandered, I caught their looks of lust and distasteful longing latch on to me. Looks that made me squirm inside. Looks that seemed to coat me with a film of grime, like someone had shaken a dirty blanket close by and covered me in their thoughts.

There came the time, one night, when Mint excused himself so he could visit the men's room and the whispering at the bar grew more insistent.

"What's your name, honey pie?"

Two men rose from their stools and came to sit right next to me.

"Ain't none of your damn business."

One of the pair lurched closer, his tongue moistening his top lip. "You godda smart mouth, but you look sweed enough to eat." I felt his hand on my knee. "You wanna come out back show me what you got cookin' under that dress? Or you gonna put on a show right here for us all?"

I tried to push his hand away as it slid further up my thigh. "Leave me."

"Whoohoo. No cause to get so jumpy."

Mint floundered back into the bar, lost in some world of his own as I was pawed and pulled in all directions until I bared my claws. I'd grown my nails on purpose - something else Dinah taught me.

"There's some gen'lemen who like an alley cat in the sack next to them. But if you ever meet one of them dirty dogs that won't take no for an answer, you got yourself some extra protection."

A rake of scratches drew blood and got us thrown out of there so quick that Mint barely had time to straighten his cap and settle his bar tab.

When we'd left the city, it had seemed, for the first month or so, that we were heading deeper into winter. The roads were still pitted with frozen ruts and pot holes, and frost burnt the sparse grass into stubble along the roadside. But the roads grew dustier and the air became drier the further south we travelled. And once we were west of St Louis and the skies opened up, it felt like there was no place to shelter or lie low. So much of it expanding in all directions.

There were evenings when we'd get to watch storm clouds in wagon trains head across the horizon. Any one of them capable of seeking us out if it had the notion. Even at the darkest hour of night, the stars seemed to keep close watch on our movements. Judging our actions from afar.

Mint'd sit beside our camp fire and tell tales of the first wagon trains that had headed even further west, through Oregon and Santa Fe in search of new lands. I'd never once imagined there were such places. Lands where the crushed bones of the earth were exposed in layers like the pages of a waterlogged book - as if there had been countless floods since the dawn of time.

"Just think what it musta been like, toots."

I did. A new world waiting to be discovered. The dreams people must have carried with them as they rode west and saw fresh wonders each day.

I had my own dreams about how things might turn out once we reached Greenwood. Mint had already promised me there would be balmy times ahead of us: filled with the intoxicating scents of magnolia and tupelo, with palmetto trees and cypresses laden with Spanish moss. He planned continuing south once the bibles were delivered. He reckoned there was a fortune to be made on the crap tables of New Orleans.

But once we passed through the swamplands and

flatlands of North Louisiana, it felt like summer had already passed us by. The Mississippi sky was laden with grey banks of sodden cloud that seemed intent on keeping tight hold of us beneath their weight.

There were floods that put me in mind of another of Mint's tales - of Noah and his ark. God's punishment for the acts committed each night inside the back of our truck, even though they'd became Mint's way of giving comfort and my way of taking it. He always said you have to sin to get saved.

"You're gonna be my lucky charm. My lucky silver dollar. I just know it."

"I thought I brung you nothing but bad luck," I said. "That's what you kept tellin' me all the way out here."

"Good luck. Bad luck. Any luck is better than no luck."

But it wasn't so much bad luck as a judgement. Forty days and nights of rain, or so it seemed. Once the sultry air of Texas and the draining humidity of Louisiana were behind us, we were greeted by floods and thunderstorms like I never experienced before or since.

Mint reckoned the balance of nature had been tipped over by the heat wave of '36 and the barren times that followed. Others, mostly the Biblers we met, said it was the wrath of the Lord sent down from above on account of Man's ungodliness. The Mississippi rains would wash away all our shame in preparation for salvation.

But mostly it was the roads that got washed away. Parts of the turnpike between Greenwood and Jackson were more than five foot deep in water. So it seemed we were going to be trapped in Leflore County for the foreseeable future, even though our work was done. That's when someone convinced Mint he would be better heading north for Memphis and boarding a river boat there.

I begged him to wait a week or so longer. He'd got paid all that was owing him and was desperate to put as many miles as possible between us and the Southern Baptists. But in the end, he agreed to park up outside a juke for three or four days, and I was left in peace to make use of the newly acquired space inside the back of his truck.

There had been weeks when all I could smell was musty paper and frayed leather bindings. Now I could shake out our blankets each morning and hang an oil lamp either end at night. This was more like a home, and I was in no rush to see it abandoned for the throw of a dice.

But each night the gentle creaking of the springs as we coupled was countered by the spatter and squall of rain on the canvas roof. Then, as Mint's drunken fumbling ended with a shudder and I was left to hold tight to his arm as it circled my waist, it became clear how things were going to be. Night after night.

If I was his lucky charm, then I figured I deserved my share of good fortune. By my reckoning, I had a year left before my sixteenth birthday. That June day would mark the end of my childhood. But it would as likely as not pass like any other day unless I could get my hands on Mint's stash.

Ma's pocketbook or Mint's wallet, there seemed to be no means of making my own way in the world without someone else's money.

- 8 -

1938 - 1939

The floods turned out to be a judgement and a blessing. Though when the engine finally sputtered and died, somewhere south-east of Leflore, it seemed they were a curse. I was forced to wade knee-deep through water in Mint's wake until we reached drier ground. Time and time again the loose earth slipped underneath my footing until finally he hoisted me into his arms and bit back a laugh. "You're as light as a snowflake, toots."

"That don't make no difference, the mess we're in."

"We'll be fine once we find some sucker to take pity on us. Just let me do all the talking."

"Why? You planning on having us hitch a ride off some hayseed and his mule?"

There had been hobos the length and breadth of the highway, yet Mint never once offered them a ride. I guessed we still had a lot of walking ahead of us.

"I told you we should have stayed inside the truck until help come."

"Honey, don't you think I took account of that? There ain't no help coming. And you see all this water? If it rises any more, it's likely to carry the truck away along with the ground it's sitting on."

So we were forced to march for miles. Seven or eight at least, by my reckoning.

Eventually the rain eased off and the feeble sun emerged from the clouds. Banks of mist began to settle in layers on the adjacent fields, and the scent of the river and ripe vegetation spread everywhere - alive enough to crawl inside your body and lay its eggs before hatching like blowflies.

I could see on either side of the road how most of the crops had gotten flattened beyond salvage. We came across men and boys, standing at the edges of their fields, staring into nothingness. Hoes in their hands as useless as unloaded rifles.

"Any mechanics round here?"

They shook their heads and laughed as they watched us tramp past.

A mile or so along we passed a group of three shanties alongside the ruins of an abandoned plantation house with smoke-blackened windows and an air of desertion. The only sign of life, two roosters scratching in the slick, green scum that coated the yard.

I was desperate to rest my bones and suggested we camp there for the night, but Mint insisted we press on.

"I got a bad feelin' bout how these people fell on such hard times."

Further south, we met a boy beating a mule with a stick.

The beast was up to its haunches in a ditch and the boy, no more than five or six years old, whipped and cursed it to Hell and back.

"Look away, honey," Mint whispered. "These folks are in even worse straits than us two."

"But can't we do something?"

"It ain't any of our damn business."

By the time we reached the Hardy farm, I was about dead on my feet. Mint put on his Bible face and told the lady of our plight. She was reluctant to offer him the time of day until I spotted the child peering round the corner of their cabin.

"Is that your little girl? Look pa, ain't she the sweetest child you ever seen."

Mint's curse became his blessing, and for once our lies bore fruit.

Pike was the same age as me, give or take a month or two, but he hadn't yet learnt how to deceive with a glance. For weeks I'd catch his eyes latching onto mine then slide away some place else. As if the shame of being caught looking too close was more than he dared admit to.

His sister, Bertha, was a different matter. She had an open face and could talk until my head echoed with her Mississippi vowels long after I climbed behind the canvas with Mint.

Bertha's pa had towed our truck into their yard, and it soon became clear we were accustomed to hunkering down in the back of that rather than making do with any tent.

"Sooner or later, someone's gonna start wondering. A grown man and a child bedding down under the same sheet night after night," Mint said.

"I ain't no child, and besides they need never know if we don't let on." I needed the warmth of Mint's body next to mine more than ever now. As much as he needed mine.

"But that girl's a smart one. I swear her eyes are everywhere, like fruit flies on squirrel shit. She sees one set of bed sheets she's gonna figure out how the land lies."

So we made do with a gentle touch in passing until nights became too cold to sleep separately and Old Man Hardy let us hole up inside the patched-up cabin across the yard. With a proper door and shutters on the windows, there was little chance of our arrangement getting found out.

The smell of the river filled every corner of the building. But once we got a fire going in the grate, the idea of a winter moored alongside the Tallahatchie didn't seem so bad. Mint and I shared the same bed again and I began to accept that some things were unlikely to ever change, until Pike's close attentions began to stir different feelings inside my belly. I'd taken to accompanying him and Bertha along the creek down to the banks of the big river in search of something for the pot when pickings were slim. There were waterfowl and jack rabbits there, and Pike was a sure shot.

"I hear you're meant to be headin' off to New Orleans sooner or later," I said. "But a little bird tells me it don't exactly suit."

There were few secrets between Bertha and her brother, and what he told her she told me as a matter of course.

"There ain't nothin' worth stayin' round here for." He flashed a look of contempt in his sister's direction. "But Bertha's got no right tellin' you my business."

"I'm just makin' polite conversation. Me and my pa had entertained the idea of heading as far as Memphis when the floods came. He was looking to board a riverboat and head down the Misissippi to New Orleans."

"You won't be goin' anywhere if the damn truck can't be repaired," Bertha chipped in.

Truman cocked his head as the thought of joining us became a possibility. "I know a bit about trucks. At least what I picked up from watching my pa. Maybe I could help Mint fix it up and I could ride with you as far as Beale Street."

I shook my head. "Pa's intentions are to reach the delta and make his fortune there. Fixin' his truck means we don't need to go anywhere near Memphis."

The boy shook his head in disappointment. "I only been downriver the one time. And I tell you; you're gonna end up like a pimento unless you cover up. And there's bugs there the size of pack-mules."

So we began to make our own plans to head north. Plans that Pike took great pains to keep from Bertha. We spent nights in the back of the truck with a kerosene lamp and a page torn from his school atlas. Mint kept well out of the way, nursing a bottle of rye in front of the fire and preaching about how there was going to be another war sometime soon. Meanwhile, Bertha sulked in her room - Pike making it clear he didn't want her trailing his every step like his shadow.

"I'm still not sure I should take you with me on account you're just a kid - same as Bertha. And your pa's gonna raise the roof when he finds out we run off together."

"I'm older than you think, Parker Lee Hardy. And you don't have to listen to a word Mint tells you. That tale he's been spinning since he dragged me with him all the way from Chicago. He's been peddling it so many times now, he's beginning to believe it's the gospel truth. He's no more my pa than you are. I was doling out tricks in a cat house first time he met me."

I could tell he didn't swallow a word of that until I showed him exactly what tricks I meant. Then he was onto me even before I'd pulled my panties all the way down to my knees.

"Slow down, hotshot. Let me show you how to do this thing properly."

Pike wasn't no ladies' man, and he was no sweet talker either. The boy was as much taken by my pale skin as by my womanly wiles. He claimed such whiteness had to be a sign of absolute purity. In his head I was Eve come back to wash away mankind's sins. The colour of my skin worth more than any show of fine manners or southern roots.

"You're a gift from the Lord, and that makes you kinda special. I ain't seen anyone more perfect. You're a real life angel. It's like you were sent from heaven to save my soul."

Of course, when I found out what other business he was carrying out those nights when he was gone 'til dawn, there was no amount of clean living that could save his soul. It turned my stomach and his words echoed inside my head like a curse. But by then it was too late. There was a child on the way.

The only gift from heaven was that February storm. A blessing that it came when it did. Mint and Pike between them had patched up the truck the best they could. Mint was planning on hauling me to New Orleans with him once the days grew longer, unaware of what had taken root inside my belly. If he'd discovered what Pike and I had been up to, I'm guessing he'd have left me on the Hardy farm to rot.

Under the circumstances, I'd figured out two bucks a night was reasonable compensation for getting my ass hauled all the way from Chicago against my will. Of course, once Mint realised I'd taken my share of his earnings, it's likely he'd come after us. Cut me maybe, before abandoning me for good. But first he'd have to catch me.

The night we left Leflore County, I was tempted to plant a parting kiss on Mint's cheek as he lay coiled in the blankets alongside the spent embers of the fire. But I feared this show of treachery would be more likely to wake him than the storm brewing outside.

Pike almost drove off the road twice in his desperation to put some mileage behind us. I begged him to take more care, but he wouldn't even put on the headlights until we reached the outskirts of town. We heard something rip behind the cabin as the wind grew in intensity, and the truck gave an almighty shudder, but still he wouldn't stop to take a look until close to daybreak.

"We need to cross the state line before they find out we're gone. Pa's gonna know I'm headed north. That's no secret."

When we finally pulled into a gas station and climbed out to stretch our legs, I could see the tarpaulin was torn beyond repair and flapping like a wounded sail. I paid for fuel and food. Pike had less than thirty bucks to his name back in those days and he didn't show much inclination on spending them on me.

He'd been desperate to reach Tennessee before dawn, but fate kept us out of the Promised Land. It wasn't until winter that same year that we finally set up home in the big city. By then, I knew all of Pike's sordid secrets. The truck only got us as far as Byhalia before it pooped.

It was his lies that got us as far as Memphis.

This is where it began.

Ode to Bertha Swan Hardy

- 1 -

1938 - 1939

When it began.

There's little wonder Truman turned out the way he did. My brother, Pike, had too much ambition to be fit for fathering, and too much religion to see any need for compassion where his son was concerned. He'd been quoting the scriptures and touting politics since the moment he clawed his way out of the womb, according to Old Ma Hardy.

Of course, religion has helped many a soul in need of saving. And ambition's not a bad thing to admit to having round here, even if it don't put food on the table. I been here my whole life and I got no fancy ideas to up and leave. They can bury me in my own pumpkin patch as far as I'm concerned. But there ain't no future on the Flats if your heart isn't in the land.

Pike would spend hours lost in his story books, and I guess that's why he set his sights on the big city life long before he growed out of short pants. He'd watch the trains head north, and I swear I could see his hopes and dreams jump aboard and hitch a ride.

That long mournful whistle sometimes gave me the heebie-jeebies, but Pike'd cock his head and listen 'til it faded into the hush of the evening. "Hear that, Bertha Swan? It's callin' me away."

The same voice seemed to have called the Drago girl. She'd been skittish from the very moment she turned up here with her daddy, and their broken down truck abandoned five miles up the road. The two of them looked about ready to collapse in the dust at Ma's feet when they caught her hanging out bed sheets. The girl looked no more than thirteen or fourteen. Such cotton-white hair and the palest skin we never seen round these parts before.

The old man had stopped at the gate, his muffler rolled into his hands and a desperate cast to his face. "You know of any cheap mechanics round here, ma'am?"

Winter was on their heels and there had been floods the past month. Parts of Roebuck Road had washed away and one of the bridges across the Tallahatchie had come close to being breached. But this was no place for Northerners. For all their fast talk and fancy education, most of them had no more sense than a newborn calf and Pa was ready to send them on their way.

But something about the look of surrender in the girl's face must have made Pa relent. Maybe he saw they were both as poor as the rest of us; out of luck and down at heel through no fault of their own. He hitched up our horse to tow the wreck all the way into the corner of our grazing paddock. It kept company with Pa's rusted Chevy pickup for the next four months.

There was plenty enough space there for them to set a camp fire of sorts. Pa told them they were welcome to pump water from our well, otherwise they kept to themselves. Then, once it got too cold to sleep in the back of the truck, Pa let them hunker down inside the abandoned shack at the corner of the old tobacco field. The wooden hut had been used by his grandpappy's family when they first came to the Flats from North Carolina in the 1860s.

Now the Dragos had a proper roof over their heads, Pike and I'd go round and spend time with them once the chores were done even though my pa didn't encourage us to associate with our new neighbours. We were both curious, of course we were. Mint Drago told us how they'd driven from way up north. All the way from the Niagara Falls, west across the Prairies as far as the Rocky Mountains, then south into Texas before crossing the Mississippi. The child had little to say for herself, but a smile often crossed her face as her pa fed us more tales.

Angel Drago carried her own set of lies. How Mint won her ma in some tin-shack gambling den west of Chicago, and how they all ended up living under the same canvas roof. Her ma died of cholera two years later, but Mint showed no emotion at her passing. Mint had his own reasons to head south. His aim was to seek his fortune in New Orleans. He reckoned O'Dwyers wouldn't know what hit them when it came time to cash in his chips.

Angel was the same age as me, I reckoned, though her pa claimed he never once got around to registering the paperwork after she was born. Another lie that came to light in due course. It turns out that Mint Drago was no more her pappy than Geronimo is mine. But there were times when I'd catch her eyes, the way she stared at me without breathin' a word, and I'd surmise she was much older than she appeared. She wore wisdom like a veil. It obscured her innocence and somehow called attention to what few feminine charms she had. I'd been flaunting my bosoms since they'd first showed, proud of my growing womanhood. But Angel Drago had no cause to do anything of the sort.

My brother had finished at Greenwood High the previous summer and was set for a placement at a funeral parlour outside of Metairie, New Orleans. Uncle Box had contacts, and Pa made it clear Pike had no choice in the matter. We couldn't afford to have him live with us anymore unless he earned his keep some way other than through doing yard work. There was no regular employment to be had within forty miles of here.

Pike's shoes had always been pointin' north, so this sudden switch of direction hit him hard. I noticed a change in him the closer it came to his time of leaving. And it wasn't just a reluctance to flee our little dog trot cabin. Or the fact that his dreams of headin' to Memphis had died on the vine. Nothing like that. It was something else, and it didn't take long to figure what it was.

I was accustomed to telling my brother every mortal thing - from the boys I was ferociously in love with to the monthly cramps I'd started experiencing. And I believed he reciprocated. But lately he began to keep his own counsel. Angel had confided in me how she wanted to get away from her pa due to his drinking bouts, so it should have come as no surprise when she and Pike set off together.

Between them, Pike and Mint Drago had got the truck repaired, and our visitors were set to leave before the next full moon had passed. But many a time I'd heard Pike tell Angel she'd be a fool to follow the old man south into 'Skeeter Country' as he called it only to be eaten alive by bugs and get her delicate skin burnt red raw. And it transpired my brother had already decided he would never be setting foot anywhere near New Orleans either.

It was the third week of February when they left, shortly after the gala at our school to celebrate Washington's Birthday. I'd taken Angel along as my special guest, and most of the other girls in class were too disarmed by her delicate looks to say what was on their minds. Grace Chisholm was the one who finally spoke up, as curious as her witch of a grandma.

"Where you say you from again?"

"Chicago," Angel replied.

"Chi-kaw-go? You don't say. So does everybody up there look as washed out as you, honey?"

"Leave her be, Gracie. She's just naturally pale, that's all," I said.

"If you ask me, she needs some Mississippi sun on her skin."

But there had been no sun for weeks. The fields everywhere lay grey and sodden; mists off the Tallahatchie clawing at your hair leaving a sheen of damp if you so much as peered through the blinds.

Pike didn't have to let on to me what was on his mind. I could tell the girl had her hooks in him the same way any woman catches the man she wants. I'd seen nothing specific until now. But there had been nights when he sneaked out - and mornings when he came back, sucked dry and dead on his feet. Pa assumed he was sowing wild oats with the boys down Sharkey way, but I guessed that Pike's tom-catting was taking place a lot closer to home.

As it happened, Pa and I were both mistaken.

The night of the storm that brought down the Tippo radio mast, I caught my brother putting on his boots when any man with a morsel of sense would stay indoors.

"Can't you hear the wind out there, Pike? You knows how scared I gets whenever the shingles start to rattle."

That wasn't strictly true. I'd outgrown the custom of climbing inside his bed for reassurance a long time since. But when I got up from my knees after offering a prayer before sleep, I noticed him packing his shirts and spare pants inside a gunny sack. He wasn't just heading out to lie down a while with Angel Drago in the back of her pa's truck.

"You hush up now, Bertha Swan. Get your head under them sheets an' you won't hear a thing."

I pleaded with him but my tears were wasted.

- 2 -

1939 - 1946

Less than a year later, Ma got a Christmas card and accompanying letter. Of course, I had to read it out to her. Angel and my precious brother were safe and well, thanks to the Good Lord's ceaseless bounty. They'd driven as far as Byhalia before the engine of Mint's truck gave up for good. But they were fine. Pike had been working double shifts in a cotton mill there all summer.

They'd succeeded in getting far enough from home, but not quite crossing the border into Tennessee. This was some kind of blessing because it meant their son first drew breath in the state of Mississippi.

'You and Pa have a grandson, Truman Hardy. Born September 12th 1939. You ain't seen a finer boy.'

My pa, Abraham Lee Hardy, had passed away in his sleep earlier that same month. Some kind of balance in nature Ma reckoned, but she cursed Pike all the same.

"They wed?"

"He don't say."

"So I got myself a bastard for a grandson."

"Ma, you shouldn't talk that way."

"Your pa never laid a finger on me until our wedding night."

I held back a snort of contempt. "Well times change, don't they?"

There was no return address. Besides, neither of us had the energy let alone the wherewithal to travel north in order to hook Pike by his breeches and give him the hiding he deserved. We'd learned what he and Chester Macarthy had been up to and his name got spoken less in our kitchen as the months turned to years and the War kept us all listening to the radio for news from overseas.

Then Ma's farming days came to an end after she got herself a blister that developed into a septic heel from wearing Pa's worn-out boots. Within three months she lost the use of her leg through her obstinacy and spent most of her time propped up in bed. Once she realised it was time to start counting every day as a blessing, Ma took to religion for comfort. She had me read the Bible out loud but I couldn't get past all the names of who begat whom. I could only sit and watch Ma's eyes flicker then fade like a kerosene lamp with a wick in need of trimming.

She eventually got taken in the early hours of the morning following Franklin Delano Roosevelt's passing. That tragic news took a while longer to travel this far south, but she surely would have approved of the man who took his place at the White House. Another Southern Democrat. Another Truman.

In Leflore County I became the only one left to carry the

weight of the Hardy name on my shoulders along with twenty acres of bottomland prone to flooding, a patched up sharecropper's cabin and a fallen-down shanty close by. What little stock we had - two cows, some chickens and Pa's old horse - cost more to feed than what they'd sell for at current market prices. And Grandpappy's rifle, a Dutch hoe, rusted plough and straight-edged spade would do little to lift the debt from around my neck.

I'd inherited Ma's broad hips and ample breasts, and many a boy had tested the merchandise. But none were set on buying. My field had been ploughed and seeded numerous times, but I realised I'd likely as not end up wed to this patch of land rather than to any eligible man who might cross my path.

I was a month short of being nineteen years old, alone under the family roof for the first time in my entire life, and already I felt trapped. There was no way of letting Pike know how things stood. No way of telling him he was welcome home again, not that he had a drop of farming blood in his body. But I'd have walked barefoot to Memphis if I thought there was a chance of finding him and of some reconciliation. The farm was too much for me to manage on my own and I toyed with the idea of selling up. But again, no one was buying.

As it turned out, my luck changed the way life sometimes trips you up when you least expect it. The following Spring, almost seven years to the day when he took it into his head to run away, Pike turned up in a fancy automobile and with a pair of patent leather shoes on his feet. Claimed he'd driven all the way from Memphis that same day after eating breakfast and reading the latest issue of the 'Commercial Appeal' from front to back. Like I'd swallow such a lie, given that Pike normally looked no further than the day's Hambone cartoon.

He hadn't changed as much as one might expect. Still as lean as whipcord, hair slicked down and sporting a set of dentures that made his mouth look a size too small. But I could tell from the cut of his clothes that he was doing mighty fine. I'd often imagined him skulking outside on my porch those late nights when I added up the books and found somehow I'd managed to turn one more corner. I pictured him kicking down the door demanding to be let in to his house, which was legally my house now. Pa had travelled all the way to Natchez to make a will and disown his only son three months after the boy went off with Angel. I was prepared to show Pike the documents if he doubted my word. But he hadn't come to fight, or to spout verses from the Bible about the prodigal son.

There was a bloodshot glaze to his eyes not brought about by driving a hundred and thirty miles of dusty road. I heard the falter in his voice as he explained that Angel was gone. Left him for some hotshot in uniform. Last he'd heard, she was down in New Orleans shaking her fanny at anyone who cared to look closer.

"She took the boy?"

No. A residue of the arrogance I'd so often despised when growing up under the same roof crossed his face as if there were chiggers writhing under his skin. Truman was asleep in the back of the car. A bed for the night would be most welcome. A glass of bourbon and a sandwich with Ma's comeback dressing and he'd tell his tale - if I wanted to hear it.

I chided him for making me wait then dashed outside to collect my darling little nephew leaving Pike on the porch to get used to the idea of losing Ma and Pa in the space of thirty seconds. I could see him taking in his surroundings and weighing everything against his memory. The empty yard and broken-down fences told their own story.

- 3 -

1946 - 1948

Once the boy was settled on the collapsed couch in my living room, Pike and I retreated to the kitchen and shared a bite. He handed me the envelope while I poured us each a coffee - as dispassionately as if he was passin' me the milk. "That's for you now, Bertha Swan."

"What you mean it's for me? You tryin' to buy this twenty acres of Mississippi mud from under ma feet?"

"No, honey. You got me all wrong. It's my way of paying back what I took - all those years I should have been working to support my kin. If Pa was still around I guess I'd be handin' it over to him."

"And he'd tell you what to do with it. You just tryin' to put right what can't ever be put right," I spat out. "It's too late. Besides, how much is inside this envelope? A couple hundred bucks? Ten cents for every day we had to manage without you?"

When he told me, I nearly passed out at the thought of so much money under my roof for even one night.

"It ain't a gift. It's payment in advance. You see, I need someone to look after Truman here while I head south on business. New Orleans."

"How long?"

"Maybe a week. I've got a message to pass on, and I want to make sure it gets delivered in person."

"Fine," I said. "As long as you ain't got back into your hateful ways. I know what you got up to with that Chester Macarthy."

Some of the tales I'd heard about my brother made me sick to the stomach. Maybe I didn't move in the same social circle as Miss Lah-de-dah Eleanor Roosevelt, but I like to think we held the same values. I couldn't abide neighbours disrespecting neighbours on account of the colour of their skin. We were all of us slaves to the soil.

"It ain't nothin' of the sort, sister. This is between me and the boy's mother. And if it suits, I'll allow you to tend to Truman every summer from now on when he ain't at school."

I pictured myself in that Memphis heat, socialising and drinking mint juleps every afternoon with the neighbourhood ladies, and me not even in possession of a single summer dress to call my own.

"Much as I love this little man, I ain't plannin' on quitting Mississippi for thirty pieces of silver, Parker Lee Hardy, so you'd better think again."

His condescending laugh was enough to convince me I was getting ahead of myself. A long way ahead.

"There ain't nothing further from my mind. It's knowing

you'll never leave this damn place, not for anyone, that's made me decide. I figure it might be best for Truman to stay here each summer. Leastwise, until he's old enough to make up his own mind about what line of work he wants to follow."

"Truman come and live here?"

"There's things in the city I'd rather he didn't get involved with. This is as good a place as any to grow up in. And I knows I can trust you to keep an eye on the boy."

"What kinds of things? You in some trouble up there?"

"Just politics, sister. Nothing for you to lose sleep over."

So the plan was finalised. I'd have the boy stay here for the period Pike was away on business, then Truman would go home again with his pa. He'd return once school got out in June. Pike would send him by train as far as Greenwood and I'd receive a telegram in advance to confirm arrival times. The same would happen for the next nine summers, God willing.

A thousand bucks was a fortune back then. But I could write ten thousand words about that poor boy's upbringing and another ten thousand between the lines of what Pike told me and what he chose to leave out. Suffice to say, I treated Truman like a son - as if he was my own flesh and blood. I loved him, and cherished every day he spent here - and I confess I beat his hide whenever I felt he warranted it.

The first summer, Truman turned up with a note from Pike telling me to keep the boy away from the river. He had proved himself no swimmer and his pa was scared he'd go and get hisself drowned. The following year there was a note asking I keep a special look out for dogs. Truman had got bit, and his pa had a mortal fear of the boy contracting rabies.

Of course, the Sumpters had a couple of cross-breeds they set loose on their farm from dusk 'til dawn. But there were worse things out there to snag a young boy than deep water and rabid dogs. The note Truman brought along with him the summer of '48 spelled that out clear enough.

'On no account is the boy to be allowed to mix.'

- 4 -

1948

Marlene Cobham, Marlene Sheldon that was, had turned up at Leflore County the previous winter. I remembered her from our schooldays. A shifty, scowling girl with impetigo. She would frequently cuss those of us who stared too closely at the wildfire raging across her face.

Marlene's ma had died when she was still a baby, and her two brothers had high-tailed it to Texas as soon as they were old enough to jump ship. So there was just Marlene and her pa, 'Pastor' Sheldon. The old man had a propensity for preaching the gospel whenever he drank too much liquor. And he was more than just a daddy according to those who knew the family history.

There had been rumours her pa was taking her down to Jackson to see a skin doctor. But if that's so, the treatment must have taken its toll because neither of them came back in time for Marlene to start ninth grade, and I never once got wind of her again until she turned up one bitter winter's day with her husband and daughter in tow. Her face carried the same constellation of scabs, and once I did the arithmetic, I realised it was no skin doctor she'd been visiting.

The Cobhams were camped in a clearing along the shore of Roebuck Lake, within shouting distance of the elementary school. They'd settled there late November when most itinerant workers had long moved on. The harvesting was done, and Sammy Rae would have little choice but to head south. I'd got talking to him outside the stores one day when I was buying coils of barbed wire, and I mentioned I had new fences I needed putting up. I'd already sold the carcass of my poor old horse to Davey Moon and I intended to get myself a pair of gilts for breeding.

Sammy Rae let on how he'd been hoping to find part-time work elsewhere but was in no particular rush to move on for the time being. That was good news from where I was standing. He also knew a thing or two about rearing hogs and suggested I begin with the one sow and see how she performed. He called by a week or so later. Said he just happened to be passing. Within three days, the fencing was in place and we reached an agreement that he would continue to help me out when necessary. The pump stock of my well was needing attention, and by the time the first winter floods hit us, he was nearly done fixing the loose shingles on my roof. I'd made it clear on more than one occasion he was welcome to stay over any time he decided it was too long a walk back to Leflore after a day's labouring. Yet he always made his excuses.

It wasn't until the time I snuck up on him and stole a kiss that he mentioned the fact that he and Marlene never once got properly wed. Not with a judge and such like.

Give him his due; he could have used this oversight as an excuse to tumble me on my back porch. I'd forgive him. He'd not be the first man to stray onto my patch, married or otherwise. But he didn't even allow me time to cover up my embarrassment, explaining how Marlene's daughter, Donna Mae, had got sick from bad water. The only reason they'd stuck around Leflore long past Fall was because she needed to build up her strength.

That's when I mentioned the shack at the corner of the wet paddock - Pa's tobacco field as we always called it. It had stood empty since my pa gave Mint Drago a ride en route to New Orleans eight years previous. Mint had figured out it was no coincidence Pike had chosen such a wild night to drive off with his daughter. No one would hear the rattle of the truck's engine above such a storm.

I'd been tempted to pull the cabin down and find an use for the lumber, but the grey dust of family history clung to its low rafters like ghostly admonitions, and Truman had taken a fancy to playing in there when the sun and skeeters got too much for him to endure. Within a fortnight, the Cobham family moved in. Sammy Rae agreed to work the paddock and the two half acres either side of the creek in exchange for a share of the crops and four walls and a roof. Marlene took her time to get used to the idea of being beholden to me, but she had no choice in the matter.

Her daughter was a sickly, sweet-natured child. She had her momma's bird-like frame and the set of her mouth would sometimes put me in mind of Marlene's tinderbox temper. But she took to me from the first time she ever set foot inside my kitchen. I'd had a stew of ham and black-eyed peas simmering on the stove and intended taking a portion for my new neighbours once it was ready, but she must have followed the scent all the way from across the yard. I heard her tentative tap on the screen door. "You in there, Miss Hardy?"

"Who dat? De big bad wolf?"

It was a silly game, but one we continued to play together until she grew too old to wear pinafore dresses. Her laughter never once failed to soften my heart back then.

"No. It's Donna Mae."

"Donna who? Don't know anybody round here called Donna Mae."

And so it went on until I handed her a glass of warm milk and a cookie. "Take this for now honey. Then once the soup's done, you can be first to try some. Yeah?"

"Mhmm. Okay."

I could hear sawing at the side of the house. Sammy Rae. "Shall we go find Daddy?"

I put on my heavy jacket. The wind was raw and buffeted the tarpaper I'd stuck over the windows to keep out the chill. There was always hot coffee on the hob, and I poured him a cup, guessing he'd welcome some warmth.

"You knows how to bring a smile to a man's face, Miss Bertha Swan."

I couldn't stop myself acting like a foolish schoolgirl when I was anywhere near him, despite the fact that he had no intentions of cheating on his so-called wife. It was the simple fact that I was close enough to touch his lips. Lips I'd already kissed once. Close enough to catch the scent of sweat on his work-shirt, and to register the secret smile and slightest dip of the head he always tendered my way in thanks for the least show of kindness.

For all my amorous exploits, I'd yet to capture the imagination of any man as worldly wise as Sammy Rae. He'd worked the stock yards at St Louis and dug coal with his bare hands from the abandoned mine at Coal Glen in order to survive. He'd also spent time in prison for breaking the jaw of an US marine in some bar in Oklahoma City. I was just some hick farmer's daughter with a wide beam and a tight mouth.

Deep down, most of the men I'd bedded were as unadventurous as me. They'd lived here all their sad lives and done nothing more daring than fire buckshot at road signs or drop their breeches outside church. The strangers passing through, whose names I'd long forgotten, were mere tumbleweed that helped scratch an itch. But this flesh and blood man with a history and an attitude to match was within whistling distance every single night I lay alone in my bed and thought my thoughts.

I don't believe Marlene suspected anything. She had somehow managed to dig her claws into him despite the encumbrance of a fatherless child at her breast. It seemed they had a perfectly acceptable domestic arrangement. Whatever affection they felt for each other was supposedly rationed to the hours they spent together in private. There's no doubt Sammy Rae worshipped the daughter, but on the surface, at least, he treated the mother with the same lack of concern one might pay a worn-down broom. Or in Marlene's case a rusted scythe that had lost its edge. She was functional, but it was difficult to feel any emotion towards her.

That was my excuse for relentlessly pursuing her man.

Early summer stretched like a tarpaulin over the river - its weight keeping the bugs drowsy and making my skin crawl with heat. I'd been chopping out weeds all day and smelt as ripe as a dead dog left to moulder at the roadside. Donna Mae was kicking about in the dust with her ma's chickens and she came and watched as I filled the pail at our pump.

"Hey there, honey."

"Watchu gonna do with that, Aunt Bertha?"

I'd got her to call me 'Aunt'. 'Miss Hardy' made me feel like some dried up old schoolmarm. I hadn't long turned twenty-two, yet sometimes I could sense the lonesome years that lay ahead closing in around me. Especially during those nights when I sat with a book and watched the flicker of the kerosene lamp behind the window across the yard. Or stirring in the dark and hearing nothing but the wind in the eaves and knowing there was no one out there who cared whether I woke in the morning or not.

"I'm plannin' on sluicin' away the dirt. Make myself smell sweet as you."

I hauled close on fifteen bucketfuls into the dog trot passage between the bedroom and my living quarters, filling the tin tub almost to the brim. Then I grabbed a bar of Ivory soap, stripped off and climbed into the water.

I could hear Donna Mae chattering to herself at the end of the porch, poking her head around the corner once in a while to catch a glimpse of me then laughing as I poked a finger in her direction.

"Hey, missy. You keep them peepers pointin' the other way."

It was one of the few pleasures I looked forward to in the summer: washing away the dust and sweat and cooling off when all the chores were done. I reached down for the jug so I could pour some water over my hair. That's the part of me that always gets to smell the worst after a day labouring under the Mississippi sun.

The air was motionless, yet I swear I could smell his skin on some imperceptible breeze. The big bad wolf I longed for had come calling. That was surely the same oil he sometimes combed into his hair. And the Luckies he'd always smoke in the doorway late at night. If I watched carefully, I'd get to see the red tip hang by his side before he lifted it to his mouth and sucked in the smoke.

His voice came closer. "You hiding from me?"

"No, I'm right here, Poppa."

I put a hand either side of the tub and hoisted myself to my feet. The water ran down my body in frothing cascades. I reached down for the jug and rinsed off my breasts and stomach and shoulders and back. Turning all the time. Listening for a step on the porch that never came.

"Was that little show for my benefit?" Sammy Rae said.

I'd wandered down to the river bank once the fireflies had replaced the skeeters. The heat of the day had finally seeped into the soil, and the temperature was more tolerable despite the scent of baking dust everywhere.

Baking dust and the hint of burning tobacco.

"Were you watching me all along?"

"I was fetching Donna Mae in for her supper. Why would I be watching you, Miss Bertha Swan Hardy? You think you got something I ain't never seen before?"

I let my gaze drop to my boots. "How's a young woman meant to answer that?"

"Well take it from me. There ain't no way without embarrassing yourself further."

I could feel something like a live gopher frog clawing at the back of my throat, struggling to climb out. "So. . . d'you not approve of what you saw?"

He nodded and seemed to take the measure of me with his eyes. "Maybe I do."

"Only maybe?"

- 5 -

1948

Three weeks later, the boy returned for his summer stay and my affair with Sammy Rae Cobham, if that's what it amounted to, appeared to be over. Yet I swear Truman knew there had been something going on. As if he could pick out the smell of a stranger's body cooling off on the unwashed sheets. Smell my heat whenever I thought of a man in my bed under my own roof, his hips driving against the core of me, whispering my name with his woman less than thirty yards away darning his shirt collar or rinsing the dirty supper dishes.

Of course, there was a scene once Truman found someone inside his precious shack. "What are they doing here?"

"Now, Truman. Ain't you got no manners? We got ourselves some neighbours."

The boy ventured closer and stared as Sammy Rae lit a cigarette then tilted his hat. "You planning on staying here all summer?"

"That's right, if it's okay with your aunt. You got yourself a problem with that?"

Truman retreated behind me as I tousled his hair. "He's not used to having anyone else here. That's all. There's been just the two of us for the last two summers."

Then Donna Mae skipped into the yard, and as soon as their eyes met she seemed to freeze in mid-step.

"And what's that?"

"Truman!"

Sammy Rae laughed until he was almost choking. "Ain't they got little girls where you come from?"

That seemed to break the spell. The children wandered off together towards the creek and Sammy Rae tipped me a wink.

"So that's how his father brings him up? To be distrustful?"

"It's his Memphis ways," I ventured. "Give him a couple of weeks of Mississippi air and he'll be fine."

My sow farrowed early in July. Sammy Rae had told me all sorts of lurid tales: of mothers reabsorbing their own litters or dying a painful death due to bad blood. But when he saw them for the first time - eleven new mouths eager to feed - he reckoned I'd done well enough for a first-timer. It would only take four or five weeks to wean them then they could be fed on kitchen scraps. Along with the supplement Davey Moon stocked, they would be fattened up in time for fall.

This was the task Truman took upon himself - feeding the

piglets and making sure they all got to gain weight. As far as Donna Mae was concerned, the job was too much for one boy to manage alone. Besides, she had eleven new babies to cosset and cuddle. She even took to giving each of them names until Truman pointed out that she couldn't tell them apart.

"What you planning on doing with them when they get too big for the pen?" he asked one evening.

"Well, Truman. They're only here to serve one purpose. When they get to be a certain size, I guess I'll have to sell them. Mr Moon will come collect them and take them to market, and then they'll most likely be slaughtered and made into ham and bacon and pork belly."

I'd expected him to reject the notion, but the thought didn't seem to bother him. Quite the opposite. He couldn't wait to go outside and explain all this to Donna Mae the next day - sneering at her despair.

She cursed him until her face was purple with rage then ran in to Marlene and we never once saw a sign of her for the rest of the day. Not until the following morning when she must have heard Truman hitting the sides of his two pails with a stick to get his charges to gather round for their feed.

"You finished yo' tantrums now, young lady?"

"What's that to you, city boy?"

I thought she'd come out to help, but instead she must have slipped through the fence and unlatched the high gate at the back of their paddock.

The piglets were happy enough chasing Truman around

the yard for their breakfast, but the sow took the opportunity to escape and by the time we noticed the gate was open she was long gone.

For the next four hours we wandered up and down Roebuck Road in search of my pig. We must have covered every acre between my yard and Hooper's Crossing, but there was no sign of her. Donna Mae had been given a whipping by her ma and told not to set foot back inside that house until Big Bertha was found. That's the name they'd given the sow without me knowing it.

Truman came with us, of course, hollering every few yards and waving his stick like some Civil War general fixin' to go into battle. But our efforts came to nothing. By the time we got home, we were tired and dirty and ready to curse whoever crossed our path.

"You need a proper scrub down, the pair of you. You got more dirt stickin' to you than my grandpappy's old plough."

They were both covered in dust and streaks of mud, as if they'd been rolling in the pig pen.

I dragged the tub onto the front porch, drew enough water to half fill it, and ordered them to get undressed. It was likely Donna Mae had caught a glimpse or two of the local boys marking their territory like wild dogs along the turnpike. But she still gawked at Truman before pulling off her drawers. As curious about what he had growing down there as he was about what she had lacking.

"Quit staring, you two, and get in this tub."

Once they were covered in lather and splashing about together, they got over the novelty. I helped rinse them down then towelled them dry: the pair writhing like landed fish as I rubbed their skins until they almost gleamed.

"Now go get decent, Truman, while I see that Donna Mae gets home."

I wrapped the girl inside the damp towel and carried her into the shack. But as soon as Marlene caught sight of her daughter, I could see her anger brewing once more. I told her there was no need to fret. The girl had done her best to help us find the sow - we'd got her cleaned up and I'd see to the laundry.

"Don't go hard on her. She can come round for supper with Truman once she gets dressed."

But Marlene had no room in her heart for joy or compassion. Some reckoned she was born just so she could get buried. "Not tonight, thank you Miss Hardy. The girl don't deserve your charity."

"It ain't charity. And she's just a child. She didn't mean no harm by what she done, I'm sure."

"She wilful. Just like her pappy, God rest his soul."

The animation seemed to drain from the child's face, scolded into silence by her own mother's lack of compassion.

"Don't you fret, Donna Mae. I'm sure big, fat, old Bertha will come squealing home for her tea once she gets hungry."

But it was another twenty-four hours before my sow returned. We heard the commotion from inside the house. Truman had been busy cutting up pictures from old newspapers for a scrap book he was compiling.

Two boys herded her into the yard. The younger Macarthy boy from the Roebuck Lake side of the tracks, and Gospel Fry. I'd known Gospel's mother from the time she used to wash dishes at the diner.

"Dis your sow, Miss Hardy?"

"Why, bless you, Gospel. And you too honey. I thought we'd lost her for good."

"She was sleeping in Pa's barn."

Then, without warning, Truman raced into the yard, my straight-edged spade raised above his head as if fighting off an imaginary assailant. "You, boy! You get off our property right now. You listenin'? We don't want no nigger boys round here. Now scoot!"

This is when it began.

Ode to Mint Drago

- 1 -

1939 - 1941

How it began.

I was raised in the city, so it's no wonder things turned sour between me and Pike long before our baby boy arrived. Mint's truck broke down for good a mile short of Byhalia, and I'd already lost the appetite for life on the road. Pike kept his wallet closed tight and I figured out Mint's money wouldn't last for ever. But no amount of that farm boy's ambition or gospelling was going to provide a roof over our heads anytime soon so it was up to me to take charge until we got settled.

To his credit, Pike got taken on by a local cotton mill that was hiring for the summer and I found a two bedroom apartment that we were forced to share with three other families. But the cramped conditions didn't suit Pike for long. He took to playing cards at night, losing money more times than bringing home any winnings. Many a night I lay awake waiting for his return while listening to our neighbours' drunken fights and domestic arguments. I began to wish I'd never left Greenwood and I made my feelings clear to Pike more than once.

Finally, when I let on how we were down to our last forty bucks, it got too much for the both of us. I packed a case while Pike collected his last paycheck and we jumped a freight car running north through Olive Branch. Pike thought it was romantic. After three days touting for work from one aircraft hangar to the next along Lamar Avenue, we begged another ride as far as Victor-Kerr in the cab of a flatbed stock truck, and ended up inside a diner some place along South Parkway with less than thirty bucks between us. My waters broke shortly after midnight and Truman Hardy was born on the floor of the restroom. To Pike's eternal shame, his son first drew breath on Tennessee soil. But that didn't stop him writing home to tell his ma and pa different.

When I first saw Truman laid out on those tiles, slick with my life's blood, he looked no bigger than a freshly plucked yard bird. I couldn't believe something so small could draw breath and scream so loud; that something so small could be the death of me.

I clung on to Pike while one of the waitresses cleaned me up and he muttered prayers of gratitude. I needed him to hold me a while - to tell me he loved me and how I'd done good. But instead he picked up the child and carried him out into the dining area. I could hear him telling anyone who'd listen that Truman was nothing short of a miracle. He was duty-bound to shepherd the boy along the path of righteousness, the same way Abraham had raised Isaac.

"We got more churches in Shelby County than we know what to do with," someone called out. "So you're safe here in the Good Lord's hands." But the Good Lord's hands proved to be less than reliable. I bled for three hours until those in attendance decided I might not die after all. Maybe that's the reason one of the waitresses finally took pity on us. She put us up in her apartment until I was strong enough to walk again. Pike had heard the assembly plant at Riverside was hiring mechanics and by then it had become clear he'd have been happier if I'd died in childbirth.

Truman claimed my entire life now and I swear Pike felt I'd somehow cheated him. Somehow gone back on an unspoken promise made when we left Greenwood. Maybe that's what lay at the root of his hateful ways. For all his Christian chest thumping, Pike's determination to rise above the flood of poverty at all costs exposed the canker in his soul. "We're not meant to live here with this heathen mob. It's in the Good Book."

I'd seen my share of deprivation in Chicago, and our shack in the neighbourhood Hooverville complete with cardboard flooring and sheet metal door was no poorer than most. So I took him to mean those worse off than us; the scabby children and the winos who lingered in the alleyways, and the flighty women that sometimes hung around the drinking dens close to the waterfront. There were so many lost souls without a roof over their heads, forced to hunker down in this clapboard city where every window leaked and every door let in the wind-laden dust. But I felt closer to them than to anyone else in a long time. I'd become just as accustomed to the layers of smoke that turned the sunsets red as fire and the gutters running with fresh water clean enough to rinse your face in one day and clogged with human sewage the next.

Everywhere, I came across beggars with creased faces; their hunched bodies clothed in ragged shifts and moth-eaten pants that did little to cover their filth. I heard voices, hoarse with hunger and fatigue and hopelessness. Begging for scraps. A crust. A dime. A barbed curse and a snarl of warning if I drew too close with empty hands. Barking at shadows like feral dogs. I saw men as old as Mint sucking at bottles held inside paper bags as if they contained their mothers' milk. The sour smell of unwashed flesh and rain-sodden clothing hung like a veil over them all. Other eyes, palsied with age, barely acknowledged my passing. Life seemed to have been scraped from their faces like a supper dish hastily wiped over by a dirty wash cloth.

The cry of hawkers and the hustle bustle of daily life became music inside my head, and I had no reason to seek escape. I'd made up my mind to count each day a blessing. I'd learned long ago how to bite down on despair and couldn't imagine what might make some poor souls throw themselves off the Harahan Bridge. But Pike saw our predicament as something altogether different. "I'll get us out of this fix, Angel," he'd say. So many times he repeated the same words. Soon, the least setback had him cursing our luck, and slowly it pulled us apart.

There came times, mostly in the early hours, when the shack lay quiet apart from the splutter of the lantern. I'd recall my journey south in Mint's old truck. The dance of light on the mottled ceiling brought back memories of the rippling canvas we slept under. The rattle of wind through the chassis. The tick of insects outside in the desert night. My body curling against Mint's after we made love and he began to scatter promises as rash as any campaigning politician's. Promises I'd taken as gospel truth.

He'd told me he would shower me in jewels and gold dust and smother me in fine silk dresses one day. Mint Drago the king of Chicago and me, his princess daughter.

"My snow white princess." Those words clung to me like a curse. A curse brought back to life the day I got my hands on some pumpernickel. Two cents worth. Pike took one look at it and swept his plate to one side. "You tryin' to poison me now, woman?"

I thought maybe he was sick.

"You tellin' me there ain't a single slice of decent white bread out there?"

For the flash of a second, I was reminded of Ma and the day she went out in search of a loaf. I couldn't check the tears as I tried to explain. "I got it off of the German bake shop up near Central Station." I'd spent the best part of two hours shopping for food. Searching for bruised fruit and shrivelled-up greens and whatever else we were forced to make do with until next pay day.

"There ain't no German I know who'd ever stomach this," he said. "I've studied history. Enough to tell you've been tricked."

"Tricked?" I laughed at the absurdity of what he was saying. But then Pike explained how it must have been some Jewish baker who had sold it me, even though I knew different. "I didn't bring us all the way up here to have you associatin' with kikes and Polacks and coons. I've got a reputation to maintain."

His reputation in these parts meant no more than his

habit of putting oil on his hair, as far as I could see.

"I associated with a lot worse in Chicago," I said.

But Pike had already erased my shameful past long before we crossed the state line into Tennessee. "This ain't Chicago. The devil might rule the roost up there with the gypsies and faggots and nigger landlords. But it was never God's intention we follow that city's depraved ways."

I'd had more than enough Bibling from Mint. "There's nothing I recall in the scriptures about how folks are meant to live in Memphis let alone any place else."

He gripped my wrist and I had to fight back the urge to pull free. "You don't contradict the word of the Lord. And you don't contradict me, woman. You never contradict me while you're under this roof."

I nodded, dumb with fear.

"You heard all about the Garden of Eden? It's writ there in Genesis."

"Yeah," I whispered.

His mouth inches away from my face as he explained. "We're destined to rise above the animals. But this damn place. Can't you smell the sin out there? Even the way they talk ain't civilised. It ain't dignified. I'd set fire to this whole shanty town if I had my way."

"Burn your own neighbours out of their homes?" I knew how he'd answer. He'd bragged about doing that often enough long before we left Mississippi.

"Damn right," he sneered. "I already gone and done my share of burning, and I'll do it again if I have to."

1941

When the auto plant announced there were going to be lay-offs, Pike suddenly found himself a new mission in life, or so I thought. We moved into a three-room apartment on Pigeon Roost Road, close enough to Lamar Avenue and the freight line for smuts of soot to blacken the drapes and spot the washing on my line, but a step up from Hooverville. It suited me fine, and Pike continued to promise it wouldn't always be this way. Things would steadily get better. But the gloss on our relationship had already faded.

There was barely room for the two of us to sit around the dining table, let alone hold an union meeting. Yet some nights, there'd be a dozen or more men crammed inside the kitchen. Pike had taken to holding get-togethers with his co conspirators: other men who'd already been laid off and claimed it was on account of black workers taking their jobs for lower pay. The air would hang grey with cigarette smoke long after they left, and I spent many a morning swabbing tobacco juice from the floor.

That's how I ended up walking the streets with the child in

my arms, night after night, until the cars were gone and I knew the coast was clear. I'd keep Truman pressed tight to my breast and hum him to sleep. A song Ma had sung to me one time, when I had a fever maybe. I forget.

Pike claimed it was union business - nothing more. But I didn't trust the smug looks on some of the faces that turned up. Or their fancy cars and city suits. They'd have looked as out of place on the assembly line as I'd have inside the Queen of England's bed chamber.

Then out of the blue, Pike announced he'd gotten himself a position with an export firm, arranging shipments of cotton bales and tobacco from the fields to the big stores out east. I don't know how a boy his age found the wherewithal for wheelin' and dealin', given that he had no more a head for figures than I had for fancy French talk. But Pike had a way with words when it came to selling himself.

His ability to get noticed by 'people in the know', as he called them, helped pay our way into a rented apartment and allowed him to wear a clean shirt every day along with a fancy seersucker suit and a broad-brimmed hat. I know if his sister, Bertha, saw him dressed that way, she'd have bust her breeches laughing.

Pike had always been a vain man. Vain enough to believe no woman would turn her back on him and walk out. But I came round to entertaining thoughts that maybe deep down Pike didn't trust me anymore. Especially on those balmy nights when I came in later than usual and caught the look in his eye. One particular time comes to mind. The air heavy and humid and Truman more fretful than usual. It had taken me the best part of an hour to settle him down before heading back for home.

"You meet anyone while you were out walkin' with the child?"

"No. Why you askin'?"

"Just the look on your face, that's all. Like you got some fancy man out there whose payin' you more attention than what's decent and natural."

"There ain't nobody. Now let's go to bed."

He grunted, as if he had no fight left in him. I could smell the liquor on his breath and I led the way into the bedroom.

"So take off your shoes and let me look at you, honey."

I kicked off my house shoes then lit the candle on the nightstand and turned to face him. I was tired and in no mood for his drunken talk. "So go ahead and look. But I'm fixin' on calling it a day and getting me some shut-eye."

"I said I want to look at you, so take off your damn clothes."

"But Pike. . ."

He pushed me onto the bed and began to unfasten the ribbon at my throat. Then I felt his fingers take hold of the hem of my dress and tug it up towards my waist.

"I'm too tired for all this tonight, Pike."

"Off."

I swallowed a knot of dread as he leant over me until our faces were touching. But then he calmed some and allowed me to work the dress up over my head. Then the shift. "That do you?"

He shook his head, more in wonder than denial, and one

finger slipped under the strap of my brassiere. "Now take this off."

I sat up and unclasped the fastening at the back then gently released my breasts before lying back down. Then I felt him tug at one leg of my bloomers.

"And this."

I began to fight for each breath as my chest tightened and my skin grew clammy. Slowly I raised my buttocks and slid my underwear down to my knees. He helped me as it got snagged on one of my feet. Then I lay back and waited for him to climb on top. But instead he reached for the candle on the nightstand and sat himself at the bottom of the bed, worming his way between my legs.

"I always knew you'd been sent for me."

"Right." I'd heard it all before.

The shadow of his arm moved closer as he played the light of the candle over my thighs. "I ain't looked at you properly since God knows when, woman. Ain't realised how blessed I am."

I held my breath, desperate for it to be over, yet dreading his touch. But Pike was in no hurry tonight. I could feel his fingers tracing the skin from my knees to my ankles, and he began to whisper as if there was someone else in the room listening to our conversation. "I knew Mint weren't your pa, honey. I seen through his lies right from the start."

"Mhmm. I already told you that, didn't I?"

"I didn't need no telling. I could see you ain't got his colouring for one thing."

I flinched as his hand moved up towards my belly. "And when I saw all this and you told me I was the first one, sweet Jesus."

That was a lie. I'd told him often enough how there'd only been one virgin in the back of the truck that night. The way he'd fired his shot so quick.

A blob of molten wax dropped onto my thigh and he wiped it away. Then his fingers began to knead the flesh above my knee. The touch of his fingernails sent a shudder through my innards. "It was as if you'd been sent as a reward for my carrying out God's work."

"You call that God's work? Humpin' in the back of a truck?" I couldn't help myself. I laughed and he pulled his hand away and I felt him climb onto the bed until his body was poised over mine.

"I don't mean the tom-cattin' and you know that well enough. I mean the other business we got up to."

The number of times he'd left me in the back of Mint's truck in his pappy's yard with barely a word of affection. Buttoned up his breeches and climbed out into the dark. His sister asked me one time whether Pike was spending all night in my company and I nodded. "Some nights he stays over, but there ain't nothin' to it."

Bertha said no more on the matter. She was old enough to realise different. But she didn't know the whole story either. Pike had other matters to occupy the dead hours between midnight and cock's crow, and none of us discovered the truth 'til the Friday morning before we left.

On the surface, Pike was just another teenaged white boy, seething with misplaced self-righteousness. But his true colours blossomed the first time he accompanied Chester Macarthy on one of his jaunts. That had been January 1936. They'd chased down a coloured boy who'd been seen acting suspicious outside a town house in Greenwood.

"The house belonged to a white lady and he'd been caught peepin' through her blinds," Pike told me. "He didn't confess to it until we beat the truth out of him. But once he done that, he left us no option."

Three of them had hog-tied the boy before throwing him in the back of Soggy Carmichael's old Packard. They'd taken him to an abandoned lumber drying shed and strung him up to one of the timber cross beams.

"I watched that boy dance on the end of a rope and I knew justice had been served."

Months before Mint and I turned up at his pa's property, Pike had been out most nights looking for any excuse to cause trouble. He confessed there were times when he lost control. A sharecropper's cabin got burned to the ground out of pure devilment, and two boys who'd done nobody any harm were whipped senseless the same week we arrived just for failing to tip their caps when passing Pike in Greenwood's main street. A week later, a young black teacher woman was driven out of Webb late at night and left to find her own way home. They'd stripped her naked and painted her all over in lime-wash.

In total, Pike owned up to playing a part in seven killings - including two drownings and one accidental death where a man threw hisself off a railroad bridge rather than end up getting caught.

"I lost count, but there must have been more than twenty

burnings," he told me, as if treasuring the memory. "It was more than a game, if you must know. It had become a sacred mission to clean up our neighbourhood. It wasn't my fault some people took more persuading to leave than others."

Then early one February morning, a farmer caught Pike and Chester returning home, high on bravado with their shirts torn and blood-spattered and their sleeves blackened up to the elbows with wood tar.

When challenged, they'd said, "Been dealin' with vermin. That's all."

But later that same morning, a minister was discovered tarred and feathered and tied to a makeshift cross outside a small church in Grenada - a coloured minister who refused to identify his attackers. By lunchtime, Pike's pa had got wind of the situation and figured out what had been going on all along.

"It's you who saved me, Angel Drago. D'you know that?" He straddled me and I felt his fingers stroke my breasts. "Pa already had his suspicions when he heard I was spending time in the company of Chester. So as soon as he heard about that minister, he swore I was to be packed off to Louisiana the next day. The thought of losing you. . ."

He kissed me on the lips - no more an admission of love than a punch to the face. His words and the hard liquor on his breath left a bitter after-taste. Then he sat up again and ran his fingers down towards my belly. "Just look at this. I ain't ever seen skin so clean white. So pure. Every inch of you, every mortal inch."

He slid down the bed until he was laid between my legs

once more and I felt him begin to spread me open. "I could never plant my seed in tainted ground, honey. You know that, don't you?"

I managed to control the tide of acid rising inside my guts a while longer. It swilled like a whirlpool, but I held it down until Pike was done. Then he sprawled next to me, spent as a match, and I watched the candle flame dance shadows on the bedroom wall until I heard his breath still. Somewhere a cat yawled. The room shook as the clatter of a freight train grew louder; slowing down with a click-clack of wheels as it crossed the points. I pulled myself upright and reached for my shift pooled on the floor next to the bed. I'd have given anything for a tub of Miss Lily's hot water and her scented soap to scrub away the touch of Pike's fingers and the slime of his passion. But I knew I could never wash away the taint of those words he'd mouthed in pretence of love.

I took the candle into the bathroom and squatted in the dark. Then I wept. I knew if Pike heard me he'd pay me no heed. My sobbing came unrestrained enough to scald my throat. I rinsed my face in the kitchen sink and crept back into the bedroom. It stank of him.

I realised that as long as I stayed here, every room would carry the stench of Pike's hateful intolerance. Truman could never thrive under the same roof as a man who harboured such hatred in his heart. Pike would kill me easy as slap down a coloured man for looking him in the eye if he suspected my loathing for him ran so deep. Deep enough to steal his son and make my own way in a strange city.

- 3 -

1941

I chose a day when I knew Pike would be out of town 'til late. He'd mentioned a trip to Bartlett with some advertising literature. An associate of his, Mortimer K Sweeney, owned a white convertible that Pike sometimes got to drive for business purposes. Mort was a fashion plate with an eye for the ladies. Some said he kept a mistress out of town, a mulatto, but Pike never once let that rumour tarnish his admiration for the man.

Pike got himself a pair of stitched leather gloves the same as Mortimer's and wore them whenever he was required to drive any great distance. That's how I knew he'd not be home before dark. "What you got planned today, honey?"

I smoothed the collar of his coat and straightened his scarf. Octobers in Memphis were turning out to be unseasonably cold, otherwise I'd have taken Truman across town to feed the ducks at one of the parks.

As soon as I mentioned my reservations, I could tell from the look on Pike's face he detested the mere thought of weakness in his son. "You coddle the boy too much."

I might have been Mint's lucky charm, but deep down I knew Pike felt cheated by what fate had dealt him. I'd not fulfilled the role he'd mapped out for me. With his dark hair and brown eyes, Truman was a long way from being a purebred albino.

The old walnut-cased clock on the mantelpiece kept good time. But the ticking seemed to have slowed down as the shadows moved across the linoleum floor of the scullery. I watched the minute finger skitter around the dial. Twenty before three. Fifteen before three. My mind was made up. I'd not set foot outside the house the entire day. The thought of having to unlock the door and step back inside when all I wanted to do was to run kept me trapped inside our apartment until the appointed time.

I waited for the smaller hand to pass the hour, anxious in case Pike's plans suddenly altered and he arrived home for his dinner. I'd even prepared his favourite meal, eggs and fried ham, so he'd see they were ready for heating up as soon as he walked in the door and not fret too much if I wasn't home to greet him. Then finally at ten minutes past three I picked up Truman and we walked out.

I carried a small shoulder bag that contained a few essentials for the two of us. Truman had spent most of the afternoon asleep on our double bed and I hadn't the heart to wake him. I buckled my street shoes up to my shins, put on an extra apron, even though there was no need, and hoisted him onto my shoulder. I'd already put on a tight, red cap with most of my hair pulled up and pushed inside it.

Imagining the meal laid out in the cold frying pan like a parting gift, I closed the scullery door and I touched my fingers against the doorframe one final time.

- 4 -

1941 - 1942

"What you planning on doing next, honey?"

I didn't have the faintest idea. I'd made friends with Myrtle Buchanan some six months earlier. When we first met, she'd been scrubbing steps outside one of the rooming houses close to the Dummy Line where streetcars ran down Cooper as far the Parkway. Myrtle was a plain looking girl with rounded shoulders and a lazy eye, but we'd each seen another kindred spirit. Another woman looking to survive without a man in her life.

Myrtle had her own troubles where men were concerned, but recently she'd gotten herself a position working afternoons at a drapery store on Madison and was looking for someone to share the rent on her new apartment close to the station.

"I'm gonna have to get together a heap of money before I can leave Memphis," I said. "Then I guess I'll head north - the further from Pike the better."

"Stay as long as you want, honey."

"Much appreciated. But I gotta do something about my hair."

So Myrtle took out her shears, and when Truman saw how I'd shorn it short as a man's, he near broke his little heart. I barely recognised myself in the mirror.

"It's Mama." I soothed him as best I could but he kept staring at my deception all the same. My disguise would maybe attract more attention out on the street than it was meant to. I knew Pike was sure to be on our trail before too long, and the thought of what might happen if he found me tied my stomach in knots each time I stepped outside Myrtle's door.

She told me I still looked as white as a china doll. "You need to put some blusher on your cheeks. And there ain't no way to cover up your hair colouring unless you intend going the whole hog and start wearing a hat like a man."

My thoughts switched to Momma and the way she used to darken her complexion. Pa's Cherokee bride. "What if I got a long jacket with a hood to cover my head?"

"That would work. I can get you good discount."

But the truth was, I had less than ten bucks to my name. I laughed as I recalled asking Pike for a dress allowance one time. The look on his face had been enough to teach me my place. "Don't I buy you perfume to smell nice?"

He'd bought me a 'Country Club' make-up set the previous Christmas that wouldn't have looked out of place in a Chinese whore house.

"Yeah, but my clothes are near enough worn to tatters."

"The finest perfume is all I need any woman of mine to

wear. Besides, Ma used to see to all our needs by making and mending. If that's good enough for Ma Hardy, it's good enough for you."

In the end, Myrtle dug out an old coat she'd taken to wearing in bed when the heating cut out. She also handed me a woolly hat and a pair of wide-legged breeches she'd once bought on a whim. "You've got the figure for new fashion," she said. "But these trousers make me look like a panhandler."

It was fine by me. I could scout the streets like some ragamuffin, looking for work, while all the time keeping my eyes peeled for Pike. Within a fortnight I'd gotten myself a position - night shift work in a factory carroting felt. It paid a buck fifty a week and was a sure means of grinding a body down if you were planning on spending any length of time there. But this life was only temporary, as far as I was concerned.

Once Truman and I reached Chicago, things would be different. I knew I didn't have the temperament or the smarts to work behind a bar. Pike told me often enough I was a plain Jane with the courage of a mouse, and that role served me well when it suited. But I aimed to prove him wrong on every account once I left Memphis.

Myrtle agreed to watch over Truman on the five nights a week I spent at work. Like a slave cut free from his chains, I struggled to get used to my new-found independence. Three months, fingers worn raw and a stoop to my back. Three months looking over my shoulder, expecting to feel Pike's claws dig into my throat at any moment. Demanding his son. Demanding more than I was prepared to give in exchange for a roof over our heads.

Then, one morning mid-January, I ran into a man loitering outside Myrtle's apartment. He seemed well-dressed. A soft, black hat square on his head, a cane, and one of them eye-glasses on a chain attached to his lapel. He stepped aside to let me in, and as I slid the key into the lock he offered me a crisp new dollar note to feel my snatch.

That was the kind of language he used, and my insides heaved as I dashed inside and slammed the door closed. His voice sounded no different from those I'd heard calling out from between Mama's sheets. His hungry smile exactly the same as those I'd studied in the mirror at the end of my bed once they'd spent their passion in my momma's arms.

By the end of the month, I was taking home six bucks fifty a week. He'd be waiting for me most mornings at the end of my shift, but I never once let him inside the apartment. We conducted our business in one of the alleyways that ran parallel to the main street. I'd freeze as soon as I heard his voice. But I still let him tug down my trousers and probe his fingers between my legs before we even got around to wishing each other a good day. Then he'd mount me from behind, and we'd make out like a pair of dogs in heat while all the while he cursed me and used Bible words I remembered hearing in those woods out beyond Broken Corner.

But he never once hurt me. And there were times when I entertained the thought of asking him to take me and Truman away with him. Then one morning he gave me a rose. I felt so sickened afterwards that I trampled it into the cobbles. Tears that I couldn't begin to explain coursed down my cheeks. Momma had taught me that no man was meant to be this gracious. And when I got inside the apartment, I was tempted to tell Myrtle everything, even though many a time she must have guessed what I'd been up to from the high colour in my cheeks and the muddy imprints of the cobbles on the knees of my pants.

By the time the hackberry trees were in bud, I had close on fifty bucks saved, sewn up inside one of Truman's soft toys. Bowzer - a threadbare puppy dog with floppy ears and a long, red velvet tongue. The days were getting longer and I knew it was time to think seriously about heading north. Maybe find my way back to the Lavender Garden hotel. I'd already given Myrtle notice that we were fixing to leave before the Easter weekend.

But things came to a head sooner than I anticipated. The Japs had been running riot in the Pacific for the best part of February, and on the morning in question, all I could hear on my walk home from work were the news vendors on every street corner announcing the fall of Singapore. It was a sign. Human nature had somehow become corrupted beyond hope. Evil was destined to triumph over good.

I sensed something was wrong even before I took the key out of the lock and pulled off my shoes. The apartment had a hollowed-out feel about it. The drapes at the front had been left wide open from the night before but the air inside the hallway was stale. There was a lingering smell of fried onions, and the monotonous drip of a tap somewhere close by that no one had bothered to close tight.

Truman generally stirred once I stepped inside our room, but all was silent. The bed empty, though there were signs he'd been sleeping there. The sheets were barely warm but I could still make out the imprint of his head on the pillow. The warm, sugary smell of his skin grew stronger as I knelt to pick up the rumpled sheet from where it lay on the bedroom floor.

Sometimes he'd creep into Myrtle's room during the night, and I'd undress and slip into my own bed. Glad of some momentary peace before she woke and had to fix herself ready for work.

I stripped down to my brassiere and panties and padded bare footed into the kitchen. My throat was parched, and I was hoping there was enough milk left for me to steal a glass. I could hear the early morning honking of traffic as soon as I entered the room. The sash window was pulled half down, and the chopping board had been pushed to one side as if someone had stepped onto it to climb through the broken window.

My heart screamed, yet I didn't make a sound. I dashed back to our room and grabbed something to cover myself. That's when I noticed Truman's dressing gown wasn't where it normally hung on the door next to my robe. They'd taken everything. His tiny pair of brown canvas shoes. The sailor suit Myrtle had got him in the sales. The stuffed puppy dog with my life savings sewn inside it.

I felt my way to Myrtle's bedroom, legs already expecting the apartment to capsize once I confirmed my worst fear.

Her shades were still down, but I could see well enough to make out that the sheets on the bed had been pulled all the way back. Maybe she'd thrown them aside to get more air. Or something had disturbed her sleep. Someone.

Myrtle sat hunched up on the rug between the bed and the wardrobe. Blood darkened the front of her slip, and I thought the worst. But as she raised her head and struggled for breath, I could see she'd survived the beating.

"Where's my boy?" I screeched.

She seemed to uncoil like a broken spring as I helped her to her feet. "Two men came in and took him away. I couldn't do anything."

Pike. Who else could it be?

"One of them said, 'Tell the bitch this ain't over'. He'll be back and you'd better be ready."

"Did he hurt you?"

She shook her head. "Not in that way. And it's no worse than my no-good husband used to dish out whenever he craved more liquor."

They'd come for my boy and I hadn't been there to stop them. Instead I'd been kneeling in an alley less than a block away with a dick in my hand and the taste of sin on my lips.

"This is all my fault."

"No, sugar. It's your man who's to blame and no one else. I never seen such rage."

I began shivering as I tried to figure out what to do next. I'd let my guard drop and somehow Pike had found out where I was staying. Presumably he'd expected to find me at home when he came calling. A couple of weeks later and it might have been a different story.

"I daren't stay here another night," I said.

"But where else you gonna go, honey?"

I had enough in my pocketbook to catch a train north and ride as far as the money would take me. Chicago if I was lucky.

"I've friends in Chicago. It don't matter where. If he comes back, it's best you tell him you don't know my plans."

"Don't worry. I'll not let on."

"I know. But I don't want him to hurt you again if he discovers I've fled town for good."

Myrtle wiped the blood from her mouth. "He ain't got no fight with me."

"Maybe not." But if Pike could kill a poor black boy out of devilment, there was no knowing what he'd do if he thought I'd got the better of him. "I should have it out with him before I leave town. It's not right that there are things unfinished."

"Your home ain't safe any longer, honey, so don't go getting any damn fool ideas. He's got the boy and there's no way you're gonna change that. If you go back to him, you're as good as dead. I say get as far away from here as you can before he comes back looking for you."

The thought of leaving my baby boy in that brute's hands almost tore my heart in two.

"And if it eases your conscience," she said, "leave a note. I can hand it over to him the next time he comes calling. You have to tell him you're out of Truman's life now for good."

I didn't have time to consider the implications. We composed a letter and I pressed it into Myrtle's hand before leaving for Central Station.

But my stubbornness got the better of me once I'd slammed the street door shut. Truman was as much my flesh and blood as Pike's. I took a tram way past the Pinch then walked the mile or so to our old apartment. It looked no different from when I'd walked out almost six months earlier. I could hear the clock on the mantelpiece strike the half hour as someone opened the door.

"Pike at home?"

"Who's askin'?" The young girl looked me up and down. She can't have been more than fourteen years old, and she wore a check shirt and fawn trousers like a tomboy. Then she must have noticed my hair and caught the Chicago twang in my voice. "You must be the boy's ma. The albino Pike keeps cursing."

I nodded. "They inside?"

"Pike's away somewhere the other side of Olive Branch. On business. He's left me looking after the property."

"He took Truman?"

"Why? You plannin' on stealin' him again?"

"That ain't none of your damn business."

She smirked. "I can tell you're not here to climb back inside his bed. But for your information, I already got that covered, sugar. And yeah, he took the boy with him. Though why he takes that shitty-assed cry baby anywhere, God only knows."

"Don't you lay a finger on that boy, you hear me? And you can tell that cocksucker I'm gone for now, but I won't forget the way he mistreated me. He's gonna pay. Make sure you use the same words I just told you. And look out for yourself, if ever he turns mean."

- 5 -

1942

Cabs lined the street when my train arrived at Chicago. But it was after midnight, and within the hour the forecourt of Union Station was empty. I'd been tempted to jump inside one and have the driver take me to a rooming house where I could put down for the remainder of the night. Myrtle had given me a ten dollar bill for emergencies. She called it a forever loan. But I had less than six bucks left in my purse now, and no clear thought in my head how to go about surviving. The chances of finding a friendly face offering me a dish of fried chicken and French fried potatoes were slim.

I could hear pigeons roosting on the high ledges above where I sat, and dark shapes scuttled in the gutter. The bench gradually prodded at the bones of my spine until sleep became impossible. Twice someone walked up to me and asked if I was open for business. But I cursed them the way Mint taught me. Even by Chicago standards, my language could be coarse enough to strip paint whenever my nerves were shredded.

Some time around five o'clock, with a grey light pearling

the sky, a policeman came up to me and ordered me to move on. "Vagrancy's an offence in these parts."

I picked up my shoulder bag and began to shuffle in the direction of the dawn. Maybe something in my demeanour made him follow me. Maybe he was more accustomed to abuse than mute acceptance.

"You waiting here on a train?"

"No. I got in late last night. Too late to make plans."

"It still ain't right for a woman to be sleeping on the streets. How old are you, miss?"

"Nineteen." I could tell from his sneer he thought I was a good deal younger. "I used to know people up near Hammond. I'm gonna head that way now it's getting light."

"You're a long way from Hammond, miss. Is it family you have there waiting for you?"

"No more. No."

"Well, there's a couple of places in the West Loop neighbourhood takes in young single women. The rent's reasonable enough. Or else there are church missions that might offer you a square meal and a blanket for a night."

"I ain't lookin' for charity."

He tipped his cap as I reached the street corner and surveyed the line of gaslights ahead. "I'm only looking out for you. Be careful now, and I pray you find what you're looking for."

A church? A mission? Neither fitted in with what I had in mind. I was hoping I'd somehow find my way back to Miss Lily's. After all, that's where this lie I'd been living began.

But three days later, there was no further need to seek out Miss Lily, or Dinah and her ma.

- 6 -

1942

That first night in the shelter, I barely slept. The unfamiliar smells and sounds kept me awake until the early hours, and once I heard a child wailing for its ma all I could think of was my baby boy. The next day one of the volunteer ladies put me to work in the kitchen - explaining I had to earn my keep if I intended spending another night here. It beat wandering the streets until I found my bearings, but then on the second night I got into a scrap with a foul-mouthed Negro woman who claimed I'd taken her bed roll.

"What's a sorry streak of bacon rind like you doing in this part of town anyway? Your sugar daddy throw you out on the street, did he?" She stank of piss, and her scalp showed in dry, flaking patches through her shorn hair. "If you're plannin' on a new career sucking Chicago dick, let me give you a few tips. 'Cause if I ain't mistaken, you'll end up sucking your fair share before this month's out."

I dragged my bed roll to another corner, but she made a grab for my bag, and that's when I lashed out. She was little more than a bundle of sinew and bone but she was quick as a sewer rat. Her hands clawed at the strap as I ducked and barged my way past her. "Now what you got in there that's so precious?"

"Leave me be."

Someone else close by began to curse and chide. Then a light appeared behind the flimsy curtain separating our sleeping accommodation from the men's. "Quit the catfight. Some of us are tryin' to catch some sleep."

She paid them no heed. She had me cornered now between two rows of reclining bodies, hands reaching for anything they could get a hold of. "Fuckin' spoiled bitch. I can see your fancy silk stockings and shoes under that coat. You don't fool me. Show me what else you got."

"It ain't none of your damn business what I got."

I felt a hand grab the collar of my blouse and someone else kicked out at one of my legs. Then before I knew it, I was flat on my back on the filthy floor.

She was straddling me and I could feel her hands grabbing between my legs. "Maybe you should let us all take a proper look at what you're peddling before they throw you back out on the street. 'Cause I know you're a fucking whore. I can smell it on you. Every inch of you. A filthy, cock-sucking whore."

More voices began to call me names as, one by one, the other women woke up.

"I said cut the noise."

The light came closer and two men waded through the sleeping forms. By the time they pulled us apart, my stockings were torn and my legs were scratched and bloody.

The strap of my bag had been cut clean through by a blade as well and I'd managed to lose the heel from one of my shoes.

- 7 -

1942

I spent the next two days following the tramlines from one part of the city to the next, hoping to find a familiar sight. Charlie's bar maybe, or the footbridge in Harrison Park. Apart from a burger and a bottle of root beer, nothing passed my lips for the next forty-eight hours. But by dusk on my third day in the city I was no nearer reaching Hammond or Miss Lily's. I felt dirty and weary and hungry, and that's the only excuse I have for letting someone take me inside a hotel room. I was past caring.

Both my shoes were gone - left behind in the scuffle as they threw me out into the street. Somehow I'd also managed to misplace my pocketbook. The image of Momma setting off to buy a loaf of bread came to mind again. It seemed life had set out the same pattern in our stars.

Carlo was little more than a kid, but he had the city swagger Pike tried to imitate whenever his big-shot friends came calling. And he wore a fancy suit and a pencil-thin moustache that made him look like he knew his way around a block or two.

The hotel room smelt of mildew and dirty carpet. No worse than the flophouse in Hammond.

I told Carlo as long as he didn't hurt me, he could do whatever he wanted with me. I needed money. I needed shoes on my feet and something to eat and maybe an hour to freshen up. I rinsed out the only remaining set of underwear I possessed and hung it to dry while I waited for the water in the hand basin to get warm. He'd promised to go get us a sandwich and a half pint of liquor, and told me to make sure I was cleaned up before he returned. He locked the bedroom door behind him, but I thought nothing of it. The bed sheets were fresh and untorn, and even though the pillows were as flat and hard as kerbstones I counted my blessings.

I was already in bed when I heard the key in the lock again. "You decent? 'Cause you better hadn't be."

I turned onto my side and watched as Carlo unlaced his shoes. "You found any drinking glasses, sugar?"

"Don't see any."

He threw me a pack of pastrami on rye, then handed me the unopened bottle, unhitched his braces and began to unbutton his shirt. "In that case, ladies first."

The metal cap gave a snap as I untwisted it then took a mouthful and near enough choked as soon as the raw spirit scraped the back of my throat.

"Hold on, sugar. That's not cough medicine you're slugging back."

I'd never once been tempted to sample Mint's bourbon.

The smell had been sour enough.

"If we can find a glass somewhere you should add some water. Takes away the taste of kerosene."

"That's okay. I've had all I want."

"Suit yourself, honey."

By the time I finished my sandwich and got back under the sheets he was down to his skivvies. He slipped in alongside me and I felt his cold skin press against my body. "You ain't gonna mind if I have myself another little drink before we get down to business are you?"

Once he'd had his fun, I managed to fall asleep for the first time since climbing off that train. The thought of what we'd done, what I'd let him do, of no concern in the twilight world between guilt and desperation. I'd arrived in the city with precious little, and now I had nothing left, not even my pride.

Traffic sounds carried up from the street long before I heard him get up and use the hand basin. A trickle of water then the full force of the faucet. "Beats pissing out of the window."

I could still smell him on every part of me. But it felt good.

"There's no need for you to leave just yet, sugar," he said. "This room's paid for 'til ten. But after that they're gonna throw you out whether you're dressed or not." He sat on the bed to put on his shoes. That's when I noticed the holster.

"I've left a little something for you on the bedside table." I could see a five dollar bill and some loose change.

"What line of business did you say you were in?" I said.

"I wheel and I deal, sugar. Same as you, I guess." Echoes of Pike's short-term business plan.

He placed his hand on my bare shoulder and leant forwards for a brief kiss. "So are we gonna meet up later, or you got someone keeping your book?"

I didn't know what he meant, but I could figure out what he thought I was. Not so far from the truth.

"I got no one."

"So why don't we continue this later? There's a bar two blocks down from here. The Millhouse. I'm usually in there between seven and eight."

"Maybe."

By then he must have noticed the state of my stockings. "Tell me your shoe size and I can get you a little something on commission."

I pulled the blankets tighter around my shoulder and coiled inside the heat of the new morning as he pulled the door to and went off into the day. Then I wept until I had no tears left.

- 8 -

1942

The Millhouse was no different from any of the other bars I'd been in all those times I'd accompanied Mint on his travels. It could have been Charlie's, the place we first met, except for the layout of the tables and the overpowering smell of stale cigar smoke.

I sat on my own in a corner booth beneath one of the stained-glass windows featuring French dancing girls waving their skirts in the air revealing frilly bloomers and high-heeled boots. Red and gold panes forming the top half of the window allowed the sunlight to paint the wooden flooring like flames.

I took another sip from my half glass of beer and tried to work out what I'd do if Carlo didn't show. Two men in work clothes stood propping up the bar, but neither looked the type to buy a drink for a five buck whore.

Then I heard the rumble of a familiar laugh as three men walked in. Matching black trilby hats, brown suits, dark spats and polished brogues. Mint looked in good shape. He seemed to know his way around the bar too, collaring the barkeeper and ordering a round of drinks as if he owned the place. Then he shepherded his two associates to one of the spare booths adjacent to mine.

I'd turned my back on the door and covered my face with one of my hands, desperate in case something about my expression gave me away. I reckoned I'd aged more than one might expect in the two and a half years since I'd left him. Shoulders hunched, face lined with worry. My time with Pike had taken its toll.

But Mint told me later he'd recognised me as soon as he walked into the bar. It just so happened he'd had more pressing matters to attend to.

"You know how it goes. Always business before pleasure, toots."

Carlo turned up fifteen minutes later. A grand entrance if ever I saw one. His overcoat was slipped over his shoulders like a cape and he carried a Wieboldt's paper bag in one hand and an unfurled umbrella in the other.

"Hey, sugar. I got delayed but I managed to pick you out a little something before they closed for the day."

He handed me the bag and I peered inside. He'd bought a pair of dark blue court shoes with kitten heel attached. "There's a whole sheet of green stamps in there too."

"I guess I owe you."

"You gonna try them on for me?"

"Here?"

"Unless you got somewhere else in mind. But I need a drink. I got a raging thirst, so you planning on joining me?"

I shook my head and peered sideways in the direction of the neighbouring booth before sliding each foot into the shoes. They were a loose fit, but that was fine. I'd grow into them as Ma always told me when passing on her hand me downs.

I could hear muttered voices to my left. Something about War Bonds. Then Carlo returned with a glass of bourbon and a pack of Chesterfield Kings. He opened the packet and eased out a cigarette, pointing it in my direction.

"I don't smoke."

"No kidding?" he said. "Well maybe you oughta start. You sound like a Sunday school teacher despite your Chicago manners. Time you acquired a little grit to wear down the silk, if you ask me."

"Not really."

"I swear, these Chesterfields are a damn sight better than Lucky Strikes if you're ever planning on taking up smoking."

"You won't ever catch me smoking." A promise as simple as all the others.

Carlo pulled out a cigarette and lit up. "So how long you in town for?"

"What makes you think I'm just passing through?"

He grinned. "There ain't no other conceivable reason why someone with your looks would be wandering the streets of Little Italy all hours, barefoot and without an overnight case, unless someone's on your tail."

"You were watching me?"

He shrugged his shoulders. "I followed you, that's all.

Making sure you didn't come to any harm, let's say. Because as soon as I saw you I knew you were in trouble. So am I right or am I right?"

I shook my head.

"A jealous husband maybe. Or you got money troubles. Not that I give two hoots what you're running away from. But if it's the Mob, then I think you owe me the decency of some truth."

Truth? That was something I'd stopped peddling a long time ago.

- 9 -

1942

It got late, the bar filled up and I lost count of the number of cigarettes Carlo smoked. He also managed to down half a dozen shots of bourbon before the barman called time and began dousing the gaslights strung above each booth. That's when Mint made his move.

"You gonna introduce me to your boyfriend?" Mint had managed to slip in to sit alongside us without me noticing.

Carlo slid his hand inside his waistcoat but Mint was quicker on the draw. "Hold on there, cowboy." He pinned Carlo's arm to the table and began to press down hard.

"Leave him be," I gasped. "He's just some random guy who bought me a drink."

"So you ditched the farmer boy once you crossed into Tennessee, same way you ditched me back in Mississippi. Gone with the wind, just like your ma."

"It was nothing like that," I said. "I don't owe Pike nothing. We had our differences and I figured it was time to come back home."

"So you're here to pay your debts," Mint said. "That's gratifying to hear, 'cause you still owe me a buck or two, remember?"

By now Carlo was leaning against the back of his seat, shoulders slumped and a smirk on his face. "This your pa, honey? Or is he the one keeping your book?"

"I already told you once," I said.

Mint laughed. "If I'd raised this scheming little whore as my own, I wouldn't be wasting my time on polite conversation. I'm here to settle some unfinished business. Right, honey?"

I shook my head. When I cut loose from Mint back in Mississippi, I'd figured he owed me two hundred bucks for my company on the journey south. But Pike somehow managed to squander most of that long before the baby arrived. He kept reminding me that he had to dress like a city boy to fit in.

"It's Pike who took your money, so you ain't got no beef with me. He even stole what little money of my own I had saved. I only got back in town a couple of days ago and I'm already down to my last buck."

"So that's the way it's gonna be." Mint shifted his hand from the table and grabbed my shoulder then began to squeeze.

Out of the corner of my eye I saw Carlo rise to his feet. "I got this, sugar." That's when I noticed he was drunk.

But Mint didn't flinch his gaze from mine. "See the two guys at the bar? I suggest you park yourself back on that bench and sit tight or you might end up wishing you'd picked another bar to get slewed in."

I motioned to Carlo. "This is between me and Mint. If it makes you feel any better, hand me one of them damn cigarettes."

His face paled, and I steadied his hand as he lit a match and held it to my lips, then I took a couple of drags before speaking. "It was never my intention to finish things the way we did. But Pike's pappy had it in for him, and by the time we decided to sneak off there was a baby on the way."

That made Mint relax his mood. "You've got a kid?"

"A boy," I said, as much to remind myself as to gain Mint's sympathy. "We called him Truman."

"Fuck," Mint laughed. "So where's your boy right now? You left him with Pike?"

"They're still in Memphis. I tried to get us far enough away, but Pike took my son back. I know he'll kill me if I ever go near the boy again."

"That ain't natural."

"Yeah, well you don't know Pike. Deep down he's a mean sonofabitch. You've gotta believe me, Mint."

Something in Carlo's body language changed, as if he'd sobered up during the last few minutes and realised he had to be someplace else. His eyes grew wider and his lips made out words I couldn't hear. Then he rose to his feet and buttoned up his jacket.

"Past your bed-time, sonny?" Mint said.

"I'm sorry, Mr Drago. If I'd known this was one of your girls." Carlo stared at me for a brief moment and shook his head. "Pleasure making your acquaintance, miss." Then he turned on his heels and left the bar.

"So am I forgiven?" I said. Mint's mouth twisted into a half-hearted sneer. "I mean, if the money meant that much to you, why didn't you come after us?"

Mint hadn't returned to Chicago after discovering the theft of his truck. He had no intention following me and Pike, and the loss of two hundred bucks didn't cost him much more than a single night's sleep. He told me he'd had more money hidden away inside the lining of his coat than I'd probably ever see in a single lifetime.

"I took a bath in '29 like everybody else," he said. "But I swore I'd earn back my cash the only way I know how. It took almost ten years, mostly racketeering, but here I am as good as new."

"So that means we're quits?" I said.

He shook his head. "Nobody gets away with anything in this life, sugar. Jesus, when Nails Morton took a fall from a horse and died from his injuries, the Outfit put out a hit on the horse."

"The Outfit?"

"I was carrying Mob papers when we high-tailed it out of Chicago," he said. "Why do you think I kept looking over my shoulder 'til we crossed into Missouri?"

Mob papers. I'd never known which of Mint's tales to fall for and which to write off with a shrug. "You expect me to believe you were stupid enough to steal from the Mob? It's crazy coming back to Chicago?"

"Who said anything about stealin', honey?" he said. "It

was documents I was keeping safe from the Feds, that's all."

"So what about the time you got double-crossed by the Mob? Collecting guns instead of auto parts?"

"I might have twisted the truth a little. I'd been sent to buy a truck-load of World War surplus tommy guns over in Buffalo, and when I handed over the payment, somehow the cash got switched."

"So you double-crossed some gun runners?"

Mint didn't have time to reply. One of the suits at the bar came over and whispered something in his ear. Then he got to his feet and next thing I knew I was being bundled through a back door into the street. A black saloon stood waiting for us outside, engine purring and its paintwork polished to an impossible gloss.

"I'm gonna have to stay away from the Loop for the next twenty-four hours until the heat dies down," Mint told the driver as he climbed in alongside him. "Take us back to the Lavender Garden and I'll telephone the boys, tell them to mop up."

- 10 -

1942

Not a great deal had changed inside Miss Lily's since the first night I walked in off the street. I felt just as lost and helpless. The foyer boasted the same gaudy wall coverings, same threadbare carpet and plush, upholstered armchairs. The same smell of hair oil and rosewater and cheap perfume hung on the air. I could hear someone shrieking with laughter in one of the adjacent rooms and the faint tinkling of piano music carried through into the foyer from the Parisienne Room.

It was late but there were still at least a dozen men hanging around, waiting to be served. One or two looked the worse for drink, and I felt their gaze latch onto me before breaking free and sliding to the floor once they saw whose arm I was on.

"What are we doing here again?" I said. "I don't need you looking after me anymore."

"You're the one said it was time to come back home."

"Yeah, Mint. But I didn't expect the full treatment. Is Dinah and her ma still here?"

My spirits rose for a moment but then he shook his head and whispered something to the doorman.

"Forget about Dinah. I've got the Honeymoon Suite booked for the weekend."

My stomach lurched. "If this is some kind of fucking joke, you got me. Bully for you. But I'm not some wet behind the ears kid anymore that you can tumble in the sheets any time you want."

"I know, sugar. You're a two buck whore with a filthy mouth. But before I turn you out on the streets, we need somewhere quiet to talk."

He took me into one of the upstairs rooms and offered me a glass of liquor from a bottle kept locked in the bedside cabinet. A dress shirt was draped over the back of a dining chair next to the bed, and once he drained his own glass, he loosened his tie and shuffled off his shoes as if he was planning in staying.

"Did I ever tell you about the night they shot John Dillinger?"

"Yeah, yeah, yeah." I'd heard him tell the same tale numerous times when bumming a drink in one of the roadside bars between Topeka and Greenwood.

"First there was Vinnie Gibardi. That could have been me lying dead outside that bowling alley on Milwaukee Avenue. But I got a feeling - call it a hunch - and I cancelled our meeting last minute. The boys called it a sixth sense. I put it down to sheer good fortune.

"Then two years later I'm sitting inside the Biograph on Lincoln Avenue, a party of five. And suddenly I felt a stabbing pain in my guts and had to walk out half way through the movie. Don't ask me why I didn't say something at the time when I made my excuses to leave. But I never got to see Clark Gable go to the chair, and next morning I hear Dillinger got shot as soon as he left the theater lobby. Three shots - pop, pop, pop."

"Why you telling me this stuff again?"

"The way I felt back at the Hardy place when I discovered you'd run, Christ. I should strangle you right here and now and have someone dump your body in the North Branch. Or have you flat on your back twenty-four hours a day for the next two years earning enough to repay what you stole from me. But I won't, 'cause you're still my lucky charm. My lucky silver dollar."

"Yeah, sure." I couldn't figure out how I was meant to process this turn of events.

"Somewhere along the way the silver got tarnished. But if I hadn't run into you tonight, sugar, I'd have been right on time for my business appointment at the other side of town. And by all accounts there were certain individuals waiting for me to arrive who weren't on the guest list."

"You mean the Feds? Or are the Mob still after their money?"

"Honey, I told you I never stole a penny from the Mob. I got my orders to keep our books hidden and head out of town until I got word it was safe to return. That's exactly what we did. Remember?"

I put down the glass and looked him in the eye. "We? What d'you mean 'we'?"

"You were part of the con. The cops weren't gonna look twice at some bum in a clapped-out truck full of bibles dragging his scrawny-assed daughter half the way across the continent. I'd seen it all before when the World Fair was due to hit town. City officials getting a sudden hard-on to wipe out organised crime, forgetting all the handouts they'd been paid to look the other way. Cops raiding paint shops, gambling joints..."

"So how did you know it was time to come back? Did the Mob send you a telegram to Hicksville?"

I could tell Mint knew I didn't believe a word of his story. He surveyed the room as if seeing it for the first time. "I had my own reasons for coming back. There was talk of a war over in Europe. Austria. Czechoslovakia. Poland. Hitler was lining them up like wooden ducks in a carney, so I figured it was time to come home, sugar. Make a killing while I could."

"A killing?" I said.

"I'm talkin' property deals. I could make a damn sight more from handling property loans than in selling hooch and contraband."

"I don't get it."

"People were desperate to raise money. The government was selling Defense Bonds to pay for the war effort and suckers were buying them up like it was a closing down sale at Macy's. So I began offering loans in exchange for deeds to various properties in the city. And I'm including these four walls, sugar."

"You tellin' me you own the deeds to this place?"

"Have done since Miss Lily came beggin'. Every pillow case and face cloth. Every gold-plated bath tap and crystal chandelier."

"So what was tonight about? You still wheeling and dealing as well?"

"I get back a percentage on every dime I loan out. Thirty cents to the buck, no questions asked. And before you start hollerin', there ain't no law against that."

He must have seen the look of bewilderment on my face. "It's called doin' business, honey. That's what I do. Business. The same reason the Pope goes to church every Sunday. But some people think they can shuffle in on the market and make a name for themselves."

"You in some kind of danger?"

He laughed and shook his head. "No, sugar. There was a temporary situation, but now there isn't."

"So what have you got planned for me?" I was imagining all sorts.

"The way I see it, this war's gonna be over in less than six months. Once we teach those Japs and Krauts a lesson or two, I'll book myself a one-way ticket out of town and there ain't nobody going to stop me. They won't catch me the same way they tapped Dillinger."

"Where you headed?"

"New Orleans. We'll be there in time for Christmas. Mark it down in your diary, sugar, 'cause once the house doctor checks you over and makes sure you're clean, you're coming along for the ride."

- 11 -

1945 - 1946

As it turned out, Mint had miscalculated. The War dragged on for another three years. Three years growing richer thanks to Uncle Sam. Three years ruling the streets between Little Italy and Greektown with bullets and switchblades. But three years growing older and sicker as well. And all the time I grieved for my baby boy. And I grieved for Dinah. Mint told me how she and her ma had left soon after the war began, looking to settle down someplace warmer than Chicago.

The cold winters had taken their toll on Mint as well. Fifty years breathing in Chicago air and suckling bottles of Jack Daniel's like they held his mother's milk had left him breathless and doubled up in pain most mornings when he climbed out of bed. He coughed up blood as well but told me it was nothing to worry about. "Clearing out the pipes, sugar. Nothing a little delta sun won't cure."

Mint waited until the dotted line was signed in Tokyo Bay before packing all our valuables inside four trunks and announcing we were leaving Chicago for good. By then I was allowed to sit front of house at the Lavender Garden while Miss Lily saw to the girls. With the European war finally over, the city streets were awash with horny soldier boys and sailors fresh off the boat. They came with money to spend and a desperate need for creature comforts. That's how I first met Marlon.

I'd grown accustomed to spending evenings in the salon, having fresh-faced men buy me gin fizzes in return for a kiss and a sisterly hug, no more. Marlon called that a criminal waste, but Mint had warned me. "Any whoring and I'll turn you out on Bed Bug Row with the same rags you wore on your back when you walked in here ten years ago."

I knew my place and made sure it would never come to that. Ma had gotten pregnant when she just was seventeen, and by the time she turned twenty-one we were trapped inside a flophouse and she made a living on the street. The threat of being forced to survive by turning tricks was enough to keep me in line, at least until we reached the delta.

Marlon and I spent afternoons at the movies. We'd sit beneath the star-spangled canopy of the Ramova and watch the latest matinee. I enjoyed playing the role of gangster's moll, with my own snub-nosed Colt 38 small enough to fit in my purse and a taste for expensive clothes and fine living, I fancied myself a less glamorous version of Veronica Lake in *This Gun For Hire*. But Marlon said I could pass as Lana Turner's kid sister with my blonde hair and flawless skin. He reckoned I'd be a Hollywood sensation.

The Ramova movie theater was only a couple of blocks away from the Lavender Garden, but there were enough darkened doorways en route for Marlon to sample my

Hollywood charms for himself. There were times when his body buckled as he held me tight and told me of the horrors he'd seen overseas. Young boys shot to pieces right in front of his eyes. Villages reduced to rubble, while goats wandered amongst the ruins. The sporadic sound of machine-gun fire and shells keeping him awake at night.

"Ssh. You're back home now. There ain't nothin' to get worked up about anymore."

There were other times when I felt him shudder as I kissed away his denials and let his fingers explore the contours of my body. He was just a boy. Not much older than Pike had been when we first arrived in Memphis, and just as naive. I showed him what I could do with my hands, and all the things he was allowed to do with his.

I was still a kid as well and had no intention of sticking by Mint any longer than practical. Just twenty two years old, yet I was already expected to drag around a dead weight who'd only brought me along for the ride so I'd make him look a success with the ladies. I played along because it kept him happy. Happy and generous.

Truth is, Mint had more money than I'd ever dreamed of owning, and I knew if I waited long enough I'd get to give him a decent burial before ditching the widow's weeds and heading west with Marlon. We'd both watched D*ouble Indemnity* at least a half-dozen times.

We finally quit Chicago late one Thursday evening, three months after VJ Day. Mint had one of his boys drive us to Union Station and everywhere I looked, handsome GIs swarmed along the platforms. Most were still in uniform, with their kit bags at their sides, their faces lined with hope and longing as they waited for a loved one to show up. Marlon had promised he'd follow me to the ends of the Earth, but I warned him to keep away from New Orleans until he heard from me.

"I'll wire you as soon as I'm ready."

Mint had booked us a master bedroom on the overnight Pullman. When I studied the itinerary for the twenty hour trip, I wondered whether I could arrange to see Truman en route. "It says here we stop over in Memphis. Maybe we could call in on Pike," I said. "It's just, I miss my baby boy so much."

Mint killed the notion stone dead. "Don't go getting any fancy ideas. It says here we get forty minutes to soak in the atmosphere of Central Station. What good would it do to go lookin' for trouble? Besides, the boy's probably doing fine without you."

The very idea made my stomach churn.

"I mean, how old is he? Six or seven? You'll only confuse the poor kid, and Pike ain't exactly going to welcome us with open arms."

So I boarded the train with a heavy heart. One of the porters explained the water had frozen in the pipes while the train had been waiting for everyone to board at Chicago and we were not to use the shower until they thawed out. Cocktails were served followed by a five course supper, then Mint and I left the dining car and retired to bed.

I barely slept the entire journey. I kept getting woken by the sound of hail scratching at the windows and the roar of freight trains passing on their way north to the Great Lakes.

I curled up against Mint's warmth and felt my skin flush at the thought of how it would feel to have Marlon's naked body lying next to me night after night. I felt the rhythm of Mint's breathing match the sound of the track and counted the minutes and hours until dawn.

Back in Chicago there had been nights when Mint's business deals kept him awake and he'd let loose his short temper on me. But on the way to the railway station he promised we'd never need to set eyes on the West Loop again. The Lavender Garden had been signed over to Miss Lily and there would only be golden days ahead. The warm sun on my skin and the sweet Gulf air would make a new woman of me. But I couldn't help recalling Pike's warnings - bugs the size of pack mules and my delicate skin burnt red like a Spanish pimento.

Ten hours after leaving Union Station we pulled out of Fulton - the last stop before crossing the state line into Tennessee. I was already getting kind of homesick. All I could see were spindly trees bordering the line and dirt tracks running alongside us one minute then veering off across the Flats the next before disappearing into the horizon. I was used to towering buildings and streets that closed in on you. But instead all I could see were unfenced fields and untidy paddocks littered with decaying shacks and misshapen hickory trees that reminded me of Pike's neighbourhood. The entire landscape seemed like a premonition of bad times ahead.

Eventually, after a stopover at Memphis where Mint bought a newspaper and a pack of cigars, I caught a glimpse of the river. That's when I knew we were getting closer to Mississippi. The next stop was Greenwood, but I had no hankering to climb off the train and visit the Hardy property. I could imagine the look on Bertha's face if I turned up on her yard. She'd curse me, likely as not, even though I'd moved up in the world since the days when a fumble in the back of a truck with her redneck brother made me bless my good fortune.

We rolled up at the Big Easy shortly after midday and Mint said we would eat first. He'd promised me a late breakfast of sugar-coated beignets and a dinner of crawfish étouffée followed by lemon and chocolate doughbash. I didn't even know what half those words meant, but before heading back to Chicago after we stole his truck Mint had spent close on six months here. He promised me I'd soon grow to love the city as much as he did.

A porter collected our cases and helped us pile into a cab. Then Mint told the driver we were new to the city and asked him to take us on a tour so I could drink in the atmosphere and the sights.

"Keep the meter running, my friend. I ain't in no hurry."

Eventually we pulled up on Frenchman Street and Mint instructed him to come back for us after five with the promise of a tip. There were oyster bars and fancy restaurants on every corner and the scent of cooking food seemed to add to the sense of entering a strange world. The intoxicating heat after weeks wrapped in furs made me catch my breath.

The hotel Mint had chosen was close to the riverfront ferry terminals and our ride there took us along Bourbon Street - loud and boisterous with more drunks and hookers than the Riverside on a Saturday night. Once we checked in, we didn't venture out of our hotel room until close on sundown. There was a private balcony overlooking a park with the river just beyond it and Mint ordered room service like he was the King of New Orleans.

I almost forgot about Marlon as I soaked in the luxury of our new surroundings. I could get accustomed to this kind of life, but I should have guessed it was too good to be true. While we nibbled at pecan coated pralines, and drank wine and Old Charter bourbon, Mint began to outline his plans.

"In case you ain't noticed, sugar, I'm dying. It's only a matter of weeks; months at best. The doctors in Chicago say the heat might help, but every time I cough it's like I'm bringing up a piece of lung."

"You might have told me sooner then I could have looked after you better."

"And risk having you walk out on me the same way you walked out on your son?" he said. "Beats me how a mother can do that."

"I'd never do any such thing. I told you, Mint. It was Pike took him away from me."

"So you say. But let's not dwell on the past, sugar." Mint poured himself another glass of bourbon. "You've got yourself a new life to look forward to. So this is the deal. I'm too old to keep you in check, sugar. I had the notion one time of spending summers on a Mississippi riverboat casino and winters sailing in the Gulf. But paddle steamers are a thing of the past, and I never had the stomach for adventures on the high seas."

"That's ok," I said. "We can live on Easy Street and soak up the sun like the doctors said. There's sure to be bars and casinos in town where you can play a game or two while taking the shade if the heat gets too much. And you've got your lucky silver dollar here with you."

He slammed his empty glass on the table. "And what's my lucky silver dollar gonna be doing while I'm playin' poker? Shaking that fanny at every passin' uniform?"

"What d'you mean?"

That's when Mint explained about the reasons behind that afternoon's guided tour. "I got your card marked, Missy. Just so you know, your GI boyfriend's packed his kit-bag and left town. The boys convinced him it might be in his best interests to forget about Angel Drago and head west while his legs could carry him."

I tried to deny everything, but Mint had eyes everywhere. He'd had us followed through the backstreets of Greektown many an afternoon.

"I know he had his fingers inside your panties while you sat and watched your trashy films. And I guess you were puttin' more than popcorn in your mouth. Don't tell me I didn't warn you what I'd do if I ever caught you whoring again."

"But it wasn't like that. We were just socialising. I already told you I'm never gonna leave you again. You know that." I could put up with Mint's mean temper a few more weeks, if that's what it would take to keep him contented during his final days.

"So you keep saying, but I know different. You need to hand over your purse before I throw you out."

My Colt 38 was in my purse, but despite all Mint's deception I didn't have the heart to shoot him in cold blood.

"You're throwing me out without a dime to my name?"

The grin that crossed his face told its own story. "You'll get along fine, honey. Whoring's not so well organised now they stopped sellin' the blue book on Basin Street. But there's a guy who still runs a house in the neighbourhood. So finish your drink, pack your bags and get your ass down to Bourbon Street. You're gonna be working the streets for Blind Billy from now on, sugar."

This is how it began.

ODE TO GOSPEL FRY

- 1 -

1954

Where it changed.

Blind Buzzard Lake, Leflore County, one hot summer's afternoon, two months before my fifteenth birthday. Bo Dean Macarthy, Gospel Fry, Donna Mae Cobham and me. We were meant to be fishing, but nothing was biting except for the bugs, so Bo Dean suggested we all go skinny-dipping.

"What you all waiting on? It's hot enough to grill crayfish out here on the spit."

"Yee-haw!" Gospel called out in response.

I watched Donna Mae as she chewed her bottom lip and her gaze turned in on itself. I had already identified her limited options. There was a low scatter of boulders set back under the ironwoods where she'd sometimes go and squat to take a leak whenever we came out here to chew blades of grass and try out new cuss words. But there was barely shelter for her to undress without being watched. And the wide apron of grey chick-gravel stretching from the shade of the trees to the water's edge would be hard on her bare feet.

"OK. But no peeking now," she warned.

Bo grinned at her sudden show of modesty. "Donna Mae, we already seen most of what you got enough times for it not to matter no more."

"Only 'cause you keep starin' when any decent body would turn and look the other way."

Gospel had already taken off his dungarees and was down to his skivvies. I tugged off my shoes and began to unbutton my shirt. I was a year or so older than the others, but hopelessly self-conscious of the way I looked. Compared to him and Bo Dean, I was still a child.

Gospel was wiry as a whip, yet the thought of standing naked in front of him with my pale complexion and spindly legs made my mouth grow dry. More shaming than the thought of Donna Mae seeing what hung down between my legs.

"Truman, I swear your arms as scraggy and milky white as a city girl's." Gospel said the same thing each time I came down from Memphis to spend the summer months at Aunt Bertha's.

Bo might still have been a few years shy of manhood, but he'd already filled out. He helped his pa in the fields most days after school, and his skin had become scorched red by the Mississippi sun. Gospel was slighter - no bigger than me

- but he'd be expected to pick cotton next month while his older brother, Forrest, fought in Korea.

Once he was stripped down to bare skin, Gospel turned to face me with a look of exaggerated exasperation on his face. "C'mon, Truman. Get yourself in the water before Donna makes a grab for yo' pecker. She like a catfish soon as she scents lean meat."

I stared at his naked body as if discovering a new continent right outside my front door. He was darker than I had expected. Under his dungarees and that torn tee shirt, I had assumed his black skin would somehow be paler. Not the colour of burnt coffee. Nor with signs of the dark curls to come already shadowing his belly where my blonde fuzz was almost indiscernible.

Bo screeched as he entered the water and the spell was broken. I ripped off the rest of my clothes and picked my way between the sharp rocks until I was up to my waist in cool water.

Water, on such a scale, was an alien concept as far as I was concerned. Since my pa had started travelling all across the state of Tennessee on account of his work, I'd spent every summer at my aunt's out on the Tallahatchie flatlands. But until today I hadn't been tempted to get too close to that swirling mass of contradictions.

The river never failed to capture my imagination as it swept past Aunt Bertha's cabin - sometimes an elegant sheet of hammered pewter, level with the surrounding fields; other times a raging curse that carried trees and barrels and broken fence-posts downstream and threatened to burst its banks at every turn. The reason it haunted me so is on account of the fact I couldn't swim. Another cause to feel inadequate.

Bo turned and gave a wolf-whistle as Donna Mae ghosted herself from the rocks to the water's edge. One arm did its best to cover up her breasts while her splayed right hand preserved the rest of her dignity until the shock of cold made her squeal and dig both elbows tight against her waist.

"Woohoo! Donna Mae's kitty got caught up in some tumbleweed."

Her body disappeared under the flat sheet of green water and she slowly crawled against the lazy currents until she was far enough away from us boys to risk surfacing. Then her head appeared, hands swiping hair back from her blue eyes as she yelled out how much of a dumbass Bo Dean was turning into.

"I'd rather be a dumbass than a smartass."

Donna Mae had a crescent-shaped scar cut into her top lip that she never once explained how she came by. She always acted as if she was better than most Leflore County girls, but we all knew she was just the same as every other poor critter forced to survive out here on the Flats.

Her folks lived in the shack next to Aunt Bertha's squash patch, and occasionally we'd invite her for supper when pickings were slim at home. She had passable manners, once she took the trouble to untangle them from her contrary attitude regarding civilised behaviour. And one time I saw her in a dress. But deep down Donna Mae wanted to fit in with us boys, I guess.

After an hour or so of fooling about in the shallows and yelling for Donna Mae to come closer so we could see her titties, we clambered ashore and put on our pants. Donna Mae took her time to emerge. "You all gotta lie face down and cover your eyes now 'til I gets decent."

I reckon Bo might have peeked as she tippy-toed past us, gasping as the stones bit at the soles of her bare feet. But I kept my own eyes shut tight.

Eventually, she came and lay next to us wearing just her cotton bloomers and a flimsy, summer undershirt that did little to conceal her developing bosoms. Thin cloud veiled the blue tree-line to our right, and slowly our skins steamed then dried in the sun. "I hope you still learnin' your letters," Donna ventured.

Gospel groaned and sat on his haunches. "Some bit, yeah. But Papa says I gotta spend more time in the fields if I'm ever gonna amount to much. He says no fancy words ever gonna pay enough to keep a body an' soul together."

I had been giving Gospel reading lessons on and off for the past six summers but he was an unwilling student. We'd sit on my aunt's back porch and work through *'Days and Deeds'* or *'Fun with Our Friends'*. But after ten minutes or so, his attention would wander. I'd finish up sprawled face-down in the hammock, dozing while he told tales of the possum nesting behind their siding or the hard winters when his family struggled to get by.

"Las' January the bootane ran out, an' all they wanna do is take yo' money, an' if you got no money they ain't gonna give you no gas."

There was something about the way he moved his hands when he got agitated. And his voice, pure Mississippi. There were times back in Memphis, when Pa was out politicking until all hours, I'd lie on top of my bed and close my eyes.

The breeze picked up and Bo clambered to his feet, flexing his arms and readjusting his pants. "I'm gonna need to shake some dew off the vine."

Gospel announced he had to go do the same. I watched them both paddle towards the dogwoods at the far side of the shoals, a hint of my jealousy wallowing in their wake like a waterlogged oil drum.

"At least they got the decency not to do it in front of me anymore," Donna Mae chirruped. "Last time he come round to chop lumber, I caught Bo takin' a leak right there against our hickory tree. Ma told him he'd better put that damn thing away or she'd cut it off and feed it the hogs."

It was my aunt's hickory tree, and Bo Dean Macarthy could do what the hell he liked with 'that damn thing' as far as I was concerned. It was Gospel's footprints my eyes were fixed upon as they led towards the waterline.

"So Truman, why'n't you tell me some more about livin' in Memphis?" Donna Mae liked to hear me describe the mule market almost as much as the stores that sold Paris fashions.

Eventually the boys returned, Gospel carrying a bunch of swamp milkweed in his arms. As soon as I saw the mass of burgundy, blossoming like a cloud of flame against his bare chest, I stopped caring about what other kind of business might have kept them away so long. I watched his ribs move as he caught back his breath. They rippled beneath his taut skin like an undercurrent, subtle enough to drag me down with it.

"I picked you a heap o' milkweed, Miss Donna Mae. Cause

I remember you said you gonna marry me once Truman here shows me how to read an' write prop'ly an' I gets a job up in Memphis."

"Why? Bless my soul. I'll be sure to mark that day down in my diary." The girl's half-hearted effort to humour poor Gospel was laced with contempt, but I'm not sure he was bright enough to see through the deceit.

- 2 -

1955

One year down the line, I'd sprouted a couple of inches but I still looked as gangly as a woodbine. A week spent at Lovelace's yard pulling out neps from cotton bales had done little to callous my hands or weather my pale skin. I was more desperate than ever to return to Leflore County. More than I dared admit. It had been a cold, loveless winter.

Down south, I was greeted by another dustbowl summer. Fields and trees had acquired an uniform palette of withered browns and greys. The secret scent of fertile soil and hot tin throbbed with its insistent beat, punctuated on occasion by the irregular punch of distant metal on rock as the Sumpters drilled another well. Our shadows were barely dark enough to take shape on the parched earth.

"You sure you know what you doin'?"

I knew damn right what I was doing. Sammy Rae Cobham had a cabin hidden behind the indigo bushes along Sharkey Road. I'd got Donna Mae to take us there the day after her pa gave her a black eye to match her smart mouth. I was mad as hell. My intention had been to pay him back.

"You really gonna go through with this, Truman?" Bo asked.

"If it makes him think twice before raisin' his fists to her again, then yeah."

"I know Pa's gonna be mighty riled when he finds his cabin burnt down. He'll likely as not take it out on Ma."

I hadn't thought of that. I couldn't have Sammy Rae's reprisals on my conscience. Besides, for all my talk, when it came down to it I didn't have the nerve.

"So what you waitin' for, big city boy? 'Cause her pa's gonna whip our asses if he even catches us anywhere near here."

"Fuck Sammy Rae." I gave the door a kick. The entire frame seemed to buckle, but it held fast.

"Truman!" Donna Mae yelled out.

I put my shoulder to the door and it gave a little. Then when I applied my foot, I felt it yield some more. Enough to reach an arm between the frame and the bottom half of the door.

"No, Truman!" Donna Mae screeched. "Pa keeps a nest of cottonmouths in there. They better than any guard dog."

"And you believe him?" I lay down, rolled up my sleeve and extended my bare arm through the gap. I knew enough about snakes to disbelieve the myth. Garter snakes maybe. But they seldom bit, and their venom was no worse than a spit of poison ivy. I felt some sacking on the floor and something rattling inside it as I groped further with my outstretched hand.

"God dang it!" They all screamed as one until I let out a laugh and my arm emerged unscathed. "You should have seen your faces."

Donna Mae stared at the two corked bottles I'd managed to extract. "If Pa knows you've been at his stash then you'd better watch out."

"So, we gonna find somewhere to drink this moonshine or y'all want to sit around here waitin' to get caught?" I handed one of the bottles to Donna Mae and we headed north towards Roebuck Road.

I uncorked the other and took a swig before passing it around. It tasted like worm medicine. And it smelled like the chemical the pest man used to spray against skeeters. But after a swallow or two, the firewater blossomed into heat and I felt something at the back of my skull dislodge then burn its way down into my stomach.

By the time both bottles had been drained, the world was on fire and tilting. Bo turned unsteadily on his feet as he swung a smile Donna Mae's way. "So you gonna give me that kiss now, Donna Mae?"

"I'd rather have Cable Datum rise from his grave an' kiss me."

Cable had been a nervy kid, the same age as me, who had died two winters ago from consumption. Aunt Bertha said he'd coughed his lungs up until there was nothing left inside his chest cavity except marrow bone.

"Aw, c'mon. After all I done for you. Just one little bitty kiss."

"What you ever done for me, boy, 'cept cause me endless

provocation?"

But then she seemed to relent - her eyes lighting up, and a twisted grin like touch-paper flaring across her face. "So long as you keep them dirty mitts of yours all to yourself this time. And you gotta kiss Gospel an' Truman here first."

It was barely a peck on the cheek. But as soon as he clamped his mouth against Donna Mae's lips I could see his eyes grow wider. She eventually pushed him away and began spitting and scrubbing her face with the heel of her hand. "Jesus wept. You got a tongue like a raccoon. Leastways, I reckon it tastes about as bad."

Gospel got down on his knees and promised to kiss Donna Mae the way they done in the movies. If anything, he'd grown leaner since the previous summer, but I could tell he was approaching manhood faster than me. Gospel was expected to do his share of the yard work since Forrest never came home from Korea. His brother chose instead to move in with some floozy outside Fort Worth.

"But you gotta kiss Truman here first, remember. That's the deal."

If anyone had seen the four of us now I know we'd have been skinned alive, moonshine or no moonshine. Our lips met with a touch as light as a wing beat. I let my tongue chase the taste of his mouth as he pulled away from my face and turned to kneel alongside Donna Mae.

"Miss Donna, you as sweet as cherry blossom honey. You know dat, sugar?" He reached out for her hand and made to kiss her fingers first, but his clumsy attempt at courtship sent him sprawling in the dust even before he could complete the deed. Bo reached out an arm and dragged him towards a mass of crushed buckweed before collapsing with laughter. "You hot stuff, Gospel Fry. You know that, sugar?"

Gospel ended up asleep face down across Bo's belly, both boys oblivious to the world around them.

"You ever seen anything more pitiful in your entire life?" Donna Mae said. "They both as swacked as Cooter Brown."

I could feel my eyes burning and my face flushing red as she raised her chin in anticipation. "So what you waitin' for, honey?"

She came closer and I pulled the curtain of hair away from her face, exposing her bruised eyelid. "How could he do that?"

She ran her bottom lip along the edges of my mouth and the heat of the moment seemed to explode from the centre of everything else surrounding us. The world grew dizzy as sensations of drowning shot through with electricity filled my head. Her tongue tasted sickly sweet; the smell of damp sweat on her skin as strong and sour as crab apples. I could feel her breasts against my chest and her fingers drew circles in my hair as she pushed her lips tighter and tighter against my mouth. Then I felt a hand slip inside my breeches and my stomach lurched.

"What's gotten into you, Truman?" she sniggered. "Don't you like my fingers playin' down there anymore?"

Tears began trickling down my cheeks as I fought for control, and once she recognised my discomfort she pulled back. Her hollow eyes were drawn by my nervous gaze towards where the other two lay asleep in the shade of the cottonwoods. "Get your breath back, sugar. I already knows."

- 3 -

1955

Aunt Bertha had a rifle. An old Merrill Carbine that had belonged to her grandpappy. We'd taken turns shouldering it years earlier when Gospel's big brother was out shooting Reds in Korea 'til Aunt Bertha put a stop to our tomfoolery. She said I had no business carrying round a lethal weapon at my age, so we ended up marching along Sharkey Road with broom handles.

But my aunt also had a stock of lead minié balls still in their original paper cartridges. Point five four calibre. I'd found them in the back of her kitchen cupboard.

Bo refused to believe a word of it until I took a pack out to show him one afternoon late August. He'd wanted me to bring the rifle, but the chances of me sneaking from the house with that over my shoulder were as unlikely as snowfall in June. Aunt Bertha had taken to watching my every move.

"So what we s'posed to do with these?"

"We can set them on the rails. Watch 'em get flattened

like dimes," Gospel suggested.

Donna Mae had already concluded we were no better than a bunch of yard boys with too much time on our hands, and she could find other things to occupy her mind.

"That's up to you," Bo snarled. "I swear, woman. Since last Thanksgiving, you behaving like you're too fisticated to be seen in our company."

We ended up heading in the direction of the railroad - following the turnpike as far as Hooper's Crossing then leaping across the drainage ditches until we were alongside the track. There were corn harvesters working the fields either side of the rails, and the air was heavy with the smell of chaff and impending thunder. Anvil clouds were banked over the dark green horizon enclosing both sides of the valley.

"So, this gonna be yo' las' summer down here wid us po boys?"

It was common knowledge, as soon as I turned sixteen in September, I'd be expected to take up work. My father had arranged an apprenticeship for me at Lovelace's yard. He knew one of the supervisors, and I was to be given the opportunity for advancement if I showed willing.

"Looks that way."

"But Donna Mae says you be sendin' for her. Right?" Gospel continued. "She says you plannin' on takin' her wid you up north, once you gets yourself a proper grown-up job."

The idea had not been discussed openly until this summer. Aunt Bertha was trying her best to make a match, even though Donna Mae's family were dirt poor and the girl was barely above the legal age to marry without her pa's consent. My aunt saw this as her last chance to straighten my ways. "You need to stop running round with the likes of Bo Dean Macarthy, getting up to all sorts of shenanigans."

Maybe this was a subtle way of warning me about getting too close to Gospel as well, even though she'd welcomed him into our yard with open arms. It wouldn't do to encourage a white boy to associate with an uneducated nigger boy now we were both grown up.

"A young man your age and reaching your station in life ought to start thinking about settlin' down. Once you're working and earning a regular wage, it'll be time to get yourself a steady wife who ain't afraid of hard work. I swear, if anyone deserves a chance to better herself more than Donna Mae Cobham, then I ain't met them yet."

Donna Mae went through with the deceit up to a point, but we both realised such talk was a sham. She had long given up the idea of ever joining me in Memphis - or anywhere else for that matter.

Bo made to grab my shoulder as he stopped in his tracks and turned to face me. "So you puttin' it to her yet, pretty boy? You get inside her breeches? Cause you practically livin' under the same roof."

I shook my head.

"You can tell us. I reckon there ain't nothin' of hers you ain't already sampled one way or another."

Donna Mae Cobham. Perfect in so many ways. Imperfect in only one. I shook my head, embarrassed by the memories flashing through my head and at the direction the conversation was taking.

"It's not like that."

"How come? We all knows you a real Southern Gentleman. But you gotta let yo' balls drop sooner or later if you meanin' to marry her." Bo had everything figured out. "It's time to stop takin' advantage of Donna Mae's affections and make your intentions clear to her before you leave."

"Maybe."

"You gotta show her you're serious, Truman. Women need a little more encouragement than just fancy talk and a tumble in the hay. She gonna forget all about you once you're back in Memphis."

I laughed at the very idea of these two farm boys giving me advice on how to do my courtin'.

"Let me an' Gospel take her out past Sumpters' Mill tomorrow. You make some excuse why you can't join us. Then directly we get to the dam I give a whistle. You climb onto the bridge where she can see you - hollerin' how much you loves her. Then you throw yourself into the river. She gonna be so hot for you after that, I promise."

Except, no one knew for sure I couldn't swim. The thought of leaping off the Tallahatchie Bridge to prove how much I loved Donna Mae was enough to keep me in the outhouse grinding sweet-corn chowder most of the evening. I could see no easy way out of my predicament until Gospel sneaked round to the cabin early next morning and I realised he noticed much more than he let on.

"You kiddin' Bo Dean, am I right? An' maybe you kiddin'

Donna Mae about all sortsa other stuff that ain't none o' my business. But I know one thing fo' sure. You jumps off that bridge, Truman, an' you're a dead man. I seen you performin' at the lake often enough, an' you no more a swimmer than I's a fancy Alabama lawyer."

That's how I ended up on the Tallahatchie Bridge later that day with a bag of maize flour and a disturbing sensation that life was slipping out of my control. Gospel had already stripped off his dungarees and shirt, and I undressed alongside him, both of us hidden by the bridge's trusses.

"They won't know any different once I puts on your red shirt an' dem dandy striped breeches."

I shivered as I helped him prepare. The numbing sensation as I rubbed maize flour between his shoulder blades and along the backs of his thighs. The texture of toned muscle beneath my fingers, and skin as warm and slick as molten molasses. He turned to face me, never once flinching as I made sure every bit of dark skin was covered up before helping him put on my clothes.

"An' you remember to count to a hunnerd at least before you takes off along Roebuck Road," he said.

I'd run the scenario through my head a dozen times on the way out here. Gospel would climb onto the parapet of the bridge, then I'd holler Donna's name loud enough to be heard in Jackson as he undressed to his skivvies and leapt into the river. A thirty foot drop, but there were deep enough pools even at low water. Then I would put my own clothes back on, make sure my hair was wet, and follow the road south to meet up with Bo and Donna Mae. She would have watched the entire display from a safe enough distance not to see through the deception. Gospel was supposedly digging ditches with his uncle Cass somewhere between Tippo and Sharkey.

I wiped the scum of flour from my fingers and lips and we crouched in the shade, waiting for Bo's signal. Then on his whistle, Gospel clambered onto the metal stanchion and edged towards the centre of the bridge.

I called her name out twice. Then I heard Gospel voice a prayer before launching himself from the bridge. His words carried such conviction that I believed maybe he would get to fulfil his dream once I returned home. That Donna Mae would realise what a noble thing he was doing. And why he had chosen to do it.

- 4 -

1955

It was late Friday afternoon before Gospel's ma got in touch. Her boy hadn't been home the previous night. Hadn't got back in time to see to the chickens or tidy up the yard.

I couldn't disguise the ragged edge to my voice as Bo Dean and Donna Mae considered the turn of events.

"She thinkin' maybe he run away from home."

Donna shook her head. "Ain't no reason why he'd ever do such a thing."

"For Christ's sake, where's he gonna go?" I said. "He's no money saved or any reason to quit these parts."

Bo stared at me as if I might know more than I was letting on. "So where is he? You sure he ain't let on anything to you 'bout his intentions? 'Cause you two was awful close."

I looked at their accusing faces. I could feel my own cheeks burning with guilt for a crime I'd not even committed. Had Gospel really run away? Shamed by the misbelief his friends had seen through the ruse right from the start? Or was he mortified by the thought that the girl he longed for had swallowed the bait? That she might join me in Memphis once she turned fifteen and damn them all?

"He never breathed a word."

"So how come you behavin' like you jus' found a rattler under your bed?"

Donna Mae excused herself, and I watched as she dragged her shadow across our yard. When I finally climbed into my bed, I couldn't get off to sleep for an age. Couldn't figure out what Donna Mae had made of it all.

Bo had done a fine job the previous afternoon of convincing her how noble my actions had been, oblivious to what had been going on right under his eyes for the last two summers. She'd responded in kind, hugging me, wiping the wet hair out of my eyes and making out like I was her knight in shining armour. But I could tell deep down she knew it was all a lie.

What must she be thinking now?

Then something woke me in the early hours as the first birds began to scuttle beneath the eaves and colour the day with song. It was outside in our yard - a sound ten times worse than a whippoorwill.

I peered through the broken blinds of my window. Donna Mae was out there in just her nightshirt, on her knees in the weeds as she clung on to her momma's legs, wailing as if she was fit to die. Someone in uniform stood alongside them and I recognised the State Patrol badge on his shirt. I thought Sammy Rae had maybe taken to beating her again until there came a knock on our screen door.

Aunt Bertha got dressed and made coffee for everyone. There was no going back to bed. Bo came by for some breakfast once he heard about the drowning. He sat with me on our back porch, and we chewed a plug or two of Mayo's Cut afterwards as we tried to make sense of events.

"You sure you never seen him there when you jumped off that damn bridge?"

"Course not. I thought he was meant to be ditching all day."

"They sayin' they found his body smashed on the rocks."

I could hardly catch my breath, head under water and the slanting hammock as slippery as a dredged-up log.

"It don't make sense. Even a city boy like you knows better than to go leapin' midstream where they found him. Them shoals are barely more than three foot under water in August, and Gospel knowed that no matter what else we might think of him."

I heard Bo calling out to Donna Mae after he left our yard but her ma sent him away. The girl hadn't set foot outside their shack since first thing. Wouldn't even cross the threshold to collect kindling or draw water at our pump. Sammy Rae cussed her once or twice about the chores, but I heard her ma telling him to let it pass.

I left her to grieve alone. I didn't have the heart to go near Gospel's family either. I couldn't face hearing them speak his name out loud or seeing the look in his little sisters' eyes. I told Aunt Bertha she'd be attending the funeral alone - I was still too broke up by it all. I reckoned Aunt Bertha knew exactly what was wrong with me but she had the good grace to keep most of her suspicions to herself.

"You were like brothers, Truman. What am I meant to tell his poor ma?"

Donna Mae refused to step outside until the afternoon of the service. There'd been a whisper that Sammy Rae had something to do with the tragedy on account that Gospel had been fooling around with his daughter all those times we'd spent playing together. But we knew this was a lie. And Donna Mae's pa had never shown much inclination to support the Klan.

Besides, he'd been driving Davey Moon's cart with load after load of grain between Leflore and Cruger for the best part of the week. He'd been nowhere near the river. And he made a point of wearing a clean shirt the day of the funeral to show his respect.

I hid inside, watching through half-closed blinds as Donna Mae finally emerged, her face drawn and pale. I could barely swallow my shame. Aunt Bertha joined our neighbours for the walk to the church, and I could imagine her humiliation as she apologised for my nervous debility. Part of me wanted to follow them to the grave side, but I knew I would let my friend down badly if I showed up.

The strange white substance found under Gospel's fingernails was only mentioned the once. Grace Chisholm's grandma put it all down to voodoo. And to the best of my knowledge, Aunt Bertha didn't breathe a word to anyone about the maize flour I'd somehow managed to work into every fibre of my soiled clothing. Another lie that never once came to light.

- 5 -

1955

A couple of days later, I arranged to walk out as far as the bridge with Bo Dean on my way to catch the county bus to Greenwood. Donna Mae turned up out of the blue wearing the same pale yellow dress she'd worn for supper one time. She had picked some fresh milkweed blossom, and as we followed Roebuck Road towards the river she spent the whole time leaning against Bo's arm.

Bo asked me why I never attended Gospel's funeral. "You got something against steppin' inside a black church? It don't make no sense otherwise."

I made up an excuse about having bad stomach cramps all week and we never spoke a single word the rest of the way. Donna Mae and I couldn't even look each other in the eye.

Once we reached the spot on the bridge where I'd attempted to show Gospel my gratitude with a fumbled kiss, I stalled in my tracks. I told them I had a bus to catch. I was heading home to Memphis and had no intentions of returning.

We stood side by side studying the water swirl below us for a while - light through the branches of the red beeches dappling the river surface and making it appear as if it flowed in both directions at once. Such grace and beauty on the surface; so much treachery below.

I imagine they stayed there a while longer to let the flowers drop over the edge, one by one. But I'd already turned my back and walked away by then.

This is where it changed.

ODE TO DONNA MAE COBHAM

- 1 -

1948

When it changed.

Truman and I had tried to run away together the first summer I spent in Mississippi. We'd planned on getting married, and I guess in those days we were still innocent enough to know no different. Truman had packed some crackers and a bottle of Double Cola in a gunny sack and warned me the previous day we'd need to get our skates on before Miss Hardy discovered we were gone. That's how Bo Dean came to catch us heading south as if our shirt tails were on fire not long after sun up next morning.

Bo reckoned it was the first time he ever set eyes on me outside of school. All I can recall is how he stood there in his check shirt and cut-offs, a switch of turkeyfoot grass sticking out from between his lips. He acted like he owned that stretch of Roebuck Road, telling us to get out of his sight.

Back then Truman was a thin, white stripling of a boy who walked like his shoes were a couple of sizes too big. And I was a scrawny-assed kid weighing no more than a cotton boll. There's no arguing that Bo was big enough even in them days to swat us aside like a pair of skeeters. I swear his hands were already as calloused as my pa's, and you could see how his chest and shoulders had burnt red where his torn shirt collar stretched open.

"Boy, you're as out of place in these parts as an A-rab ridin' a camel. Why'n't you drag your sorry bones back to Memphis?"

Bo Dean wasn't a boy to mess with, but when he made to grab Truman by the arm, I screamed at him to back off.

My reaction must have caught him by surprise because he turned to tell me to hush up, and that's when Truman lashed out. One lucky punch.

It caught Bo on the side of the jaw, and the next thing he was shaking his head like something had worked loose inside of it. "God dang it."

Bo wiped his split lip with his sleeve, and I could see anger seething like a hornets' nest behind his crooked grin. I screeched at Truman to run. I knew Bo well enough from school. He had a mean temper, and he'd bust up Truman's face given half the chance. Bo always bragged how he could whip any of the Leflore County boys with one hand tied behind his back.

We tore off in the direction of Hooper's Crossing but Truman couldn't run for sugar. I could hear Bo's curses getting closer, and the next thing he had Truman flat on his back in the grit and dust.

"You jus' leave Truman alone. You're near twice as big as he is." I aimed a kick at Bo but he didn't shift an inch.

Instead he spat out a gob of bloody spittle onto Truman's face. "Trew-man? What kind of candy-ass name is that anyway? You think you some kinda educated city boy, Trew-man?"

"You'll kill him," I sobbed.

"Hush up, child. I ain't gonna do anything of the sort. I just need to educate Trew-man here. Learn him a mess of Mississippi manners."

Truman flinched at the threat.

"He needs to understand we look out for our neighbours down here. We don't go talkin' to our coloured acquaintances like they trash or somethin' you're meant to scrape off the bottom of your shoe."

I could see Truman getting ready to speak out of turn, and I knew Bo Dean was just itching to find a good enough reason to bust his nose for him.

"There's no need. His Aunt Bertha already done settin' him straight."

That got Bo's attention. "She the one always dresses like a man?"

"She does not," Truman managed to snarl. "She's a farmer woman."

"That so?" Bo laughed and sat back on his haunches. "So how'd she set you straight, Trew-man? 'Cause I reckon that's a man's job."

"She whipped his ass," I said. "Pulled his pants all the way down and took a belt to it. You never saw such a ruckus. We could hear him yellin' from across the yard."

Truman gave me a look sour enough to turn fresh milk. "You could not. And besides, that ain't nobody else's damn business."

Bo hauled Truman to his feet and stood aside as he dusted down his fine corduroy breeches. "So that's why you're in such a darned hurry. Cause your sorry ass is still on fire. Where you two whelps headin' anyways?"

"We're running away," I explained. "We plan on getting wed somewhere on the way to Jackson."

Bo snorted with disbelief as Truman raised a fist in my direction. "Don't you start spreadin' any more of your damn lies, Miss Donna Mae Cobham."

I wrinkled my nose at him and gave Bo the gist of the tale. I'd got a beating for setting loose that old sow, and the following afternoon Truman had been punished for cursing Gospel the way he did before chasing both boys off Miss Hardy's yard with a spade. She'd threatened to take that same spade and paddle the seat of his pants until he'd not be able to sit for a week.

"So you walkin' all the way to Jackson?"

Truman nodded, a smirk tailing his words. "Looks that way. But once I get in touch with my pa by telegraph and tell him the way you stump jumpers been treatin' me, he'll get in his car and. . . Well, you'd just better watch out then, that's all I'm sayin'."

"Your pa's Pike Hardy. Right?"

I could see Truman's face swell with pride. "That's right."

"Well, he hardly gonna drive all the way down here just to get his hands dirty on a Mississippi mud puppy like me."

That seemed to make Truman think twice. "You don't know my pa."

"Maybe not, but I heard enough talk. From what they say, he got more than enough reason not to show his face round these parts."

I carried my own gunny sack in one hand and from the other I'd been trailing a length of red ribbon. I began to wrap the ribbon around my wrist, wondering how come Bo knew so much about Pike Hardy's business.

"My pa's got as much right to be down these parts as anybody," Truman said after pondering a while.

"So why'd he run away to Byhalia with his tail between his legs?"

"He's a businessman. I bet you don't even know what that word means."

That's when I remembered my own pa's words. "Pa says Parker Lee Hardy ain't got no business bringing up his son the way he does."

Truman snatched the ribbon and tugged me towards him. "You take that right back, Donna Mae."

"Let go."

He pulled the ribbon tighter and the sack slipped off my shoulder onto the ground.

"What in tarnation you got in there, girl?" Bo said.

A small, pink snout had emerged from the neck of the sack.

"Betty Lou. That's all."

He began to laugh. "You brought a darned pig with you? Jesus wept. How you planning on feeding her? You gonna put her to suck one of your titties when she starts crying for her feed?"

I picked up Betty Lou and held her to my breast.

"Why don't we have us a hog roast instead?" he continued. "There's hardly enough meat on that runt to go round the three of us, but there ain't no harm in trying."

I knew Bo didn't mean what he said, but I didn't appreciate the way Truman began laughing along with him.

"Come on, baby. Let's get away from these boys." I turned and headed for home.

"Where you goin' now?"

"I'm takin' her back. If you're plannin' on runnin' away and gettin' married you're gonna have to do it all by yourself."

- 2 -

1948

A week or so later, Miss Hardy invited me, Bo Dean and Gospel to her place. She said it was Truman's idea, but that was soon shown to be a downright lie.

The five of us sat around her kitchen table like we were meant to be having a proper tea party same as the church ladies gave us at Sunday school one time. There were plates of sandwiches cut into triangles and sugared cookies and even soda pop with paper straws. But before we were allowed to tuck in, she announced that Truman had something he was required to do first.

I lowered my head expecting him to say grace. But instead he began to apologise to Gospel for calling him a nigger. It looked as if every word that passed his lips tasted like poison. Then he apologised to Bo Dean for splitting his lip. And again the expression on his face was hardly convincing. Finally, staring at his plate, he whispered a half-hearted apology for getting me to run away with him.

I said it was no matter. Under my breath, so only he could hear, I suggested maybe we go off on an adventure again one day. But he didn't have the good grace to keep his mouth shut once he was done. Instead he looked across in my direction and raised his nose as if he could smell something bad. "Pfft. I already told you, girl. It weren't my idea you tag along. Why would I stick around with a scraggy-assed chunk of gator bait like you?"

"Now that's enough, Truman," his aunt warned. "You're old enough to know better, no matter whose idea it was. I'm just giving you the opportunity to set things straight round here before you head home to Memphis. Otherwise I'll have to think twice about welcoming you back again."

Truman's bottom lip jutted out until it looked even more swollen than Bo's. "I don't give a hoot. Just you wait until my pa gets to hear about all this."

That's when Miss Hardy's face turned white and she slammed her fist on the table. Gospel gave a jump and Bo Dean and I suddenly sat up straight as if we were back inside Miss Grady's school room.

"You breathe one word to your pa that puts me or my neighbours in a bad light, young man, and you'll not set foot inside these four walls again. You clear on that?"

A smirk played across his face as he reached for a sandwich but she slapped his hand away and rose to her feet. She wasn't done.

"And you can forget about sitting round this table with our guests. You're not even fit company for the hogs in my yard unless you cultivate a mess of manners. If you think you're going to be treated different in Memphis, then you go ahead and call your pa. Let's see who else he can find to look after you all summer long and put up with your shameful behaviour. Likely as not you'll spend it hiding under the skirts of Miss Du Pree, attending afternoon teas or helping her maid water all the plants in her hothouse. Is that where you'd rather be?"

His face flushed red as Bo bit off a laugh. That's how Truman came to start teaching Gospel his letters as penance for his sins. And how he came to spend two afternoons a week in Ross Macarthy's fields cutting back weeds for the rest of the summer.

By the end of his stay in Mississippi, the four of us had formed a strange alliance. I took to wearing dungarees so I could join in their adventures, attaching myself to Truman's shadow like a lost soul. Climbing trees and fishing with the three boys out at Blind Buzzard Lake instead of dawdling in our yard with my patchwork dolly and skipping rope.

There were times, during the weeks that followed, when we still teased Truman about his fancy accent and dandy clothes. But I'd already figured out, even back then, that the longer I kept company with him whenever he was around the more likely the chance he would grow sweet on me. I was gonna marry Truman one day for real. That was a fact.

- 3 -

1949

There were days when the stifling heat and the rotten smell from that damn river frayed all our tempers. That's why Ma did all she could to discourage us children from skulking around the yard unless I had my chores to do, even though it was rightfully Miss Hardy's property. Ma was convinced, if we waited long enough, the Devil would come out and play.

More often than not, we ended up hiding in the long grass at the back of Gospel's yard. The two boys would lie there, chewing plugs of tobacco, while I practised spitting. Then we'd toss rocks onto the tin roof of the outhouse whenever one or other of Gospel's little sisters went inside to answer a call of nature.

But there was more fun to be had hiding away in Bo Dean's yard. It was like another world - one abandoned by mankind years ago. The rusted chassis of a wagon sat on cinder blocks in one corner, and sumac and poison ivy had invaded the cab. Their devious fingers had been allowed to take tight hold of the spokes of the steering wheel from about the same time Ross Macarthy gave up any pretence of being a farmer.

Next to the wagon stood a mouldy trailer where Bo's older brother, Chester, hunkered down with his latest floozie whenever he was sober enough to find his way back to the farm. We'd often reach in through one of the busted windows in search of cigarette stubs or empty beer bottles. And at the back of Chester's trailer, a broken-down steam-shovel had been left to stand and rot. Its cabin provided welcome shade whenever the heat hit the high 90's. We'd pretend we were riding the wagon trains west. I was always the frontierswoman forced to give birth to my rag doll on the oil-stained floor between the rusted levers and pedals while the two men stood outside on the side-rails, firing their imaginary rifles at the Indians who attacked without mercy.

"You gonna have to take off your drawers if you're doing it properly," Bo said one time. He reckoned he'd seen Lacey and Patty Belle's baby brother get born inside Chester's trailer and knew all about midwifing. "Then when the baby comes, one of us is gonna have to cut its cord and pass it to you so you can nurse it."

I only did that the one time. Gospel and Bo turned quiet once I'd laid myself down and pulled down my dungarees. We never did get around to the birth itself. I chickened out, and after I got home, I threw up as if I'd eaten a handful of inkberries. Ma gave me a cup of wormwood tea to purge my stomach then put me to bed with one of her dog-eared '*True Detective*' magazines. '*The Crime of the Century*' featured on its cover - about a little baby being kidnapped and killed in New York a long, long time ago.

The following day, I recounted the entire story to Gospel and Bo as we hunkered beneath Miss Hardy's porch. The early May heatwave had broken, and rain fell in sheets.

"Why'd they have to go and kill that poor baby?"

Bo gave Gospel a pitying look. "That's what they always do if you don't pay for the ransom note."

"Or maybe they got sick of it yellin' all the while," I said.

"How come you know so much about babies all of a sudden?"

"I don't. I just wish I could have found it first," I continued. "I'd have took it home to its ma and pa, and they'd give me a reward and I'd be in all the newspapers."

Gospel decided maybe we could earn a buck or two searching for kidnapped babies if we put our minds to it - already imagining the fortune we would make whenever we found one. But Bo Dean had a better idea.

"Truman's pa must have plenty of money. The boy done told me he bought a green Lincoln Zephyr right out of the showroom."

"So?"

"Well, we could maybe kidnap Truman next time he comes here to stay. Keep him hid somewhere and send his pa a telegram."

"And Pike Hardy's gonna send us money in the mail?" Gospels's eyes lit up.

"We don't know for a fact how Truman's pa's situated," I said.

"That boy likes to shoot his mouth off, given the

opportunity," Bo added. "He ain't short of a buck or two."

"So what if he won't pay up? Does that mean we get to kill Truman?"

Bo gave Gospel another of his looks. "His pa's sure to have a couple of hundred bucks burnin' a hole in his pocket. And I know for a fact, Pike Hardy ain't likely to drive all the way down here again if he knows what's good for him."

Over the next four days we made our plans. Plans which took account of Truman's partiality to hushpuppies and the hen house belonging to Gospel's pa.

"How you plannin' on keepin' the boy in there?" Gospel said. "Cause I just know Truman gonna holler like his throat's been cut."

"Not if we put a gag on him and make sure we fasten him up properly." Bo Dean's gaze tugged at the clothes line attached to the side of our neighbour's cabin. "I knows where I can get a length of twine that's good for hog-tying."

I'd hung a couple of my ragdolls on Miss Hardy's washing line. Strung them up by the necks. We'd been practising hitting them with rocks from the creek bed until Truman's aunt told me to quit messing up her siding.

"Donna Mae Cobham? Who put you up to this?"

"It was Gospel and Bo Dean told me. We're having a lynching party."

- 4 -

1949

Both boys chased me down Roebuck Road until we reached the gates to the old Mason property and I had to stop and catch my breath. From the turnpike, there was little to show it had once been prosperous before the Civil War. The smoke-blackened shell of a house and a couple of ruined shacks were all that remained of the plantation. Set back under the trees, they had lain empty for years and everybody reckoned the yard was haunted by a young Confederate soldier left to die of his injuries right there outside on the steps. The blighted crops and fire that followed were nothing more than the result of a curse placed on those that left him there to rot.

"I just thought of somewhere better than pa's hen house," Gospel said.

I had no inkling what he had in mind. I was happy to stay on the roadside and pick flowers to thread in my hair but Bo gestured for me to follow them into the yard.

"I'd rather stay put."

"I swear, Donna Mae, I ain't seen anyone get the jitters as often as you do. Stop being such a cry-baby."

Squatters had taken root here during the last rainy season when the surrounding fields got flooded. But now the building was empty, each wall stamped black against the grey sky and surrounding flatlands. Its windows had been worn away into yawning mouths of splintered timber, and sparkles of broken glass glittered like diamonds in the dirty yellow fabric of the alluvium laid down by the deluge.

Buried treasure Gospel called them. He and Bo each found a stick and began to poke.

"You jus' gonna stand there and watch?"

"Maybe I will, and maybe I won't." I'd found a length of chain attached to one of the house walls by a large metal staple. Its other end had got buried in the silt and I started trying to tug it free.

"Let me," Bo came closer and began to claw at the ground with his stick. "If I can dig it up we can maybe use it to fasten up Truman."

"Fasten him up outside to this wall?"

"Maybe."

"But you can't just leave him out in the open where anyone can see him," Gospel said. "Someone might call the sheriff."

Bo swung his stick at the sky as if the answer would magically appear. "Quit pickin'. We can cut the chain and tie him up inside."

I shivered at the mere thought of entering the ruined

building. Even the shapes of the stones put me in mind of death and decay. Then I smelt it. The deranged stink of rot and corruption.

"Jeezus, Bo Dean. Smells like you digged up someone's body," Gospel gasped.

Flies hovered then swept en masse onto the tangle of bone and skin as the two boys tried to haul the chain free from the yellow mud. Something the size of a raccoon was attached to it. Empty eye sockets searching for escape. Its grin trapped between misshapen teeth.

Bo let the chain fall to the ground and we ran for our lives.

Of course, we had to return the following day to make sure the dog was still dead.

Gospel had been instructed to remain home and tend to his ma's vegetable patch. I was happy to stay behind and help, but Bo was having none of it. My nerves got the better of me, and by the time we reached the ruins I was desperate to take a leak.

"You're gonna have to go inside now anyways 'cause I'm not keepin' watch if you're aimin' on doin' it out here."

I lingered long enough until the urge passed. A rising curtain of mist softened the rain slanting against the faded walls of the ruins, my hair hung wet in my eyes and I could smell the carcass even though my gaze was fixed on the doorway rather than on the grave Bo had disturbed the previous day.

Much of the roof had fallen through, but I could make out drier sections inside. I figured the smell of burnt timber and damp would be preferable to what lay out in the yard. Yet it's the stench of mildewed plaster and smoke that haunted my dreams for many nights later. That and the acrid smell of my piss-soaked dungarees.

Bo left me there for dead.

- 5 -

1949

There were more than a dozen rooms occupying the ground floor, their walls blackened by fire and mildew. And I could see through the collapsed ceiling to the scorched rafters where the roof had caved in after the blaze.

We explored the abandoned kitchen first. A huge stove stood in one corner with its smoke pipe disconnected, tilting like a toppled tree trunk. And there were two faucets for hot and cold water. Both were seized tight shut. Bo tugged at the pipes attached and one broke loose. A dribble of rust trickling out like blood. "They're no good. We're gonna need something stronger to tie Truman up against."

Then he found the wooden staircase and began to climb to the first floor. "Come on."

Few of the upstairs rooms were intact. All had been ransacked empty apart from what looked like a child's nursery with a single, twisted bed frame - its springs holding it together. Rats' droppings, long-abandoned birds' nests and the leavings of its previous tenants were strewn across the bare floorboards. Broken bottles, empty cans, torn rags and chewed up newspapers, abandoned as if a storm had passed through.

"I'll need to put a blindfold on you, Donna Mae. Pretend you're Truman."

"What you talkin' about?"

"Well, someone's gonna have to make damn sure our plan works."

He'd already found a length of tattered burlap and ripped it in two. I'd never seen such an evil grin cross his face before he fastened the sacking around my head and took hold of one of my wrists. "I'm gonna have to tie you up too. Make out like we really kidnapped you."

"No way." I tried to struggle free of his grasp.

"Quit tuggin'. You ain't gonna start actin' like a scaredy-cat all over again, are you?"

I wasn't fixin' to let him find out. I managed to pull myself free and aimed for the doorway. One hand clawed for the blindfold, but I'd already set off too far to the left. My shins scraped against the wrecked bed, and as I fought for balance I felt myself falling. Then my entire world came to pieces.

I was never more scared of the dark than during that night. I'd not been one to stir when the wind rattled the tar paper in the window frame or whistled through our cabin door. But the moment I came to in that strange place, I figured out my circumstances had changed. Maybe Bo had somehow managed to chain me up after all because I couldn't move. I lay there watching the hours extend like branch shadows across the walls. Sifting the sound of the rain spattering against the withered honeysuckle for clues.

There was something out there. Something sucking at the mud and hauling at that damn chain, desperate to pull itself free. I knew for certain I'd been devoured by the same river creature that had swallowed the dog whole then spat it out. I remembered the stories. I'd been left as some kind of sacrifice; destined to suffer the cold embrace of that dead soldier.

I called out for help. Called out for Bo but he was long gone. Called out for my ma but she was nowhere near. My body ached, and it felt like I was tied inside a tangle of chicken wire that screeched whenever I tried to move. My mouth throbbed worse than anything, and I could taste blood sweet in my throat. I could also sense an unwelcome warmth envelop my crotch.

The storm seemed to intensify as I struggled to my knees and managed to disentangle myself from the twisted bed frame. Somehow I was downstairs and there were broken laths and grey-white plaster scattered beneath the gaping hole in the rotten ceiling where the entire upstairs floor had fallen through.

What seemed like an age later, I turned up on Miss Hardy's door step. My own home was in darkness and the lantern in her porch looked like it was waiting for me to call by. I couldn't explain what I was doing out in the middle of the night or why I'd not returned for my supper once it got dark.

"Look at you, child. Where on Earth have you been to get in such a state?"

She held me close to her breast and let me cry myself calm.

"You're safe now, honey. We just need to get you cleaned up. See what's hiding under all this dirt. I thought you was a ghost come knocking on my door."

She led me into her kitchen then undressed me and washed me all over with hot soapy water and a face flannel. I couldn't help whining as she cleaned and dressed my cut lip, but once I was wrapped in a warm blanket and placed inside her bed I could feel my eyes grow heavy.

"You settle down there while I go and find your ma and pa. D'you realise they're still out there searching the river bank for you?"

I still have the scar from where Nurse Chisholm stitched up my lip the following day. A crescent moon as mystifying as the look Ma gave me when she came to take me home, or the scent of Miss Hardy's shampoo on Sammy Rae's shirt when he hugged me close next morning and told me how much he loved me.

Bo never once spoke of what happened or why he abandoned me the way he did. He suffered little more than a scraped knee and a torn shirt. But he seemed anxious to take extra special care of me during the months that followed, and the plan to kidnap Truman was never discussed again.

- 6 -

1949 - 1950

1949 was the year the Ruskies exploded their first atomic bomb. I'd heard Pa speak often enough about the Red Scare, and the teachers told us in school there would be war soon, and that likely as not we'd end up dead in our beds. Like much of what we were fed back then, it turned out to be a lie.

1949 was also the year the Greenwood Dodgers won the Cotton States league. That same summer Truman arrived at Greenwood with a brand new baseball bat. He talked about nothing else, telling anyone who had the patience to listen how he intended joining the Boston Red Sox when he was old enough. But Truman was no more a baseball player than me. He was more concerned with wearing the right kind of cap, knee breeches and long stockings than in learning how to hit a ball instead of swinging at air.

This dream faded like so many of Truman's plans. He'd never shown an aptitude for sport or a fondness for hard graft, so while the two boys worked the fields he seemed contented enough with my company. I can still recall the nights we camped out at the edge of the Tallahatchie and listened to the tree locusts in the ironwoods. He told me one time how their sound carried along the wires strung between each telegraph pole all the way to Jackson if anyone were to listen.

Many a night when I struggled to capture sleep, despite the oppressive heat I'd often find myself creeping closer towards Truman's blanket until somehow I was underneath it, pressed against his body and listening to him breathe. I'd imagine resting my head against the telegraph pole at the junction of Tippo Road and Roebuck Road and somehow whispering my thoughts to Truman when he was all the way away in Memphis.

I'd also dream of living in a big fancy house and raising Truman's children while he went out to work in the office each day. We'd have us a boy and a girl. I even gave them names. James for a boy - never Jim or Jimmy - and Shirley for a girl on account of my sharing the same birthday as Miss Shirley Temple. But that was no more than a childish fantasy, and Truman made it clear he wanted no part of it.

The following summer, he took to exploring his own aspirations and it became increasingly clear I would play no part in them. The three boys hung around in Ross Macarthy's barn most days studying copies of the Marvel comics Truman hauled all the way with him from Memphis. They spent hours reading about the exploits of their made-up heroes, and that's probably when Gospel first passed on tales of his brother's exploits overseas. Forrest Fry, Gospel's big brother, got sent to Korea to fight the Commies and had already gained enough medals to weigh down a pack mule according to Gospel's pa. I swear that's when Bo's dreams of soldiering began.

The boys continued playing war games for most of that summer. Truman's great grandpappy had owned an old rifle left over from the Civil War, so he claimed, and I'd join the boys marching up and down Sharkey Road as if we were on patrol until Ma cottoned on and put a stop to our shenanigans. That's how I ended up on the Kennedy property one August afternoon when I should have known better. Patty Belle Kennedy had promised a bunch of us girls she'd show us what we needed to learn to function as a wife.

I guess I thought I'd pick up some tips on how to impress Truman and turn his mind away from guns and killing and the like.

Patty's ma had been widowed for more than four years by then, and she often spent nights in Chester Macarthy's trailer, leaving Patty Belle and little Lacey to fend for themselves. Their baby brother, Zachariah, was two years old, his face covered in scabs, insect bites and a vacant look. We found him crawling around in the mud close by while Patty Belle's younger sister helped their ma hull buckweed at the back of their shanty. He wore a grey, misshapen undershirt and little else underneath.

"I'll get him washed. You can stand by and watch."

Everyone who knew the Kennedy family said they lived like animals. We were all poor, but the Kennedys were dirt poor. I remember how Patty Belle often came to school without her lunch on account that it wasn't her turn to eat that particular day.

We watched as she hauled a bucket of water from their neighbour's pump then held the child at arm's length and stripped him naked. The boy yelped and squirmed as she took a wet rag and began to swab his body from the scalp downwards.

"Hush now, chile."

She lathered his hair, then his neck and arms, then rubbed his belly in gentle circles until he quieted down.

"See what he got sprouting down there?"

I'd seen one or two in my time, whenever Bo or Gospel took a leak or stripped down to go diving into the pool next to the weir at Sumpters' Mill.

"Well I can make it get a whole lot bigger." She tugged it back and forth, squeezing and stroking. Then she put her hand between his buttocks and began to soap him down there. "You loves this, don't ya, hon?"

It began to resemble a bird, shorn of its feathers, slowly extending it's neck and twitching as her fingers moved more insistently. I was convinced it would break free and fly away once she removed her hand.

"Now you can all get to play with his pecker, if you wants. But it's gonna cost you two cents a time."

I had more chance of meeting the president than finding two spare cents. I'd not seen a five dollar bill 'til the summer Truman turned up with a brand new pocketbook and his spending money for the vacation. But Patty Belle eventually took pity on me, and I was a quick learner.

- 7 -

1951 - 1952

By the time I'd turned eleven, I had Truman Hardy firmly fixed in my sights. I swore I'd love no other for as long as I drew breath, yet my blood still runs high whenever I recall the things I did when Truman was away in Memphis. Truth be told, I was beginning to grow increasingly confused by the way my body was behaving. I was unsure whether the boys would want me sticking round in their company once they noticed the changes unless I could give them good reason to let me stay.

I already had a precocious tongue and a wicked smile. Ma said I was gonna be a heartbreaker, and I took that as a compliment. My own heart might have belonged to Truman, but it was Bo Dean who laid claim to it first. He'd been takin' boxing lessons from his brother, Chester, who in turn had been shown a move or two by Mo Kennedy long before that drunkard ended up getting hisself killed in a barroom brawl.

Bo fancied himself as the next Rocky Marciano. He'd strip off his shirt and show everyone his muscles, and I confess my heart missed a beat or two even though we'd seen each other stripped to our undergarments often enough. I lost count of the times we lay on the Tallahatchie's gravel banks in the shade of the trees and told each other stories, maybe passing round one of Pa's cigarettes if I got lucky. Sometimes we'd reach out to slap one another's butts, or bunch up and grab whatever else was on offer. But it was nothing more bothersome than that until the day Bo told me I had the cutest pair of titties he'd ever seen.

I couldn't stop myself from blushing. Not that I felt flattered by this observation for long. I figured Bo'd had less experience of girls than he was letting on. But increasingly he kept finding excuses to get up close when Gospel wasn't around, and once or twice his fingers found their way inside my shirt. I slapped his hand away; of course I did. I wasn't lookin' to gain that kind of reputation just yet.

Despite the fact that we were all growing up fast, deep down, we were still children. But what we got up to inside the ruined Mason property was another matter.

The second time Bo took me back inside that dreadful house, my stomach near enough flipped as soon as I registered the familiar smell of rot and saw the wreck of the bed where it had fallen through the ceiling. The entire roof had fallen in upon itself since the previous winter, and most of the glass from the few intact windows was gone. Bo Dean had made sure of that. He'd also borrowed his pa's lump hammer and chisel and hacked away the chain that tethered the dog's carcass to the wall. Then he hauled away the shrivelled mess and dumped it in a ditch a hundred yards or so down the turnpike. I can still remember the stench as if it was yesterday.

Bo had begged me to tag along, promising half a pack of cigarettes if I let him put his hand inside my shirt. It was no big deal. I was still trying out my tenth year for size, had no need of a brasierre back then, and didn't know the first thing about decent behaviour where girls were concerned. I lay still while Bo teased my nipple until it got hard. It felt good. It tingled and tickled, and Bo began to tug at it the same way I'd seen him milk his pa's nanny goat.

Then I felt an urgent need to take a leak and I swiftly covered myself and made my excuses. As I walked out on him, my cheeks burning red with shame, Bo called me a name I'd heard the boys in the playground use. But all was soon forgiven. A month or so later we were back inside that same building.

This time Bo had invited Gospel along and I could tell Bo was desperate to show his friend what we'd been up to on our previous visit.

It was a sweltering hot day, and Bo had with him a bottle of Chester's moonshine. We passed it round a couple of times then I stripped down to just my vest and panties. Bo made to reach for one of my breasts, but I swiped his hand away. "You don't get to touch 'til I say so."

It might have been the drink, or maybe the heat. But my head felt like it had grown to twice its size and untethered itself from the rest of my body as I sat on that wide windowsill and reached down for the hem of my vest. I could feel the sweat running down the back of my neck, yet my mouth was as dry as a sandbox. I licked my lips once then raised the garment over my head and leant back against the wall.

I can still recall the look of yearning on their faces as the play of shadows and sunlight danced across my body. "Who wants to go first?"

Gospel's fingers barely grazed my skin, yet I swear he sent a thrill through my entire body. Maybe it was the knowledge that if we'd got caught together there'd be a lynching before the day was done.

By the following year my monthly bleeds had became more regular and Ma warned me not to let any boy near me for fear of spreading the curse. I didn't have the faintest notion what she meant, but I made sure to keep myself to myself whenever I felt the stomach cramps. No boy was going to get to touch me whenever the red rooster came calling.

But then one day I got hold of an old copy of *McCall's* magazine, one with the cut-out paper dolls still intact inside its pages. I thought Patty Belle's little sister might appreciate it, since money was tight and Chester Macarthy didn't seem inclined to spoil the brood of children he'd inherited since setting up home with Cara Kennedy. Lacey snatched it out of my hands without a word of gratitude then Patty led me by the hand to the paddock at the back of Ross Macarthy's barn and offered me a Lucky Strike.

"You ever smoke these?" she said, as we sat on one of the railway sleepers stacked outside the building.

"Once or twice, whenever I can lay my hands on one. Sammy Rae leaves a pack lying around on occasion, and he don't always keep account of its contents."

Patty Belle was three years older than me, and word was she'd regularly pull down her drawers in one of the empty shanties out along the backroad to Sharkey and charge fifteen cents for any boy needing a closer look.

"What you wrinkling your nose at?"

"Nuthin," I said.

"It's Stopette. Keeps me sweet, if you know what I mean."

I didn't.

"So, is it true you and Chester's kid brother have started foolin' around?"

My throat closed up tight at the very notion. "You mean Bo?"

"Who else would I be talkin' about?"

"I can't imagine why you'd say that."

"Something I heard, that's all. Only, I know Bo's got a sharp nose for snatch, same as his big brother." She blew out a ring of smoke and pulled the hem of her skirt down to her knee. "He got wandering eyes as well, and I have to keep my legs crossed extra tight whenever he comes callin'. Bo Dean's forever sniffin' round Chester's trailer hoping to get a closer look at me and my kid sister, if you know what I mean."

Lacey was only six years old by my reckoning, so it was more likely Patty Belle who was the attraction.

"But he a fine lookin' boy. He built big for his age and I wouldn't turn him out in a snowstorm. Gets me steamed up just thinkin' about what we might end up doing if he ever crept into our trailer at night and snuck into my bed."

I'd been having the same feelings where Truman was concerned, but there was no way I was going to let Patty Belle Kennedy steal Bo Macarthy right from under my nose.

- 8 -

1952 - 1955

The summer Truman turned up at his aunt's with a camera began innocently enough. I'd been sunning myself outside on our stoop in just my shift, sleep gritting my eyes and my hair a tangle, when I heard a click like the cocking of a pistol. I near enough jumped out of my skin.

"Who's there?" I covered my chest with my right arm.

A moment's silence passed before I heard a voice call out from high up in Miss Hardy's hickory tree. "Hi, Donna Mae."

He climbed down awkwardly.

"Hi yourself. What you doin' sneaking round without tellin' anyone you even arrived here?"

"It was late last night. I could see your light, but Aunt Bertha said to leave any greeting 'til the morning. I'm just fooling round. Pa gave me this before he put me on the train."

He showed me how to work the two buttons on his camera, as if any of that mattered to me. I was more interested in the way he'd filled out. Almost a fully-grown man now, bearing a smile that rekindled the imaginings I'd harboured through all the previous winter while he was back home in Memphis.

"I can't believe you went and took my picture when I ain't even properly dressed. Not even got my shoes on."

"It don't matter. You look pretty enough for a mud puppy."

Truman began carrying his camera with him everywhere. Taking photographs of the three of us at Blind Buzzard Lake and out near the Tallahatchie Bridge. Gospel wriggled as if he had beetles inside his breeches, desperate to see whether he looked like some film star. But Truman burst his bubble and the novelty soon wore off.

"Just so you know, I ain't planning on getting any of the films developed 'til I get back home. Howard Beech is going to do it for me, 'cause his pa owns the local newspaper and he'll print them on top quality paper if I ask him to."

"So our pictures are gonna be inside a Memphis newspaper?" Bo said.

My heart did a somersault at the very thought.

"That ain't what I'm saying."

"So how do we even know you got any film in that camera?" Bo couldn't hide his frustration. "Let me take a look."

But Truman put the camera back inside its case and tried to explain how you couldn't just take the film out and see the pictures right there in the daylight. He said the film had to be developed first, and that was probably too technical for Bo to understand.

"You don't know anything 'bout technical, Truman Hardy," Bo said. "I reckon you're only carryin' that camera round with you to look as out of place as every other city boy who ever come to Mississippi to stare down their noses at us."

To be fair, three months after Truman returned home, an envelope arrived in the post with a Memphis postmark. I still have the photograph Truman took of us that first time we visited Blind Buzzard Lake together. For some reason he'd cut Gospel out of the frame completely, but Bo Dean stood there stripped down to his skivvies and my vest and bloomers clung to my wet body, barely covering my modesty. That's what made my thoughts turn into a runaway train. There were other photographs - the ones Truman took inside the Mason property - and I began to wonder what ever became of them.

It's like that building held a curse over me. I only have to trace the scar upon my lip to recall what happened the first time Bo Dean took me there. And I can recollect the look on Bo Dean's face when I let his fingers make my nipple grow hard as a cherry pip for the first time. Then there's the afternoon I let both boys squeeze my breasts, or the time they each paid me a quarter to pull down my lace-edged drawers and part my legs. It was as if I'd cast a spell on them both - turned them to simple yard boys again.

My mouth turns dry as kindling when I think back to the day I took Truman there and picture myself squatting inside that large bay window, the devil's invitation shining in my eyes. It's like my body is all arm and leg bones and nothing much else. Even though my knees are drawn up and pressed together, and I wear a smile as if butter wouldn't melt, my feet are splayed wide apart, and I know Truman can't help but see how I must have mislaid my undergarments earlier that same afternoon.

It was just another mid-August day with the humidity making my skin slick and turning my hair to river weed. Gospel and Bo had been appointed to help Gospel's pa take down an old Aeromotor windmill on the Sumpters' property. Truman intended recording the event for posterity but was told to get from under their feet and to take that blessed camera with him.

We made for the river and the shade of the ironwoods. I was sodden with sweat and ended up rolling my trouser legs up to my knees in order to take a paddle in the shallows. Truman sat under the shade of the trees, and I heard him clicking away as I tried to pretend I wasn't posing for some movie magazine.

"I should have brought my straw hat and wore a summer dress."

"You look fine just as you are, Donna Mae."

My head swelled and I felt my cheeks glow with the compliment. "Why don't you let me take your picture?" I said. "Then you can send it me once you get back to Memphis and I can keep it next to my bed."

He put the camera back in its case and I started thinking Bo Dean had been right all along. Then he turned to look at the patch of reeds where the river took a sharp twist to the right. "There ain't no need. Pa's already had my picture took in a proper studio, if that's all you're after."

I picked my way through the gravel towards shore, gasping as I reached a strand of baking hot shingle.

"Maybe we should go home," he said. "It's too hot out

here to even think straight. You can lie on Aunt Bertha's hammock and we could drink iced lemonade."

Maybe. But I was hoping for somewhere more private. "You ever been out to the Mason property?"

"Where's that?"

"I'll show you, but first I'm gonna put on somethin' more comfortable."

By the time we reached the end of the drive to the old plantation house, my head was throbbing and not just with the heat.

"It'll be much cooler inside." I led him into the shade of the ruined building and waited as he got his bearings. It didn't take him long to begin taking photos of the ruin.

"It's bigger than any other house I've seen in these parts," he said. "How come it ended up this way?"

All I knew was that somehow or other the outcome of the Civil War had suited one mess of people better than another. "That's the way things turn out sometimes. There's a big kitchen at the back. The pipes are all dried up. And there's a ballroom over there with a huge fireplace and big fancy windows."

Truman didn't show much inclination to spend any longer than necessary inside. But then I led him to the big bay window, hoping to snag his attention the way I knew best.

"We could sit in the sun here a while longer if you like," I said, taking off my shoes and spreading my legs so he could see for himself how much I'd changed.

"Suppose."

"Don't you have a heap of plantation houses like this in Memphis?"

"Some."

"What kind of place do you live in, Truman?"

He began to describe the white, wooden house his pa owned. It stood opposite a Baptist Church on Davis Street - with yellow flowers growing outside on the wall. Then he talked about the local school and the boys who reckoned he was nothing more than a hayseed who'd arrived at Memphis inside the back of a truck. His pa spent much of the time away and an old neighbour lady would come to sit with him at night. Miss Du Pree smelled of lavender and moth balls and she painted her lips as red as the fire hydrant outside his house.

"What about your ma? She not at home?"

She was long gone. "Pa says she walked out on us one day, and good riddance. I don't remember much about her."

He didn't seem to make a great deal of his loss, but I could tell by the way his voice wavered that being abandoned that way must have hurt.

"And you ain't ever seen her since then?"

He climbed onto the sill and rested his back against the crumbling plaster. I chose the opposite side where the sun cast shadows onto the faded curtain hanging from a broken length of wire. I like to think the golden light streaming through the window and my flimsy, cotton dress, made me look prettier as he took up his camera again and aimed it my way.

"Pa says I'm not to mind her. She was no better than

trash."

"But your ma. Surely your pa had feelings for her one time."

"Can't rightly say."

"Didn't he ever try to find her and bring her back?"

His voice faltered as I dug deeper. "He acts like she never existed. Tells me we should forget all about her. And sometimes, when I see that look in his face, I'm glad for her sake that she never came back." He put down the camera and looked into my eyes. "I used to think she was an angel. A real angel. Maybe because that's what Pa always calls her."

"An angel?"

"Yeah. When I close my eyes sometimes, I can still make out her hair, tied up in a ribbon or hangin' loose down to her shoulders. How fair it was. And the way she smiled. There's the smell when she held me close - maybe her perfume. I don't rightly know. I can even recall her voice if I pay attention. Saying my name."

"But you don't know where she got to."

"Pa won't say."

He sat with his head in his hands. I didn't speak another word for a long while. I shuffled across the sill until I was settled inside his lap with my head resting against his shoulder. That's when I told him what little I knew about my pa.

"I thought Sammy Rae's your pa."

"Not 'cording to ma. She says my real pa was the Devil.

And she reckons I got his blood runnin' through my veins."

He placed an arm across my chest and pulled me closer. "That can't be right."

I turned to kiss him on the cheek and felt his body shudder as our faces met. Then he let me go, raised his head until it was pressed back against the bare wall and held one arm across his eyes as if trying to shade them from the sun.

"D'you remember that time we tried to run away together?" I said.

He began to laugh. "Course I do. You were gonna marry me, so you reckoned."

"And d'you think that's ever gonna happen, Truman? Us two? One day?"

"I ain't ever gonna marry anybody, Donna Mae Cobham. Least of all a Mississippi fluff bug like you."

I turned to kneel in front of him and ran my fingers across his bare chest where his shirt was unbuttoned. He sucked in his flat belly and I could make out something gaining size inside his pants. Then I leant back against the opposite side of the sill, pulled up the hem of my dress to reveal my nakedness, and it didn't take long for him to get even more worked up as he stared at my body and watched me touch myself.

And curling up in bed that same night, my head reeled and my breath galloped in tiny bursts as I worked my fingers into the salty seam between my legs once more until my insides trembled. I realised I was getting sweeter than cotton candy on Truman and I foolishly believed our love match would become a done deal now he'd got to sample the goods first hand.

No matter how I tried, I couldn't hide my feelings any longer whenever we were together. Even when he was back in Memphis it was difficult to get him out of my head. I began looking forward to his return more than I dared let on. And Bo Dean began to notice how preoccupied I'd become whenever Truman's name was mentioned.

"Time you stopped day-dreaming, Donna Mae. He only playing you, 'cause Truman's got his sights set higher than on the likes of you."

I'd heard him and Gospel whisper about girls only being after the one thing, and I could tell by the way they looked at me that they assumed me and Truman had already done our share of fooling around with each other. But neither had the nerve to come out and say that to our faces.

"You got a sweetheart waitin' for you back in Memphis?" Bo asked one time when he noticed Truman's occasional show of awkwardness in my company.

Truman shook his head, and the dread of such an idea was enough to make me sick to the stomach. "No one particular."

"Is that why you're spending more time with Donna here than with me and Gospel?"

"I still do my tutoring, don't I?"

That was true. I'd continue making bug eyes in Truman's direction as I peeled potatoes for Ma or bite my nails to the quick, watching him and Gospel on Miss Hardy's porch, laughing at some tale or other. But there didn't appear to be much schooling going on, and there were times when I felt I'd become invisible to them both.

There's little doubt Truman's aunt was keen he and I get together. I even went to the trouble of wearing my Sunday school dress for supper one time she invited me around. But by then Truman was becoming altogether more circumspect about the whole thing.

He'd tell me about the latest fashions: the silk dresses and fancy hats the town ladies wore. Their parasols. The cafes where they'd drink lemon-scented tea out of china cups.

I was more interested in the barroom fights and the drunken steamboat sailors who sometimes ended up falling into the river and drowning. Even the mule market was more appealing than what he termed 'Memphis society'.

But his intentions became clearer the summer before Gospel drowned. By then Truman and I shared little more than a glance, even though it was like electricity dancing across my skin whenever our fingers brushed against each other accidentally. I'd still glow inside whenever his name was mentioned. A smile would keep me floating for hours, and I continued to entertain all kinds of notions.

Then Sammy Rae caught me stealing his cigarettes one time and I threatened to tell my ma how he kept makin' eyes at Miss Hardy if he let on. I ended up with a black eye and Truman swore he'd pay him back. But that came to nothing, and by the end of that summer I got more than a notion that Truman might be turning into a sissy.

- 9 -

1955

My whole world turned upside down when Gospel went and got himself drowned. The poor boy seemed to have grown especially fond of me, right up until that dreadful day. I know how much his ma and little sisters doted on me but hadn't figured out why until the day of the funeral.

That was the saddest day I can recall in a long time. I felt as helpless as that little child wandering along the turnpike with a pig inside a sack and an empty-headed boy for company. When Gospel's ma told me he used to say a prayer for me every night - and that she knew what a good person I was - I couldn't look her in the eye a second longer.

Gospel had finally got to kiss me the way they do in the movies at the Thanksgiving bonfire the year previous. We'd found somewhere quiet, away from prying eyes. That's all I let him do, but we were both getting all hot and bothered and I had to tell him it should stop right there. He'd be skinned alive if anyone caught us together.

Gospel's death was nothing more than a dreadful accident, even though Maisie, who did Miss Hardy's laundry, wouldn't stop snivelling and whining about the lynchings in Alabama. There had been talk on the radio about whites and blacks failing to get along more than usual. Most folks put that down to the summer heat when tempers got high. But none of that applied down here. Pa reckoned we were all of us slaves - coloured or otherwise - all prisoners to the soil.

So it felt fitting that the three of us who survived that summer should grieve for Gospel together. But Truman decided to keep his feelings to himself, or that's how it seemed. He couldn't even bring himself to show his face at the funeral or pass on a word of condolence to Gospel's family.

"What the Hell's gotten into Truman? I thought him and Gospel were real tight."

I shook my head and held onto Bo's arm as the casket was lowered into the earth. "I'm too afraid to ask him."

Less than three days later, we heard Truman was planning on heading back to Memphis. This departure was two weeks earlier than expected. We'd not seen each other since the day after Gospel disappeared. When Bo called on him, Truman reluctantly agreed to come with us to see where the drowning took place and maybe pay his respects. I could tell something wasn't sitting right on his shoulders as soon as I caught the look on his face. He never once spoke a word to me the entire time it took to walk out to the bridge.

Then, as we watched him traipsing back to the river bank then turning right towards the turnpike, I realised how heavily he carried his shame. He'd been too mortified to even say goodbye properly. I'd expected a reassuring hug at least. A gentle gesture in response to the farewell kiss I planted on his cheek. But it was like we were strangers.

"What you gonna do now he gone?" Bo asked.

"Who d'you mean?"

Bo never replied, and I figured his question could apply to either boy. "Likely as not Truman'll forget we ever met. He's made it clear he ain't got no time for the likes of us no more."

Truman left Mississippi the same way he arrived - a stranger with no real place in our past or in our future. Bo and I stayed a while longer to watch the blossom spread like drops of blood as I let each flower spray tumble into the river. But neither of us could speak for a long time. Besides, silence seemed the surest way to keep the bindings of our shared loss intact.

Then like that blessed river, memories of better times resurfaced as we began to dredge up the same old stories. We recalled the innocent fun the four of us enjoyed during the summers that followed Truman's arrival. An innocent time when we were still children and the colour of our skins meant nothing.

It was almost dusk by the time Bo escorted me back to Miss Hardy's yard. We'd spoken only in whispers, surprised at how many years had passed since we first got together. Laughing at the time we got drunk on Pa's moonshine and the three boys tried to make a pass at me. I never once breathed a word about how Truman reacted. And I made no mention of the way he'd cut Gospel out of his photogaph - the same way he seemed to have cut the poor boy out of his life.

It was a long time before I thought of Truman in quite the

same way again. By then the balmy years had blended into one long summer haze. We thought they would never end. But like everything, even the sweetest honey turns bitter when it's left to decay. The tang of tupelo and the smack of clean air off the river became a distant memory.

Now that Truman had left for good I re-examined my options. I was a plain looking girl with a tomboy figure, no money or prospects worth a second look. Farmboys were two a penny in these parts but none had the brains or the gumption to look further than the end of their noses. Maybe that's why Bo and I ended up together. We were two lost souls with the same low expectations from life.

Likely as not that's also the reason why our relationship was doomed. Bo had his own set of troubles and no amount of soothing on my part would change the situation. The night I told him I hoped we could have children one day, he broke down in front of my eyes.

"You don't want no child of mine, Donna Mae." Bo came close to tears as we sat beneath Miss Hardy's hickory. "And don't go looking to take on my name, you hear? My name's infected, same as my blood. That's what they all say, and there ain't no helpin' it."

"Hush, Bo Dean. Their talk don't mean nothing of the sort."

There had already been whispers. I'd even heard Ma and Pa arguing about the Macarthy boys late at night when they thought I was asleep.

Another poor black boy had been found floating in the Tallahatchie, but this was no accidental drowning. The State Police hauled in Chester, and although he was released that same afternoon, we all knew he'd somehow been involved. Many cursed him to his face - him and his kin. Others took him aside and praised him, even though he continued to deny his involvement in this particular crime. Denied ever knowing what went on in that barn or ever meeting the two others charged with the murder. But next thing we heard, Chester had left the neighbourhood.

Bo Dean never set foot in Leflore County School again after his brother's departure. I reckoned the boy's pa kept him home purely on account of the shame. But Sammy Rae explained to me later there was a simpler reason. Now that Chester had abandoned Cara Kennedy and her brood and headed east beyond Starkville in search of work - or, as Ma reckoned, in search of harder liquor and looser women - they were a pair of hands short on the farm. Bo was strong for his age and his pa found more than enough work to keep him occupied.

Besides, no one else had been in a hurry to hire either of the Macarthy boys in the past. Most were quick enough to forget the times Bo had helped Gospel and his pa around their property, toting a six-foot picking bag over his shoulder when it was almost twice his own height.

Most nights after supper, I'd read the front pages of the local newspapers out loud to Ma and Pa. The boy that drowned had come from Chicago - visiting kin by all accounts. His smart city ways had likely as not got him noticed. Maybe he'd not had the good sense to avoid making eye contact with a pretty white lady - but nothing excused the way he'd been left for dead in the river. It was a few days later when we discovered he'd been shot then strangled with fencing wire round his throat. Pa heard tell there was a photograph of the body in some nigger paper in

Chicago that no white woman should ever have to look at.

Meanwhile, there were reports of regular fights in the Fleur De Lee - Bo setting out with the mule cart on more than one occasion to drag his pa's drunken bones back home. And I knew there were occasions when Bo visited the same bar to watch the dancing ladies and take his own share of hard liquor.

But then there came the day when Bo refused to help his pa anymore. Refused to lift a finger even though their farm was running to ruin all around them. Talk had resurfaced about what Chester and Parker Lee Hardy had been up to before we were even born. And it became clear Ross Macarthy had known of this all along.

The Klan was mentioned, Chester no more than fourteen years old and Pike the same age. They'd gotten up to all kinds of mischief, and things came to a head when Pike's pa gave the boy his marching orders. But he ran off with his tail between his legs to avoid being shipped south, and Old Man Hardy signed Pike out of his will a week before Memorial Day, by all accounts. Most considered the fact that he'd stole a truck and made off with Truman's ma when she was just a child was more than enough reason for Parker Lee Hardy never to be made welcome in these parts again.

Of course, these matters were never discussed in Miss Hardy's hearing. And Bo Dean had little to say on the matter now I'd begun to spend all my free time with him. He seemed amenable to the arrangement. If I had an itch that needed scratching, Bo's the one I turned to. There was no shame in doing what our bodies were designed for. Ma set her mouth in a pout once she saw how close we were getting, but Pa put her straight.

"Donna Mae's a grown woman, Marlene. There's not many out there willing to take her on, far as I can see."

- 10 -

1958 - 1960

Ma passed away during the spring of 1958 and her body had barely gotten cold before Sammy Rae moved in with Miss Hardy. By then Bo had started spending more and more time with Buck Moon, a boy with a reputation for wandering hands and restless feet. I was left to set up home in our old shack and many a night I'd end up crying into my pillow. Bertha didn't take long to notice my red-rimmed eyes each morning.

She convinced me I should stop grieving for Bo. He would return home with his tail between his legs once he'd worked the contrariness out of his system. The same thing had happened to Pike when he was old enough to cut loose. He only made a name for hisself when he left Mississippi.

But I was carrying Bo's child, and with her pa nowhere to be seen, Katie Jo was born in Miss Hardy's kitchen on the 8th of August. Sammy Rae said I should count my blessings. I'd got myself a beautiful daughter, and our child would grow up in a home where she would never want for love. But I longed to share this new blessing with Bo.

He'd watched my belly grow, marvelling at how my breasts had gotten so big. I was afraid he'd hurt the baby growing inside me when passion got the better of us, but somehow he knew when to be gentle. His unshaven face would scrape the skin of my throat red raw and his fingers would squeeze my breasts so tight I was sure he'd leave bruises. But in other ways, the steel inside him would turn to molasses. That's the memory I'll always keep closest to my heart.

That's why I like to tell my little girl about her pa. About him being a hero around these parts for a short while before boys were getting brought back in body bags every week. It's my way of reminding her that her daddy would never have turned out the same as his no-good brother or her grand-pa Macarthy, no matter what happened. Despite what people say behind my back, Bo was a decent man even though he never got to set eyes on his daughter.

Lord knows, it was hard bringing up a child on my own. Her pa had confessed how one look at his beautiful, little daughter would break his heart in two. He had to put as much distance as possible between us before she became part of his troubled world. Bo had plans that didn't include raisin' a child at the age of eighteen. "That child's got family enough to look out for her. Chances are she better off without me as her pa."

"So where you planning on going in such a Goddamn hurry?" I asked.

"Wherever the four winds take me," he said. "I got Buck Moon for company. We're both of a mind to put this Godforsaken place far behind us before the Mississippi dust gets under our skin and turns us to stone same way it's done to most of the other poor critters who try to make a decent living round here."

"You talkin' about my folks and Miss Hardy?"

"Not particularly."

"And d'you ever plan on coming back, see how the two of us are faring?"

"No promises for now. I'll maybe make my fortune then send word for you to join me."

But the long and short of it is, Bo was running away from his responsibilities. And in my book, running away never did anyone any good.

Less than three months after Bo left, Ross Macarthy's farm was reclaimed by the Sumpters. The old man was given a stall to sleep in at the back of one of their barns and he became one more white farmhand to add to their roster of labourers, even though slavery had been abolished years ago to all intents and purposes.

I'd moved in with Miss Hardy and my pa during my confinement, and for the next few months Katie Jo and I shared the bed Truman had slept on when he used to stay. We got word before the end of the year that Bo and Buck had been working on a lumber barge down as far as Wilkinson. Then a year later, Buck Moon came home with reports that Bo was helping catch shrimp on a scuttle bucket of a trawler out on the Gulf between Galveston and Lake Jackson. Before that, he'd been slaving in a diner and picking scrap in some metal shop on the way to the Gulf. But there was no talk of any fortune being earned en route.

I'd imagine Bo's skin baked dark as burnt sugar and his

face hardened by graft, with that mean turn to his lips I'd sometimes catch. The silken touch of his fingers had already become a distant memory. It almost felt as if I'd done wrong carrying his child - as if I'd driven him away out of a misplaced feeling of guilt. Responsibility for a child he didn't even get to meet.

As the months turned to years, I grew certain Bo had never loved me. All those soft words were nothing more than a lie. Buck Moon eventually confessed to me how Bo had found himself a coloured woman and was as happy as a hog in a Mississippi mudbath. That's when all the hours I'd slaved for Miss Hardy, holding tight to the hope he'd turn up today, or tomorrow, or the day after that, evaporated. I suddenly realised I'd been sustaining another childish fantasy.

Bo Dean had a wife down near Chalmette, and I was just some white trash Cotton Ball queen who'd spread her legs for him when he had the same craving most men have. He'd already made it clear I would never become his wife whether I carried his child or not. "Marry you, Donna Mae? Why would I need to do that?"

"I just thought now there's a child on the way. . ." and my words dried up. The look in his eyes worse than a slap across the mouth.

"You know it don't do anyone any good spendin' too much time thinkin'. You're a woman, and a woman's got no place to be thinkin'. It puts lines on her face and dries her up inside."

"Yeah, but I'm talkin' about you and me together. We could become a proper family."

His silence told its own story.

When days turned dark, and no amount of kind words from Miss Hardy could cure my solitude, I'd take to believing I'd driven him away on purpose. Bo had high hopes, and he knew I'd hold him back. I'd lost my looks as well, though they'd never been much to brag about. After Katie Jo arrived my ass shrunk so much that Pa said I was lookin' more and more like my ma each day. All skin and bone with nothing much worth grabbing a hold of.

Pa told me he'd been joking when I asked him outright did that mean no man could ever find me attractive again. He took me in his arms and said I was still the sweetest cotton bud that was ever picked and that Bo Dean needed his head examined if he thought any different. Pa kept telling me how none of that mattered to a boy with Bo Dean Macarthy's temperament. His mind had been made up to leave long before my desperate marriage proposal.

- 11 -

1960

The summer Katie Jo turned two years old, Chester Macarthy hauled up on Miss Hardy's door step one day, asking if he could sit inside her kitchen a while and get some shade.

"I got some leftover fried pickle and ranch dressing I was gonna feed the pigs, if you're partial," she told him. "But I don't want you to get the notion you're welcome in these parts. It's only on account of my brother I'm lettin' you on my property."

Chester asked after Cara, and we talked about Bo and his roving ways while he lit up one cigarette after another. I could smell the sour sweat in his woolen undershirt as well as the taint of stale tobacco smoke. There was a haunted look in his face as he confessed he'd ended up in the Drunk Farm again.

"You planning on getting yourself straight, this time round?" Bertha asked.

"This is mighty kind of you, Miss Hardy. And, yeah. I plan

on getting' cleaned up and maybe stick around a while longer."

"There's word Davey Moon's hiring," Bertha continued. "I hear tell he's looking for someone to help haul timber down to the Sumpter's new barn."

"I'll maybe call on him in the morning. I ain't afraid of hard work and Davey knows that."

I saw Chester's lie for what it was. His guilty look slid down to the floor and I could detect a tremor in his hands as he tried to smooth down his trouser legs. I realised then that both brothers were cut from the same cloth. Chester didn't intend staying round these parts any longer than necessary.

"They treat you well out in California?" I said.

"If you call being sermoned to morning, noon and night and being fed fried beans and rice eight days a week is any way to treat a body, then yeah. Best hotel I ever stayed in."

"So you're off the hooch."

"Seems that way, Donna Mae. I kept dry all the time I was out there. That's the deal. No booze, or they throw you in a cell and you takes your chances with the judge. And I hear they don't take kindly to us southern boys trashing up their town."

"So you caused a ruckus," Bertha said.

"Same old story. Too much liquor, another pretty lady and a husband with a bad attitude."

"Another pretty lady?" I said. "D'you think Cara would like to hear you talk that way? I bet you ain't seen that child of yours since you took off last time. When was that exactly?"

"'53, '54. Don't rightly recollect."

"I heard it was '52," Bertha said. "You got thrown out of a bar in Sharkey and high-tailed it across the border with the sheriff on your heels."

"Well, you probably got a better memory for other people's business than I got for my own. All I'm sayin' is, I didn't come all the way back here for another sermon. If every man thinks I'm after stealin' his woman whenever I'm being sociable, well that ain't my fault."

"Sociable? Is that what you call wrecking a bar and beating some poor guy half your size with a pool cue?" she continued.

"So you heard about the falling out I had with Soggy Carmichael," he said, stubbing the end of his spent cigarette inside his cup. Then he laughed. "Soggy don't know how to treat his woman. That's what started it."

"And I'm presuming you set him straight by demonstrating your finest Southern Boy manners," I said.

"It ain't a crime to take something from someone when they don't respect it in the first place, that's all I'm sayin'."

That line of reasoning put me in mind of a conversation I'd had with Bo Dean - here in this same kitchen. "If you ask me, you never showed an ounce of respect to Cara. And in case you ain't heard, you can't own another person now they abolished slavery."

"Maybe it's Bo you should be lecturing," he said, a grin etched into his face like a scar.

"What's Bo got to do with this?"

"My little brother's a worse bird dog than I ever was. He'd chase snatch way across the county line if he caught scent of a woman in heat. Why d'you think he high-tailed it out of Greenwood?"

I felt my face flush red. "That's a lie. Bo's a better man than you'll ever be, despite spending his entire childhood listening to what you and Pike Hardy got up to. Turning decent black folks out of their neigbourhoods for sport. That's what drove Bo away from his own home and his family. He couldn't bear decent white people thinkin' you and him were woven from the same yarn."

"Oh, my. There's a lot you don't know 'bout Bo, sugar." He threw the stub of his dead cigarette to the ground and rubbed both hands down the creased legs of his trousers. "Maybe it's best you keep those kind of thoughts to yourself."

"I know him well enough."

"So he told you 'bout the lynching he attended, eight or nine years ago it must have been? I know Bo was just a pup, but you should have seen the way he swung that ditching spade. The smile on that boy's face near enough split his face in two."

This is when it changed.

ODE TO BO DEAN MACARTHY

- 1 -

1951

How it changed.

I tell you, I only ever got to watch one lynching, and I recall it as being ten times worse than anything I witnessed in Nam.

I swear to God, the look on that po' boy's face once he realised he was beat. The sounds he made as they strung him up. The glint of satisfaction like a fever in my brother's eyes as we watched him die. I was twelve years old.

Our pa came from a long line of functioning drunks, but after my ma passed on he decided the farm could run to ruin without any help from his own sorry ass. Pa claimed it wasn't worth the effort of breakin' sweat. The Sumpters ended up takin' back most of their land and we were left with a single patch of ground at the back of the barn that I managed to keep free of weeds. God knows why I ever bothered.

Some days Pa would crawl out of bed and till it some. We grew squash and pumpkin. Maybe that's how come Chester chose to pay the Nelson family a visit while Pa was stayin' overnight in Madison.

The bank had asked him to call in on account of some legal papers he was required to sign. A loan that never got repaid, as it happens. Chester had called him a fool to his face and spent most of the day laid out inside his trailer with Cara Kennedy. But then, close to nightfall, he crossed our yard with his old Daisy 25 shotgun slung over his shoulder. Told me he was taking me hunting. I was expectin' we'd be roustin' racoons out of their dens, or trailin' deer in the scrub at the back of the shack. But Chester just laughed at me when I asked why we needed to take the truck.

"Just watch and learn, little bro." Then he handed me a pick-axe handle. "Watch and learn."

We set off along the Sharkey road. Chester said we were to collect a couple of acquaintances en route. Soggy Carmichael and Jefferson Munro. Two drinkin' buddies. I noticed the strong smell of liquor on his breath and guessed him and Cara had been layin' into pa's moonshine while restin' under the covers.

The track down to Jefferson's shack was badly rutted and I had to hold onto the back of my seat as Chester steered the truck from one pot hole to the next. Then once we reached Jefferson's yard, Chester swung us round in a half circle and tooted his horn. Both men came out and gave a rebel yell. Soggy carried a loop of rope in one hand and a ditching spade in the other.

"We gonna be diggin' for rackoon?" I said.

There was a wild gleam to Chester's eyes as his two pals climbed into the bed of the truck and tapped onto the roof of the cab signalling him to drive off. "Hold onto your balls, boy. We're huntin' coon tonight, not rackoon."

Soggy slid open the window at the back of the cab. "You got a name?" he asked.

"I got an address," Chester replied. "Some jumped up jigaboo who's been sellin' pumpkins and melons at the side of the road. Far as I know, he ain't got no permit to do anything of the sort in the state of Mississippi."

"So we gonna put him straight," Soggy continued.

"Damn right," my brother roared. "He ain't got no right cuttin' into our trade if he ain't paid his dues."

We drove for another quarter of an hour. Soggy had brought along a bottle and he passed it through the back window.

"You wanna swig, boy?"

I shook my head, my stomach already churnin' at the thought of Chester's intentions.

"Well, you can keep a tight hold of it 'til we get where we're headin'. You might need a little comfort before we're done."

South of Roebuck, Chester doused the truck's lights. Up ahead, on the left side of the road behind a stand of trees I could make out a feeble light.

"That the place?" Soggy said.

"There ain't no number on the letter box, but I smell coon," Jefferson yelled in reply.

"This is the place, right enough." As Chester let the truck roll to the grass shoulder our headlights swept across a tacky, cardboard sign advertising carnival squash for sale. "You all set boys?"

I opened my door but Chester grabbed my arm. "You stay here, Bo, and keep your eyes peeled. If you see the sherrif's car, you fire her up and hightail it back home. You understand?"

I did.

The three of them trooped along the track to the small clapboard shanty behind the trees. There was a half moon and I struggled to follow their shadows before they blended into the dark.

Time seemed to crawl past. No other traffic. No sounds apart from a screech owl somewhere close by. Then I heard voices. A baby wailing. Chester's bark and then other sounds as they made their way back to the truck.

Four men now. Chester, Soggy, Jefferson and some poor black creature no more than sixteen years old and scrawny as a scarecrow. Someone had tied a bandana across his mouth. I could hear him groanin' with each breath. Then close by I heard the sound of digging.

"You smashed them all?" Chester asked.

"I done gardenin' for tonight, if that's what you mean," Jefferson replied.

They tossed their captive onto the bed of the truck and Chester climbed back into the cab.

"Hand me that bottle."

I passed it over. Then he started up the truck and we aimed north again.

"You got the stomach for what's coming next, Bo?"

I wiped the tears from my eyes and nodded.

"The wife squeals like a pig. And I tell you, the boy thinks he some kind of boxer. But you can help us beat the fight out of him when we reach where we're headin'. Earn yo'self some Macarthy pride."

The truck rattled along for another mile before Chester turned on his headlights again. My brother had tricked me. This wasn't the kind of huntin' I'd had in mind, and I knew we had another call to make before we reached home.

Soggy's grandpappy had an old lumber drying shed out in the woods. It took us another ten minutes to walk there from the roadside - three lanterns and five shadows. Soggy led the way, tellin' battle stories as Chester and Jefferson followed with our hostage on the end of the rope.

"You ever hear tell of that nigger they caught out at Roscoe Wire's yard? He'd been caught stealin' kindling from Roscoe's store of timber, so they set fire to him to help keep him warm. But the boy broke free and ran across the paddock in the direction of the river, flames shooting out of his sleeves and him yellin' like his balls were caught in a bear trap."

They laughed and I felt sick.

"Took him more than an hour to die once they caught him and hauled him back to Roscoe's yard," he continued. "You could smell barbecued spare ribs for miles around."

"I ain't intendin' to barbecue this one," Chester said. "I seen more meat on a lubber."

Up ahead stood a wooden structure near enough the same size as Pa's barn, but closer to fallin' down than remainin' standin'. They hauled the boy inside and Chester released the rope pinnioning his arms behind his back.

"You said your prayers yet, son?" Jefferson asked as he held the lamp to his head.

He didn't reply immediately and Chester reached for the pick-axe handle I'd been instructed to carry and prodded it against the boy's chest. As he staggered away, Soggy dealt his head a blow with edge of his spade and a spray of blood spattered the four of us. I felt it wet on my cheek. I knew I daren't wipe it away for fear of being branded chicken.

"Got your attention?"

The boy nodded, strugglin' to his knees, and I could see his bloodshot eyes ablaze with fear.

Soggy passed the spade to Jefferson. Then Chester took a swipe. By now the boy was laid out on the ground, but made no attempt to protect himself.

"Bo? You're next."

Part of me died that night in that drying shed. I could only watch as they hauled him to his feet and looped the rope around his neck. Soggy tossed one end over a beam then pulled it tight until it held the boy upright without their support. The will to fight had already drained away from his body and he hung suspended like a sack of bones, feet scrapin' in the dust on the shed floor, blood wet on his torn shirt collar and drippin' off the fingers of one hand.

Chester gave the rope one more jerk and the boy rose free of the ground, spinnin' slowly in the feeble lantern light. I expected him to kick, or at least make some attempt to fight for air. But instead he hung there motionless. I could smell piss.

The three killers each lit up a cigarette as we watched him grow cold.

Chester turned towards me and there was something about the way he smiled that made me wish we weren't the same blood. "Our secret, right, bro? 'Cause what Pa don't know, Pa won't fret over."

As if I wanted to share this memory with anyone. These three men were less than human, and somehow Chester thought I had ambitions to be the same. He assumed I'd take the same pleasure from watching a poor black boy die for tryin' to scrape a living. God knows, we all needed to scrape what we could from the soil. There was plenty to go around, as Miss Bertha Hardy said often enough.

"Cut him down," Chester said.

Then he took hold of Soggy's ditchin' spade and sent me back to the truck while they dragged the boy's body behind the trees.

When they returned, they acted as if nothin' out of the ordinary had happened.

"Them damn coyotes been scavengin' here again?" Chester asked.

"Did I tell you, I seen a pair a couple of weeks ago?"

"Spread yourself some Red Devil Lye. Sure to keep them away."

Maybe the carcass is still there now, moulderin' underneath the soil. I knew that if I stuck around with Chester this would be the first huntin' expedition of many. That's how come I spent most of the remainin' summer months in the company of Gospel and Donna Mae, pretendin' the lynchin' was nothin' more than a bad dream.

Gettin' to fool around with a sweet little cotton bud like Donna Mae Cobham made life sweet again for a time, but I soon realised nothin' would ever take away the shame of what I did. It's likely I'll carry that with me to the grave.

- 2 -

1952

Summer days in Mississippi, there was somethin' about the heat that seeped into your bloodstream. Like a sickness or weariness you carried inside you from birth suddenly growin' in intensity until you had no control over yourself. Your temper. Your mood. The heat had a way of ignitin' unnatural yearnings. Yearnings that were hard to dismiss, especially when you got riled by just about anythin' or anyone.

For my brother Chester, it set a yearning for hard liquor and women. Or 'tail' as he called it. I was eight years his junior, and the concept of tail had never crossed my mind until the day Lacey Kennedy pulled down her drawers and took a leak right there in front of me.

My brother and Lacey's momma had a thing goin' shortly after she was widowed, and word was Chester'd fathered her a son, even though Zachariah looked nothin' like him. The Kennedys had lived off charity ever since I can remember. Old man Kennedy hadn't earned an honest buck since the day Joe Louis became World Heavyweight champ.

As far as Mo Kennedy was concerned, the Brown Bomber was no better than Jack Johnson - a nigger who'd had the nerve to marry a white woman.

Like my brother, Chester, Mo believed it went against the laws of nature for a black man to get on in the world. Mo spent the rest of his days anchored to his hammock with a bottle of bootleg rye pressed to his lips. He'd worked in a boxing gymnasium in Chicago before decidin' to leave the city with two marriage proposals pending. He also left behind two bastard offspring, a Negro and a half-breed. When he came south and took up with Cara Mountford, it wasn't long before her pa escorted them to the local minister with a shotgun at the ready.

Bit by bit, Mo retreated further into the bottle and the Kennedys ended up most weeks without two cents to rub together. When he was sober, Mo would play box with the local boys and tell us tales about all the champs who passed through his gym. He tutored Chester one time, passin' on tips on how to survive a barroom brawl. But Mo died flat on his back in a bar somewhere south of Crystal Springs. One punch is all it took, so they say.

My own ma died in childbirth, along with my baby sister, Stella Marie, who we never got to meet. Pa had taken to drink like a newborn takes to sucking the titty as soon as Ma died. At the time I considered it mighty inconsiderate of her to leave me to waste away in the shadows of a drunk and an older brother who had already developed the temperament of a rattler and the manners of a catfish. Maybe that's why I welcomed Lacey's affections when we were growin' up together.

Cara's two daughters came from the same mould as their

ma - fiery red hair and eyes as beady as a gopher's. But where Patty Belle was skinny as whipcord with skin the colour of creamed honey, Lacey carried more than her fair share of puppy fat and had skin pale as pastry dough. Mo Kennedy had been dead five years by then. Cara and her brood had taken up permanent residence in Chester's trailer and Lacey began to latch onto me whenever she saw I was at a loose end.

"You goin' fishin' today, Bo Dean?"

"What's it to you?"

"Only askin', 'cause I ain't allowed down to the river on my own, and it's awful dry round these parts."

I had my rod and line with me, but likely as not I'd end up sat in the shade of the ironwoods on the river bank and watch the river go by its own sweet way.

"As long as you don't get under my feet."

The occasional swirl of current carried blades of straw and dead leaves and we watched them float past until everythin' drifted out of sight. I often wondered where they might end up. Then round about midday Lacey started to squirm like she had fire ants in her breeches.

"You got an itch, or somethin' bit you?"

She didn't reply, but her cheeks coloured and I could sense she was on the point of uppin' and leavin'.

"If you think I'm walkin' you home, you got another think coming. Right now, that road's gonna be hot enough to burn the soles of your feet. Quit fidgetin' and go pick me some wild strawberry so we can have us a picnic."

"Need to pee."

There it was.

"So go ahead. There ain't nobody watchin'."

"But there ain't no outhouse."

I laughed out loud. "Jesus, ain't you ever taken a leak when you're a long way from home? There's no one else here, so go and squat down behind over there."

I helped her search the water's edge for a while before pointin' downriver where a couple of dried out oak stumps sat proud of the shingle.

"What if there's garter snakes?" she said.

We picked a level spot clear of bindweed and I stood back as she reached under her flimsy cotton dress to pull down her bloomers.

"You're gonna have to take them all the way off if you aim on keepin' them dry."

But instead she sat on her heels, shuffled her feet until her legs were wide apart then let nature take its course. I couldn't help but stare at the patch of gravel growing darker between her feet, and I felt myself get more and more steamed up as she began to snigger, flexing her bladder to make the stream of piss falter then spurt, falter than spurt.

Years later, I saw gook girls squat and relieve themselves the same way when we were on S & D and I thought back to that afternoon.

"You done foolin' around?"

She finally tugged her bloomers free and used them to dab herself dry but so help me, I never saw anythin' down there resemblin' a tail. That's when I realised Chester had been spinnin' me another yarn. But the sounds I'd hear inside Chester's trailer some nights made me realise I was still missin' out on some big secret. Somethin' about the look Patty Belle gave me whenever she caught me watchin' her hang around our yard made me wonder whether she already knew what her ma and Chester were up to. It made me pray that one day she'd maybe show me.

- 3 -

1954

By the time I turned fifteen I knew all there was to know about women. That's how I could tell Donna Mae was in heat the day we went swimming in Blind Buzzard Lake. I could smell it on her. There ain't nothin' surer when you're itchin' to get in some woman's panties than the scent of lust. And when she came across and lay beside the three of us in just her skivvies, rubbin' herself like she meant to start a fire down there between her legs, I swear I grew a boner the size of a corn dog.

I made some excuse that I needed to take a leak. Gospel came with me, and as soon as we were out of earshot I told him we should give her and Truman a couple of minutes before sneakin' back for a proper look. I just knew Truman was gonna have her flat on her back and stripped buck naked soon as we were out of the way.

But Gospel shook his head. "Truman ain't like that."

"Jesus, boy. Ain't you seen the way Donna Mae looks at him? She sweet as honey on the boy, and if he ain't put it to her yet, you can bet your last buck he gonna be diggin' for clam anytime soon. We both know she not too proud to spread her legs to get noticed. And young Truman's got potential."

"Po-tential?"

"Truman Hardy's goin' places. Anyone can see that. And Donna Mae's been sendin' him signals loud and clear she ripe for pickin'. Don't you think the same thing ain't already crossed his mind whenever he sees her undergarments on her ma's washing line? Or sees the light in her bedroom window late at night and catches her undressin' for bed?"

Gospel rubbed his fingers through his hair. "But Donna Mae says she gonna marry me if I learn my letters and get me some fancy manners like they have up in Memphis."

That stopped me in my tracks. "I swear, Gospel. There's more chance of them puttin' an American on the moon than of you ever gettin' inside Miss Donna Mae Cobham's panties. You lay a finger on that white girl and they gonna cut off your balls and nail them to your pa's outhouse."

"But Truman keeps tellin' me she ain't nothin' more than a cotton bud," Gospel said as he unbuttoned his breeches. "He ain't lookin' to make do with a scrawny little critter like Donna Mae when there's grown girls in his home city fresh out of college that could teach us all a thing or two."

"Is that what you think? Just 'cause Donna Mae's encouragin' you with your learnin' don't mean nothin'. She only has to sit in the sun out on Miss Bertha's yard, her skin dryin' and her hair blowin' in and out of her face, and Truman ain't got no cause to go lookin' elsewhere. That crescent scar on her top lip like the beginnin' of a smile, and her eyes sunk so deep in her head you can never tell which way she starin'. Any boy lookin' to get some action would be a fool to try elsewhere."

Gospel buttoned himself up again and stared me straight in the eye. "Sounds to me like you got your own intentions where Donna Mae's concerned. Sounds to me like you wish it was you back there with her right now instead of Truman."

I picked up a flat stone off the shoreline and sent it skittering across the surface of the lake. "You ain't got no cause to talk that way. Donna Mae plays her games with the three of us. I swear, if you asked her to pick one of us, she'd not be able to. I tell you, that girl's got a serious itch, but it don't matter to me which one of us is gonna end up puttin' it to her. She ain't worth falling out over."

I thought back to the summer when Donna Mae's titties started showin' and how she let me believe I was the boy who got to touch them first. That I was the only one she ever put on her little display for. But I'd been kiddin' myself all along. I know how Donna Mae liked to pretend I was the best looking boy around these parts for a time. She claimed to love my wild streak. My bad boy temperament. But words come easy when the blood runs high and she soon made it clear she was setting her sights higher than on me or Gospel.

Our paths continued to cross a heap of occasions before Gospel Fry got himself drowned, yet most times she showed me nothin' but contempt. So I guess Donna Mae only chose me in the end because Gospel and Truman were no longer around. She told me how she fell in love with me the first time she saw me in Leflore County School. Said she never stopped loving me since. But I know that's a lie. That's what womenfolk do. They twist things 'til you ain't supposed to remember anymore what's true and what's a Goddamn lie.

- 4 -

1960

Donna Mae once told me I could be infuriatin' as a billy goat caught up inside a barbed wire fence one day and the sweetest man she ever did meet the next. Maybe she had a point, but I don't care to show my sweet side to anyone. There's certain things a man can't abide bein' told, to his face or under the blankets. How he makes his woman feel inside is probably one of the worst. Good or bad.

Maybe that's why I couldn't help myself whenever our lovemaking was done. I couldn't hold her in my arms and say the words she wanted to hear. Everybody knew Donna Mae would never amount to much, but that didn't make it right the way I treated her. Whenever my sour side got the best of me, I'd remind her of all the bad things I'd said and done. Maybe it was shame made me turn bitter inside like curdled milk. Made me do things I'd regret long after the damage was done.

Miss Hardy said words broke no bones, unlike sticks and stones, but I'd still flinch when I sensed Donna Mae recoiling from my sharp tongue. She deserved better. So did her child

- bless its tiny heart, if it survived. The same goes for Fleece and our beautiful baby daughter, come to think of it, though my mood had mellowed some by the time my skin acquired a delta tan.

Maybe it was the letter from Truman that set me off. It arrived the week before I finally took the courage to leave Greenwood for good. His Aunt Bertha passed it on to Donna Mae, as if she was handin' her a hundred dollar bill. Truman was asking after everybody and gettin' along nicely in his new fancy job, thank you very much.

I couldn't hold my tongue. "Truman ain't nothin' more than a whippin' boy for his pappy. Everyone knows that."

"He ain't no such thing," Donna Mae snapped. "He's got a position in a fancy newspaper office."

"Really?" I watched as she folded up Truman's letter and put it away for safe keeping in the pocket of her pinafore. "I swear to God, woman. You talk about that boy as if he someone special - better than us folks down here."

"I do not. He's always been my friend, and nothin' ain't ever gonna change that fact," she said.

"A good friend who spent every summer trying to get his fingers inside your panties." She flushed red and made to leave the kitchen, but I took hold of her by the shoulder and forced her to look me in the eye. "For your information, that boy was never no friend of mine. From the day I first crossed his path, I got no respect for him, which is probably just as well."

Her gaze flitted across the room. "What's that supposed to mean?"

"I'm just sayin'. It's easier to steal from someone you don't respect."

She looked me in the eye again. "You stole from Truman?"

"Damn right I did." I grabbed a handful of her hair and mashed my lips against hers until she was forced to pull her mouth away to catch her breath. "It was as easy as stealin' bruised pumpkins from Ma Tyson's roadside fruit stall when she weren't lookin'."

All us children used to do the same, on account of the way Ma Tyson treated our black neighbours.

From the look Donna gave me and the way her shoulders gave a shudder, I could tell I'd gotten my message across. I might have stolen her from Truman, but in my mind the act of theft itself was more valuable than the spoils.

- 5 -

1960 - 1964

Gospel Fry and I had often talked about his brother, out fightin' the Reds in Korea. We couldn't get enough of hearin' about Forrest's adventures as a sniper. So I guess some part of me had always wanted to follow in his footsteps once I was old enough to sign the papers. We'd marched up and down Sharkey Road with our broom handles on our shoulders. Then when Truman Hardy joined us with his grandpappy's rifle it seemed that game would never end.

It was nothin' to do with wantin' to fight the damn Commies or make a name for myself as a war hero. I didn't care for any of that. Maybe I had a death wish even back then. There were times Pa claimed he didn't know what made me tick inside. Didn't know whose blood ran through my veins, or what notions sent me into those darkest corners of my mind until I could barely draw breath anymore. Truth is, I didn't know any of that myself. I put it down to the way I was made. Somethin' about my pedigree that had marked me for life.

That's maybe why I chose to get as far away from

Greenwood as I could, once I realised there was a child on the way. Another link in the chain. I knew there was no danger of anyone associatin' the child with the rest of my kin if I headed far enough south. No fear of it being tainted with the Macarthy name once I left Leflore County.

Sammy Rae had told me often enough how Donna Mae was already capable at sixteen of making her own mistakes without any help from me. That's another reason why I walked out on her as soon as I heard she was carryin'. Bertha and Sammy Rae would see her right. I had a different agenda in mind. I aimed to make my fortune before I turned twenty.

Farms were getting foreclosed left, right and centre so work was hard to come by. But Buck Moon reckoned there were plenty hirin' between Baton Rouge and the delta. We were young and built tough, so there was nothin' to stop us working our way to the Promised Land.

As it turned out, we barely earned enough money to keep a body and soul together for the first few weeks. But I feasted on more than my fair share of lump crab and shrimp. All earned through hard graft. Food had never tasted better.

I spent three months servin' burgers and fries in a roadside truck-stop on the outskirts of St. Gabriel - facing the levee on one side and the clean livin', pocket-book farms of Iberville on the other. That's where I met Fleece. She washed dishes and worked behind a bar on her days off.

Her grandpappy's grandma was an Indian squaw, by all accounts. She'd belonged to a tribe that settled on the Bayou Bouef outside of New Orleans, though Fleece was born and raised in Texas close to the Sabine River. She was thirteen when her pa began takin' an unhealthy interest, and she and her ma moved to that part of the delta where bit by bit the water takes over from the land.

My next move was to Chalmette, Louisiana. I got a summer job at the aluminum plant, humpin' scrap metal and casting a long look at the river close by. The way it stretched into the distance put me in mind of our third grade teacher, a Miss Simpson from Pennsylvania. We called her the Shrimp on account of the way she spoke. She'd remind us each and every morning how important it was to 'worsh' ourselves before attendin' class - as if anyone had the time to clean up properly after hoein' rows of beans and sweetcorn on those summer mornings when there was barely time to grab a bite to eat on the way to school.

The Shrimp had a thing for the Ohio River, claimin' it ran all the way from Pittsburgh to New Orleans and that the Mississippi should not be given credit for carryin' all that water from the heartland of the United States of America all the way to the Gulf of Mexico. I didn't believe a word of it until I ended up in Chalmette.

That's where I saw the largest gator ever, bidin' its time at the torn-off end of Marina Road one hot August evening when the crickets sang loud enough to wake the dead. I'd gone flounder gigging with Buck, and he pointed it out to me on the mud flats, as still as a washed-up tree trunk.

In the end I stuck out haulin' scrap for almost eight months before partin' company with Buck and workin' my passage on a barge way past Jesuit Bend and Port Sulphur to where farm land finally gives way to salt water bayou. Fleece and I settled in Venice on the Louisiana flats. By then she'd given birth to a little baby girl, and I knew if my Pa had seen his grand daughter, he'd likely as not have curled up from the shame. Charmaine had hair as black as charcoal and skin as dark as her ma's. In Pa's book our daughter would have been a crossbred child at best, with enough tainted blood runnin' through her body to make a pure, white man sick to his stomach.

It's partly why I could never take my new family back north to Leflore County, though Fleece asked often enough about my folks. I carried their shame around with me like a brand. Chester and my pa were no better than vermin, and it seemed their only ambition in their miserable lives had been to raise me to share their hateful ways.

How could anyone love Bo Dean Macarthy, knowin' all the bad things his family had done? In the end I was no better than them. Blame the drink. Blame my high spirits. That's how I ended up in many a fix; losing my bearings more times than I could count. It's also how I ended up leaving the Mississippi behind me and enlisting, even though I had no cause to.

- 6 -

1966

First thing you notice is the smell. The jungle has an atmosphere all of its own - some part due to the rain that falls regular as clockwork every afternoon, and some part due to the heat that floods your lungs with every breath. The energy drains out of your body soon as you get out of your hammock each morning. Your legs grow heavier with each step, like you're wadin' through a steaming swamp, filled with everythin' green and slimy wherever you look. And the trees grow so close together, you need a machete to cut a way through. Then once you come to the river, it crawls past like a slow-movin' mudslide. The colour of the water reminds me of the Mississippi down near where it joins the Gulf. But the smells and sounds tell you you're a long way from home.

There's the feelin' of being lost; a certainty that you're inside an alien world you have no part of. You can't make sense of what's goin' on, no matter how many weeks you've spent in combat. It's like the first time an FNG comes across a trip wire and doesn't think to shout a warning and someone walkin' alongside him gets hurt real bad. They've forgotten there's bad luck out there waitin' for us all. Or they never knew that in the first place.

And it hits you in the sudden twist of the gut that these new guys are as much of a fuckin' danger to you as the enemy you're meant to be fightin'. Jesus, some of the kids they're sendin' over are so young, I doubt they ever got their dicks wet with gash.

I can tell from the way they carry themselves they've never hefted timber until their bones are on fire, or worked the pipelines until their skin's as blackened and slick as treacle, or blistered their hands saltwater raw haulin' creels of lobster onto the deck of a trawler while there's a full-scale hurricane whippin' up a party less than three miles out.

I know Fleece liked to tell our baby daughter about her pa - what a hero he was gonna be. But stuck out here at the edge of a paddy field with the stench of shit and death closin' in, it don't seem brave or dutiful. It seems like we all got swept up into this situation without thinkin' things through. My pa would have called me a fool to sign up, I know that. But with no way of findin' steady work and another mouth to feed, I saw the Army ticket as an easy way to provide for my two girls. It seemed I'd made a wise choice until I began Basic Combat Training and realised how I'd swallowed the lie.

And now it's that fool, Bo Dean Macarthy, who's up to his neck in shit with the rest of Charlie Company in Operation Abilene while any American college boy with a pinch of sense is dodgin' the draft, holed up in a wigwam with a long-hair, hippy chick who's doling out free love like it's what she was born for. We've already had our third commander in less than two months, so what does that tell you? We're all plain tired of the mess we've gotten ourselves into.

No one even knows where our orders are comin from anymore. They used to call it "search and clear" - sweepin' the jungle for the invisible enemy. Now it's "search and destroy". Seventy klicks out of Saigon, we're on the heels of a Charlie Battalion holed up in a rubber plantation. But our placement is being torn to pieces by a blizzard of artillery fire, and it's clear we have a fight on our hands.

And I'm reminded of home in a flash of thrown-up earth and searing pain in my gut. My real home in that chewed-up corner of the flatlands, five hundred yards from the Tallahatchie. Tears in my eyes that time Truman caught me off guard with a smack in the mouth and Donna Mae screechin' in my ear how I was gonna kill him. The river stench of rotting vegetation and mud bakin' under the Mississippi sun. My combat fatigues stiff with two months' worth of sweat and dirt, and my own blood seepin' into the ground. The look in Gospel Fry's eyes when Donna Mae showed us what she had hidden away between her legs. The scar on her top lip that sometimes I'd get to trace with the tip of my tongue. And the promises I made but never got to keep.

This is how it changed.

Ode to Truman Hardy

- 1 -

1955

Where it ended.

Pa was already half the way drunk when I finally arrived home. I should have guessed that Aunt Bertha had telephoned in advance and told him I was on my way. Not by train but by bus. Taking my time to leave Mississippi. Taking my time to get accustomed to never going back there again. But I had no idea what else she had told him, or why he was nursing a tumbler of hard liquor in our kitchen when it was barely half past six in the evening.

I heard him call out to me as soon as I opened the screen door. I dropped my bag on the floor and pulled off my shoes. Still playing for time.

"That you, Truman?"

His voice already slurring. A bottle of bourbon half empty on the kitchen table and a dirty dinner plate and half-smoked cigar close at hand.

"Yep."

"It's okay. Bertha told me everything. You look done in, boy. Why'n't you pull up a chair?"

I was imagining what she might have told him, and what she could have told him had she known the truth. If Pa learned the entire story he'd likely as not throw me out in the street. I'd not be welcome across his threshold ever again. And I was in no mood for a fight tonight.

"You know what? I can remember the day you got born. And I have to confess you were a disappointment to me from the first time I seen you."

I'd always known that. Always felt he was expecting more from me than I could ever deliver.

"Huh."

"But not for whatever reason you might be thinking. So don't go taking what I'm telling you to heart. It's just, the first time I saw you, all red and wrinkly like a skinned muskrat, with a mop of hair as jet black as Hank Gizzi. I swear, you weren't what I was expectin' at all."

I couldn't help a snigger. "What d'you mean by that?"

He explained. How he'd expected Ma with her palest skin and finest hair to produce a child as fair as her.

"She was perfect in every way. Pure blood. Pure white skin. Never seen anyone purer."

I had no idea what he meant by that.

"Of course, it turns out she was as black on the insides as any damn nigger whore, but when I heard she was carrying my child I assumed you'd turn out to resemble your ma rather than me. It was the way I'd planned it. How God intended it to be."

I laughed at the absurdity of his conceit. And the notion of ending up like God intended was a long way from coming true. I'd read my share of the Bible at school, and knew I'd be considered an abhorrence to most so-called Christian folk.

"Your hair did fade over time. And you had your ma's delicate jaw-line and eyes, I couldn't deny that. I doubted the word of the Lord for a time. Then when she coddled you and kept you to herself every waking hour, I confess, there were times when I thought you and her were gettin' too close."

Getting too close? I was barely two and a half years old when she left.

"Maybe it's a blessing she ran off when she did and that I began sending you down south each summer. Getting you to squat inside a real Mississippi shit house instead of in some fancy Memphis boudoir with perforated wiping paper soft enough to dab your mouth on."

I'd heard this kind of talk before. Every time he set me on the train and I fought to stop from crying. "You might not understand why I'm sendin' you away like this. But I keep hopin' you're gonna come back a man, one day."

And now it seemed that I finally had become that true man he'd been trying so hard to mould me into. But not in any way I wanted to hear about.

"Bertha told me all about that nigger boy that drowned."

Head up now, eye to eye. My tongue dry as tinder. I was desperate to hear what he had to say about Gospel, but there was no way I could intervene. No way to set him straight.

"You know, I ain't never told you certain things on account of I thought you were still too wet behind the ears. Didn't want to put any notions inside your head that maybe you couldn't handle. But, Hell boy. You done proved that you more than ready to learn the truth about this mess we got ourselves into."

And as he drained the bottle my skin grew clammy and my face flared red with each poisoned word spilling from between his lips. I tried not to pay any attention to his ravings, but his voice was like a honing stone wearing down a blade. How black blood was tainted. How we all of us needed to wage war in order to make this country pure-blooded once more.

"Give 'em an acre and they'll let the weeds take hold while they sit on their nigger asses, chewing tobacco and cursing their bad luck. Give 'em a spade and they'll likely as not break it in two. Find any excuse not to be doing an honest day's work. Give 'em a saw and they'll mislay it, or hang it on a nail and watch it rust. Give 'em the vote, God help us, and they'll destroy this land of ours. They're a plague, son. So you ain't got no reason to reproach yourself for what you done."

What I'd done? What did he know about what me and Gospel had done?

"The way I see it, you must have been provoked. And so

long as nobody seen you together on that bridge you ain't got nothin' to worry about. I guess you were goaded by that nigger son of a bitch on account of your pa's reputation, and it says in the Good Book that it ain't no sin to kill under such circumstances."

My tongue had become glued to the roof of my mouth. I couldn't find the words to make him stop. To tell him he was wrong, that it had been nothing like he thought it was.

"Your aunt reckons they're calling it an accident down there. It might appear to some that you left a little hastily. Like you was guilty, but Hell, boy. . ."

He slammed his empty glass on the table and let out a laugh.

"I'm mighty proud of you, Truman. Mighty pleased you finally got yourself some fire in your blood. Some grit. There's only one thing better than watchin' a nigger drown and that's watchin' a nigger dance on the end of a rope."

- 2 -

1955

In the days that followed, I thought more than once about boarding a train and heading back south. The thought of living under the same roof as my pa began to plague my dreams; dread seeping into my bones like poison each night when I closed my bedroom door and still heard him rooting around the house. I had kin in Greenwood, and friends that meant a damn sight more than my own flesh and blood. But Pa had other ideas. I still had a lot to learn about life, so he claimed, and he intended completing my schooling before I turned up at Lovelace's yard.

We picked up Joel in a bar straight out of Catfish Row in Vicksburg. The light inside reminded me of the sepia photographs on Miss Du Pree's sideboard. Expensive silver frames containing tattered memories of better days when she and her two sisters were growing up on their pa's plantation fifteen miles outside of Nashville.

"I'd like you to meet an old neighbour of ours. Mr Joel Winters."

"So this here's your boy Truman, all grown up?" He

grabbed me by the shoulder and gave a wink. "Call me Papa Joel, son."

The mercury outside the car had continued to rise as we crossed the Wolf River and headed downtown. By the time we reached our destination I swear the temperature must have registered close on 80 degrees. My lips had become clamped shut and I could barely speak a single word in reply. "Sir."

"We go back a long way, Truman," Pa added. "This man has always been like a father to me."

Joel looked to be about sixty years old, skin creased like parchment and whisps of hair the colour of a faded tombstone. He didn't seem the kind of guy my pa would normally associate with, but what the Hell did I know?

Pa caught the barman's attention with the click of the fingers. "One root beer and a soda over here, and whatever this gentleman is having."

Joel took out a red handkerchief and wiped his brow. "Jeez, are we in Hell, boy? Or is it summertime? I'll take a cold beer as well, if I may. "

"Truman here starts work next week," Pa continued. "Thought he might benefit from an old-timer's advice since he don't take notice of a single word I tell him."

That's because Pa had no patience when it came to tutoring. He tried to teach me how to swim one time when I was five or six years old in one of the creeks feeding Wolf River. Pa hadn't traded in the old Dodge back then, and we headed off down a side road leading off Perez Avenue that soon turned to dirt after the stop sign. He let me sit in his lap and steer once we left the blacktop, and the washed-out, rutted trail took us right up to the water's edge. He let out hoots of terror each time a wheel bucked from one pothole into another but I knew it was play acting.

Then he took out a couple of towels from the trunk and we picked our way down through the sumac and brush to the sandy edge of the creek. We stripped off down to our underwear and he guided me into the river. But as soon as the water reached my waist I started screaming and he had to scoop me up and carry me back to the car. I can remember the look of shame that creased his face as if it was yesterday.

Maybe that's why he put my aunt and Miss Du Pree in charge of my upbringing shortly after. Pa would farm me out to our elderly neighbour for a day or two while attending to the business of throwing out his latest floozie whenever she began stamping her mark on our home, changing his bedsheets or rearranging his routine. He'd stressed often enough how he was an important man and had no time for fussing over the finer details of my upbringing, so I took this sudden interest in my future with a liberal dose of salt.

I slugged back a mouthful of soda and finally my tongue broke loose. "There ain't no need for anybody's advice," I said. "I'll get by just fine." I'd already spent a week the previous summer at Lovelace's weeding out pepper trash from the lint. I reckoned I knew all there was to know about cotton ginning.

But Pa had a different kind of schooling in mind. "I can't have you walking in like some wet behind the ears, candy ass college boy, Truman. There's things you need to get straight regarding how the real world operates."

"You ever hear of Tiptonville, boy?" Joel said. There were flies buzzing outside on Mulberry Street and I could hear something batting against the hot glass of the window.

"This gentleman worked the best part of twenty years out there in a cotton mill," Pa continued.

"I started out here in Memphis when I was the same age as you, I reckon. Place called Frayser. It meant getting the Covington train every day. They put me on some hick farm, working alongside a spindle picker. I wore my fingers to the bone pulling out neps and separating the seeds from the cotton fibres."

Joel turned his back to us and pulled out his handkerchief again. Then I watched as his body spasmed and he coughed. Once. Twice. Spitting a wad of phlegm onto the floor eventually, before turning to face us again.

"Once I'd served my apprenticeship I was put inside with a bunch of wetbacks and half-breeds from down south. We got modules coming in with mud and field debris on the bottom of them and it all had to be cleaned as part of the process. I got pretty darn good at picking out trash, I tell you."

There was a glint in his eyes now, and it seemed him and my pa were sharing some joke I wasn't party to.

"Tell him how it was back in your pa's days, Joel. This man's father worked on a real plantation."

"Well, they still brought in cotton for ginning from Shelby, Madison, Fayette, and other places I don't recall. But cotton was never king in Tennessee the way it been down south."

"Not since they freed the slaves," Pa said. "We all know

that once that lame duck Congress passed the amendment in Washington DC, they were as good as inviting every black man and his dog to head north to the nigger-loving cities in search of paid work. We gave them food and shelter and a taste for honest toil yet they wanted more."

"Anyhow, when my pa was a boy, there was a lynching in Tiptonville and the blacks from them parts. . . Well. There ended up a riot and they burned down thirty buildings or more."

"There wasn't a single store left standing on the main street. This man's father saw it with his own eyes," Pa said. "And that's the kind of behaviour we're encouraging now by giving these people the vote."

"They're like neps in white cotton," Joel continued. "I call it a cancer."

"Joel's pa was a great believer that the surest way to catch yourself the cancer is to pay no heed to your bowels when your body tells you it's time to flush out everything," Pa added, stoking the flame.

"Stands to reason, carrying all that poison round inside your gut can't be good for a body. That's why he taught me it was our God-given duty to weed them out. You undertand what I'm saying, son?"

"It's there in the Bible clear enough," Pa said. "'Servants, be obedient to them that are your masters' - so them uppity blacks getting ahead of themselves and trashing this fine country of ours are disregarding the Lord's word."

I'd heard Pa quote the Bible often enough to know he was twisting its words to justify his own ungodly behaviour. And now it was clear he intended moulding me into something I had no desire to be. A man who would fit into the rotten, hate-infested world he and his friends inhabited and consider himself an agent of the Lord.

Joel lived near Vance Avenue and Pa offered to drive him home. I got to sit in the back as they shared war stories.

"Back on Pigeon Roost Road, it felt like Lamar Avenue was the centre of the universe," Pa said. "The sound of them train whistles all hours of day and night. Somehow it got me longing for home."

"You got the Mississippi running' through your veins, boy."

"I know that, but I done the right thing, getting away from the farm. Even though it took a stolen truck with a twisted chassis and an engine that sputtered like a dried well to get me here." Pa laughed. "And the only thing I knew better than how to tickle for fish or turn a dust-dry acre of flatland into something resembling a pumpkin patch was the history of this blessed country. I had farming in my blood, but my ambition was to make sure I avoided the mistakes my pappy made and his pa before him. This is the land of opportunity, and I ain't gonna let no nigger folk steal it from under our feet."

I'd never known Pa speak for so long without drawing breath or with such passion. He'd always been a man of few words in my company.

"She come with you."

"The boy's mother, yeah. Led me by the balls, you might say. Pardon my language. She was expecting by then, but not showing. Soon as we got to Hooverville I set up my first talking shop in that shelter, and I'm not too proud to admit we lived like pigs back then. But I got back on my feet with the help of friends like you."

Pa turned to me and rested his hand on Joel's arm. "There's a lot you don't know, Truman. How this man and his friends hauled us out of the mire even though there were times when I got as contrary as a mule on a rickety bridge. Remember the squabbles we had at that kitchen table, Joel?"

I'd have been four or five years old, I guess, when we moved to Davis Street. There's not much I recall of the shack over at the Riverside or even the three-room apartment we left behind when Ma moved out, apart from the squares of coloured glass in the front door and the succession of young women who'd come round to cook dinner and sometimes stay over for breakfast.

"Ken Brewer and Scotty and the boys," Joel replied. "They said it would never come to this, but they didn't know shit from soda water. That's what you told them one time. And you were right. Look what we got here now. Candy-ass politicians offering equal rights just to get the black vote.

"I swear, they're stirring a pot that's gonna boil over if they don't turn down the heat. You only have to look at the situation they've created here in Memphis. Coloureds making demands. Political participation. Racial integration. It's breaking this city in two." Joel hawked another gob of mucus and spat it out of the car window. "I'm right in thinkin' the boy's ma never approved, did she?"

Pa said nothing.

"All this talk of keeping the black man in his place. I never once saw her pull up a chair and join us at the kitchen table.

You ever explain to her what you did when you were travelling?"

Pa's grip tightened on the wheel. "It never came up in conversation. Mortimer might have let on when he came collecting his dues. But I was brought up believin' there's things a woman don't need to know. In the Good Book it says wives should submit themselves unto their own husband, as unto the Lord."

"But the boy knows, right?"

"I guess he's old enough to be told."

Joel turned round to face me and began to explain why my pa spent so many days out of town. "Pike here is one of the best fund-raisers I ever did meet. He can talk ministers into emptying their collection boxes and spinsters into handing over their life savings with just a tip of his hat. And all for the brotherhood."

I felt my face flush up with shame at the mention of that single word. I knew what it meant.

"You should be mighty proud of your old man, and it don't matter what your ma thought about anything. The devil rules the world out there, far as I can make out, and a man's gotta protect his family any way he sees fit."

"There ain't nothing more to discuss where that woman's concerned," Pa said. "She took off with a wetback GI soon as Uncle Sam kicked the Japs back into the Pacific, and I swear, she would have stole the boy and taken him with her to New Orleans if I'd let her."

"New Orleans, you say?"

"That's where she ended up," Pa said. "And I hope they

lined her coffin in lead when they laid her in the ground 'cause I know she'll burn in the deepest pit of Hell for what she done."

My own memories of my ma were hazy at best, but I knew this was a lie. Momma had quit our home long before the end of the War. And Aunt Bertha never let on anything about my parents' history 'til the day after Gospel Fry's funeral when I told her I was heading back to Memphis. She told me to take care, and that I should always consider myself her son whenever the occasion demanded it. My pa had let slip how he'd taken steps to make sure my ma never made contact with us ever again, and my aunt told him what a mean thing that was to do. I never had the backbone back then to ask what else he'd told her.

"You know what this is, son?" Joel pulled out a square of silk from his pocket and proceeded to unfold it.

I recognised the hateful emblem right away.

"Take a closer look, Truman. I bet you didn't know the swastika is a sacred symbol. It signifies the centre of the world to some people - the footprint of a holy man from way back. Can you believe that?"

"Not really."

"In the wrong hands this symbol represents evil. And the same goes for the Klan. There are people out there who would rather pretend we didn't exist, because we do what they don't have the stomach to do for themselves. But we're carrying out God's work, and they'd better remember that."

"Damn right," Pa echoed.

Sleep didn't come easy that night. On the journey home Pa kept the windows cranked down, but I couldn't get the stench of Joel Winters out of my nostrils. He smelled bad - his breath, his hair, his creased shirt and his twisted politics. The interior got warmer with every passing milestone, and back at the house, the ceiling fans struggled to lower the temperature. But I had a great deal more to keep me awake into the early hours than the sound of the swishing blades above my bed and the sweltering heat.

- 3 -

1955 - 1956

Maybe it was destiny, but I never did get to set foot again in Lovelace's yard. It wasn't the summer heat that kept me awake that night. It was fever. By next morning my tongue was red and swollen and my head felt like there were jack hammers working inside my skull.

Pa brought in Doctor Gibson and he took one look before diagnosing scarlet fever. Within days my skin was rough as sand paper and covered in a fiery rash. He prescribed rest and fluids. Most of the time I lay lathered in sweat and dreaming all sorts. Gospel was here in my bedroom, tapping a switch against my pillow. One day he promised to teach me how to swim for real. The next he cursed me. "You, boy! You get off this property right now. You listenin'? We don't want no white boys round here. Now scoot!"

Then Donna Mae crept under my covers, soothing my pains with her smile, telling me how much she missed me. Memories came rushing back of the days we'd spent camping beside the Tallahatchie; that carefree life like a mirage built on snatches of laughter and the gentle touch of her fingers that grasped me tight then let go if I moved closer. Like a rope in my hands, each sensation slipped its moorings as sleep relaxed my grip. Maybe I should have fastened each dream to something more substantial, like a door handle or the bedpost.

Pa brought in our elderly neighbour to nurse me while he continued about his fund-raising. Miss Du Pree fussed around me like I was a helpless child, but I paid no heed to her most of the time. I'd spend the morning reading the previous day's Commercial Appeal and afternoons I'd take a snooze while WMC or WREC played in the background. My room seemed to have shrunk in size yet I had no desire to wander far beyond the confines of my bed. I became convinced exposure to the outside world would do me more harm than good. The hot, sticky streets of the city were toxic with the scents of baking concrete and auto exhaust, ham hocks and hoecake.

By the end of September when I showed no signs of recovery Pa started suspecting I was malingering. "I've had Moses Carey on the telephone asking me how much longer he's meant to hold open the vacancy. There's young boys breaking down his door to get a placement there."

"They're welcome," I whispered into my pillow.

I'd already sworn I'd never allow myself to become as bitter and intolerant as my pa, no matter how much he tried to poison my mind. There were men in Lovelace's who drank at the same bar as Joel Winters. Men who had the same philosophy on life. Maybe this had been Pa's plan all along - to have his associates keep an eye on me in case I developed more liberal ways. Fate took a turn that put pay to that.

I sometimes think life is a test we all have to endure from birth to the grave. Good things come along, sidetracking us from the bad, but eventually we find we've been sent hurtling down another course that's ten times worse than the one we think we've escaped. So my unexpected change of direction became as much a blight as a blessing.

"It's got into his heart," Doctor Gibson finally deduced when I showed no signs of recovery. "Truman will need to be moved to St Joseph's so we can carry out further tests."

"What do you mean by tests?" Pa said.

"The boy's showing all the symptoms of rheumatic fever. If left untreated, it will be sure to damage the valves of the heart."

Pa took out his Bible and began to search the psalms for salvation. But it was St Joseph, the patron saint of workmen, who saved me. I was spared from the daily grind of cleaning out cotton at Lovelace's by my confinement at St Joseph's and the sanatorium out at Mallory. I spent close on nine months recuperating before I was let home again. By then Pa conceded I was no longer fit enough to haul bales or breathe in the flue from cotton. Instead he decided I would go to college once I recovered sufficiently and take up accountancy. Memphis State would provide me with the necessary qualifications to progress in the life he had mapped out for me.

But less than a month after rising from my sick bed, Howard Beech and I had made other plans.

- 4 -

1957 - 1958

Howard often claimed we were tuned into a different wavelength than the rest of the world. We drank at a different bar, worshipped at a different church, buttoned up our jackets different to everybody else. It was a game we played. Two young boys with too much time on their hands.

My pal was a city boy through and through: confident and sociable where I was cautious and reticent. In Greenwood I was a celebrity of sorts, but back home in Memphis I was just another dumb kid anxious to fit in but failing at every attempt. I began to realise I was as much a Mississippi hillbilly as Donna Mae. I missed the Flats where the ground fog and chickweed often stood high as our shoulders and traces of cotton down carried on the breeze whichever way you turned.

Howard told me more than once that he'd rescued me that afternoon he turned up at the house shortly after I left Mallory, a month or so before Labor Day when Davis Street was mostly a blur of heat and dust and buzzing insects. He'd arranged with his pa for me to visit one of the print shops downtown. He told me later that his pa had seen some of the photographs I'd taken during my vacation down south and felt I showed a modicum of talent.

Howard picked me up from the house at two o'clock in the afternoon and when we got to the newspaper office he acted as if he owned the place. Once inside, he greeted everyone by their first names and introduced me as a pal from his school days which wasn't strictly true but I went along with the story. Two Remington Quiet-Riters occupied the desk in the reception area. One was clacking away while the owner of the second typewriter held a pencil in one hand and a notepad in the other, barking questions into a telephone. A telegraph machine spewed out a ribbon of paper tape on another desk, and over the entire office the aroma of stale cigarette smoke and coffee seemed to hang like drapes.

"This is where it all happens, Truman," Howard said. "The world's news arrives along that wire, someone gets to write it up and send it downstairs, and once it leaves the print shop it's ready to be sold, fresh off the press. I'll take you, introduce you to Morgan. He's the best typesetter in Tennessee according to my pa."

"Can I stick around here a while longer?" The buzz of industry had already got to me, feeding fire into my veins and igniting a spark in my delicate heart.

Howard told me later how he knew I'd discovered my calling as soon as I stepped in through the door. "That gleam in your eye. Damn, you're a natural, Truman. Same as me." But I was four years younger than Howard. He'd already been a cub reporter for eighteen months or more, and he had the confidence and drive to be a newshound whilst I was a dumb kid who still lacked the nerve to follow my ambition.

Howard's family were good friends of Miss Du Pree, and when we were boys he and I had spent many an afternoon together on our front porch or in her parlour listening to gramophone records. Both our fathers were too busy to pay us much attention, and both our mothers were no longer around. Howard's ma was still a fixture in the Beech residence, but her debilitating illness kept her imprisoned in her bedroom. Howard doted on the old lady, but when he spoke about her it never seemed as if she was amongst the living. That's one of the things we had in common.

In some ways we both looked upon Miss Du Pree as a substitute mother figure. Howard more so than I. And even though he was more than four years my senior I took to thinking it wasn't natural, a boy his age fawning over an old woman as if she was his sweetheart. But I had nothing else to compare their behaviour with. For all her cossetting, Aunt Bertha was hardly the maternal type.

Our neighbour had a fondness for Negro spirituals. 'Poor Old Joe' and 'Michael Row the Boat Ashore' would often reduce her to tears. But she was also prone to falling asleep in the afternoon, and whenever that happened the maid would close the blinds and we would be instructed to take the wind-up gramophone out onto the veranda. We'd share a smoke and Howard would play his pa's jazz records.

We also took to wandering down along the shore of Sandpit Lake or even up to View Park when days dragged and the heat got to us both. I pined for the outdoors and told Howard about the times I spent hanging around with Bo Dean and Donna Mae.

"Did I ever tell you about Mary Lou Carpentier across the street? She jerked me off once and I kid you not, she had a grip like an Appalachian milk maid."

I didn't believe a word of that. Mary Lou and I attended the same Sunday school and she got awarded a book token once for telling the class how she'd never uttered a cuss word her entire life.

"You planning on marrying that tomboy, Truman?"

I shook my head and the matter was never discussed again. But on many an occasion, Howard and I would sneak out one of Pa's pony bottles of Rolling Rock beer and play a game where we took turns choosing our future brides.

Howard said I'd probably end up marrying Miss Hayseed Mississippi 1959. I replied by telling him his perfect match would as likely as not be Miss Sniffy Smart-Ass Alabama 1972.

Soon after he turned eighteen, Howard took to wearing his hair swept back and oiled to a sheen like Clark Gable. He also adopted a way of holding a cigarette that put me in mind of Pa's hard-bitten drinking partners at the Club. I had Howard down as a lady-killer, but something about the look that passed between us when we were alone made me think different.

"We're brothers, Truman," he'd say. "Made from the same cloth, so don't you forget that."

By the time I left Leflore County for good, Howard Beech and I had become more like fellow-conspirators. I finally decided to let on why I never returned to Mississippi after the summer Gospel Fry died. Howard had already seen the photographs I took of Bo Dean and Donna Mae and he assumed I was especially close to Bo. I swear a look of genuine despair crossed his face when he heard there'd been an accidental drowning.

"Jumped off a bridge right in front of you? That poor boy." To my eternal shame I didn't set him straight even then. "If something bad happens when you're growing up there isn't an easy way to forget it. Sometimes the memories get jumbled up and you start to think it was all your fault."

Howard's family had been prominent in the city's Jewish circles for many years. His grandpa, Avi, changed his name from Bechstein to Beech as soon as the family left Ellis Island in May 1896. But everyone knew their pedigree, not least because Howard's pa, Saul Beech II, spoke his mind and printed his opinion on the front page of his newspapers each week.

Amongst these publications was the Collierville Courier, a weekly rag affiliated to the Nashville Daily Record. I started at the Courier early October 1958, a fortnight after I'd turned nineteen. They stuck me in Accounts and most of the time I took telephone orders from advertisers or chased up late payments.

Pa claimed my new position was nothing to brag about. I'd be making coffee for the office staff until the day I retired, earning buttons while sitting behind a desk and answering the telephone the entire time except for Thursdays. That was the day the paper got delivered and Pa reckoned it's when I'd be let loose in the streets. He saw me as little more than a glorified paper-boy.

But less than a year later, I was offered the position of

runner between the newsroom and the print shop. This put me at the sharp end of the Courier rather than in the backroom with Miss Grisham. Rumours were she'd worked in tele-sales since before the telephone was invented.

Not long after my promotion, Aunt Bertha wrote me a letter. Times were hard, but she was managing without any hired help thanks to the Soil Bank scheme. I wrote back telling her of my new career in newspapers. Three months later she sent word that Buck Moon and Bo Dean had abandoned Leflore County in search of better paid work, leaving Donna Mae on her own to raise Bo's child - Katie Jo born August 8th. I bit down the disappointment in my heart and sent back a card wishing mother and child well. Another ten years would pass before Aunt Bertha, Donna Mae and I met up again.

- 5 -

1958 - 1959

Saul Beech and my pa both had their faults. Neither could be accused of presenting a perfect example of fatherhood. Given his background, Saul had the strangest views on history. Amongst the framed photographs on his desk, he kept a black and white portrait of Adolf Hitler. He claimed that if Hitler hadn't persecuted the Jews so, the state of Israel would never have been created. Saul put that down to the world's collective guilt following the Holocaust.

He also said there'd come a day when America would do the same for the Negro population. We'd be forced to proclaim a separate state somewhere in the West Indies to accommodate the descendants of all the black slaves abused and mistreated during our shameful past. Maybe that's why the Courier chose to give such prominence on their pages to the Civil Rights campaigns sweeping through the state while other newspapers continued to pretend nothing of the sort was happening.

One afternoon shortly before Christmas, I got a message to report to Mr Beech's office. There were already whispers in the press room - I was either in for a pay rise or my cards. Most of the hiring and firing always took place just before the holidays. But when I arrived he offered me neither. Instead he told me to take a seat and ordered us both a cup of coffee from his personal secretary.

"Howard showed me some of the photographs you took when you stayed at your aunt's farm, Truman. I'd say you have a fine eye for capturing characters."

I nodded politely.

"I reckon, if you were given the right tutoring some of your pictures would stand the test of time. Might even end up on the front page of the nationals."

I tried to deny it all. But then he told me his plans for the New Year. I was to be taken on as an apprentice to one of the staff photographers.

"You willing to give it a try?"

"Yes, sir. Of course, sir. I mean, thanks ever so much, Mr Beech."

He waved my thanks aside and began to guide me through some of the black and white portraits hanging on his wall. There must have been twenty or more, but three in particular stuck in my mind. Jesse Owens sprinting down the track in Berlin, Jackie Robinson in his Dodgers 42 shirt taken before they relocated from Brooklyn to Los Angeles, and a black boy the spitting image of Gospel Fry, stylish in his neat white shirt, black tie and Panama hat.

"Forget about words, Truman. This is how they'll record history in the future," Saul Beech said. "These are the memories people will always carry inside their heads." Then he told me how the young black boy had been killed. "Ever hear of a place called Money, down in Leflore County?"

I felt the blood rise to my face. Of course I had. This was the boy whose body had been found in the Tallahatchie, less than a half hour's walk from Aunt Bertha's farm. He'd drowned shortly after I returned home from Greenwood with the shame of guilt still stinging my cheeks. Pa had mentioned the death in passing, as if it signified better times ahead. The boy had been caught making a pass at a white woman, by all accounts. A married woman. His punishment would be a lesson to all, and clear proof to the wider world of the need to keep black boys in their place.

Then Saul reached in his desk drawer and took out a folded up newspaper featuring a photograph of the same boy, maybe wearing that same white shirt, but without the confident smile of youth on his face. This time he'd been laid out in a casket with his head battered and grotesquely misshapen in death.

"You understand what we're part of here, Truman? If we don't show the world what's happening right under their noses, rub their faces in it if we have to, then this whole country is going to Hell."

I understood well enough. I'd be recording history the same as the other stringers on his books - not with a pen and paper but with a camera. Saul Beech made it clear to me that afternoon he wouldn't be satisfied with photographs of the latest Cotton Queen in her white lace dress on Pageant Day or pictures chronicling the demise of the Memphis Chicks. He demanded my work count for something more.

I left it until the New Year to tell my pa I intended moving out for twelve months or maybe more in the spring. He dismissed the notion with a flick of the cigarette. "You leaving just like that? My home not good enough for you anymore, boy?"

"It ain't nothing like that," I said. "Mr Beech has offered me a position out at Nashville. I get to spend some time out there shadowing a professional photographer, then if I make the grade he says there'll be a job waiting for me back here in Memphis with the Courier."

Pa took the news in his stride. "That's all fine and dandy, son. But how the hell you gonna afford a place of your own out in Nashville? You lined up yourself some rich widow woman with a fortune sewn inside her corsets?"

"I get to stay with one of Howard's cousins' family."

Pa hoo-hawed the idea. He couldn't bring himself to trust the Beeches on account of the way Saul championed the Civil Rights movement in his weekly editorials. But I convinced him it was what I intended doing, whether he liked it or not. I'd grown a backbone during my apprenticeship. I'd also figured out what I'd suspected all along since the days when I fooled around with Donna Mae and the boys. I was never going to settle down with a woman and help her raise a family.

Howard hadn't taken long to see the way the wind blew either. "It's time you started living up to your name, Truman. Be true to yourself."

- 6 -

1959 - 1960

Howard's cousins owned a sprawling ranch-style house overlooking Sevier Lake. Ed Peterson from the Nashville office took me under his wing, but Howard and I kept in touch by telephone and many a time he came over to spend the weekend in Shelby Bottoms. His pa had already bought him a Studebaker Silver Hawk for his twenty-first birthday - his pride and joy. And most nights when the weather was amenable we'd drive out to the Sparkman Street Bridge spanning the Cumberland and watch the freight trains cross the river. Howard would park under one of the high, metal trusses supporting the crossing and we'd walk as far as the river.

Or we'd sit and catch up. "Miss Steamed-up Glasses, Minnesota."

"Miss Lockjaw, Arkansas."

"Miss Bleeding Gums, Colorado."

"Miss Cleft Palate, Pennsylvania."

"Miss Skunk Breath, South Dakota."

"Miss Swampy Thighs, Arizona. Did you know we're getting drafted? You and me, the two most eligible bachelors this side of the Rockies?"

That stopped me dead in my tracks. "What d'you mean drafted?" I'd heard plenty about the draft, but Pa reckoned I'd be a code I-F if Kennedy ever declared war against Russia. I was unfit for combat - physically, mentally and morally, by all accounts.

"No need to get so worked up, partner. Before you leave Nashville, Pa wants you and me to pair up and do some scouting behind enemy lines."

I felt my face colour up at the very notion. "What's that supposed to mean?"

"He's gonna have us work as a team, reporting on the news that no one else will touch. He says there's big changes on the way, Truman. Blacks are starting to fight back. They're already holding sit-ins at lunch counters that only serve whites. Here in Nashville and at Greensboro, North Carolina. Some of them are getting beaten up on account of their principles, and Pa wants us to gather as much evidence as we can. Photographs. Witness statements."

My hands began to tremble. Almost twelve months learning the trade, and my only solo assignment to date had been to record the local Christmas Fare at the Downtown Presbyterian in blizzard conditions. A minor traffic accident had taken place while I was in the neighbourhood involving some local politician's motor car and a lamp post and I'd been lucky enough to capture the historic event on film. Howard reckoned his pa must have staged the whole thing to generate more sales, but I knew different. The camera never lies.

"It's mostly black college students," he said. "They sit at downtown lunch counters, refusing to leave or even to speak out of turn. It's their way of protesting at the way they're treated different to white folk. There's been one or two unpleasantnesses: staff refusing to serve them, and some have been given a beating without provocation. Pa says the country needs to see what's going on right under their noses."

I'd heard it all before. "When's he expecting us to start all this? I mean, you're gonna be gone back to Memphis this time tomorrow."

"Pa's given me a couple of weeks to sniff around. I'll take notes and you'll shoot the photographs. If you're gonna earn yourself a press pass, pal, you're gonna have to go into battle sooner or later. We need to make people look twice when they read the newspapers at their breakfast tables. All the better if we're part of the news because we're prepared to take risks and put our lives on the line."

This was the kind of opportunity I'd been waiting for. It thrilled me and terrified me in equal measure. "We'll be helping the poor blacks make their voices heard?"

"Yeah. Think what you father will have to say about that? You'll come home a hero."

I could just picture my father's reaction.

Howard took out his flask, unscrewed the top and handed it across. "Take a slug. It'll settle your nerves."

I shook my head. I'd seen Pa the worse for wear through drink and swore I'd never chase the bottle the way he did.

Apart from the occasional beer, Howard and I had only ever got drunk the one time on cheap red wine, and from the way we'd acted that night I reckoned it was better we stay off the hard stuff.

"I don't need my nerves settling. Maybe we should get back to the house. I've got to meet Ed early tomorrow morning."

"Ed can wait. I reckon he's taught you all he knows. Time you stood on your own two feet."

Eleven thirty at night and the residual heat from the unseasonably warm April sun continued to bake the inside of the car despite both windows being cranked open.

"It's still early afternoon in Honolulu, Truman. How about one sip just for me."

"I'm fine."

He rested his left hand on my thigh. "Unless I've misread the signals, we're heading in the same direction you and me. Right?"

I swallowed the rock in my throat as he began to stroke my leg. Then he took a swig as if to clear his mind. "We're setting off to war together, like comrades in arms. You and me. Tell me I'm right."

I had no defences in place to hide my feelings. He took another slug then he pulled his hand away. "How many other vehicles do you see parked out there, Truman?"

I counted a half dozen. Four saloons and two pickup trucks.

"And I bet there's just two people sat in the front seat of

most of them."

"So what?"

"So, d'you think they're here to admire the scenery? There must be better things to look at than this heap of rusted metal? The steel rivets rotted away years ago, and if the NBC don't look to repairing it soon it's gonna fall down into the river. The bridge ain't exactly a national monument."

"I suppose not," I said. "But it reminds me of the Tallahatchie Bridge. The pattern of cross-beams."

"That's the bridge your boyfriend jumped off. Right?"

I nodded, my face burning up with shame.

"So finally we get to the truth." The way he said it made it clear we hadn't come here to discuss architecture. "D'you think they're here to admire the ironwork? Or maybe they're sharing a cigarette and a drink with the radio turned down low?"

"Mhmm."

"Jerking each other off to while away the time, 'cause there's no one else about this late at night to watch what they're getting up to."

I didn't respond.

"You ever jerk off in a Studebaker, Truman?"

I shook my head. We'd never spoken openly about such things since we'd become grown men. Morgan in the print shop had told me all about his ex-wife and how she'd dumped him when he was caught with his pants down entertaining her sister. But he never once asked me to share my own intimate experiences. It would have been a short discussion at best.

"What about you and Bo? Or that buck-toothed tomboy down south you told me you were both hot for? She ever jerk you off?"

I thought back to the photographs I'd taken of Donna Mae - stretched out in Aunt Bertha's yard, sunning herself out at the lake and posing for me on the Mason property. Howard had printed them out when I got back from Greenwood and he'd teased me about her scarecrow body and the skimpy clothes that barely covered her nakedness; the way she stared into the lens with a look of surrender in her eyes. Or maybe lust.

"She ain't got buck teeth, and no we never did nothin' like that."

"But you told me how she let you touch her one time, and how she couldn't keep her hands off you."

"We were just kids foolin' around," I said.

"So you still sweet on her? Or was it Bo who broke your heart?"

Maybe I should have brought Donna Mae with me to Memphis like she wanted. Life offered more promise here; a future worth contemplating compared to an eternity spent hoeing the dead dust of Mississippi. But I'd dismissed her then the same way I dismissed her now.

"I keep tellin' you she never meant anythin' to me. Last I heard Donna Mae was courtin' and there's a baby now as well."

"So it's just you and me, lover boy."

"Me and you?" I said. "Why would you say that?"

Howard gave one of his dismissive gestures; a smirk followed by a shake of the head. "Deny it all you like, but I never saw you once chasing Nashville skirt all the time you spent away from under your pappy's roof. There's been nothing stopping you hook a Tennessee broad, unless you've got other tastes."

"I know that," I said.

"So what d'you propose we should do about this delicate situation you're in?"

I didn't know what situation Howard was referring to. Then I felt his left hand on my thigh again and I pressed my head against the back of the car seat and slowly slid my hips forward so he could unbuckle my belt and unfasten the buttons on my pants.

- 7 -

1960

It didn't go unnoticed, to those who knew us best, that Howard and I had grown closer while I'd been away in Nashville. I'd taken to growing my hair long and wearing the same Palmolive after-shave lotion as he did, even though the stubble on my face was barely worth shaving more than twice a week. Saul Beech started calling us Ethel and Albert. I never did work out which of us was meant to be Ethel.

In private, Howard told me I'd need to take care because I was growing more like my pa each day. He'd noticed I had the same style of walking, like my shoes were a size too large, and the sloppy way I'd swivel my shoulders whenever I came into a room made it look like I was trying to slip free of my jacket. If I looked in the mirror I'd see the same curl of lip and the same snake eyes. I'd even adopted Pa's scowl to perfection. Twenty-one years old and already wishing I were dead.

Pa didn't comment on my physical appearance apart from the length of my hair. He was more concerned about my moral and political welfare. I tried to explain why it wouldn't work out my returning home to live in Davis Street now my training in Nashville was complete. "I'll be working long hours, catching meals on the road whenever I can. And Mr Beech expects me to call in at the Collierville office most nights to deliver fresh copy."

"Is that fresh copy you're chasing or fresh cooze?" As far as Pa was concerned, if there wasn't some floozie involved, I had no business leaving home for good and living the bachelor life. But I no longer considered Davis Street home, so there was nothing he could do to change my mind.

"They've put us up in a couple of rooms out at Olive Branch for the time being," I said. "Me and one of the cub reporters. It's a condo - not much to look at. But once I'm settled and earning a proper wage, I'll be looking for somewhere closer to the city. Then you can come visit."

"I suppose that means they're paying you peanuts," he snarled. "You should look at finding work with a respectable newspaper not some kike-run rag. Saul Beech makes a fortune out of peddling lies, and I know for a fact Jews don't like parting with money."

I changed the subject. I had my Nashville portfolio with me and I let him take a look at some of the black and whites I'd shot. That was my first mistake.

"They pay you to take pictures of darkies?" He continued to flip through the pictures. "It don't make sense."

"Ain't you heard of civil disobedience?" I said. "It's happening all across America, and Mr Beech wants to make sure we get both sides of the story. There's white students tryin' to support what the blacks are doing. And there's others there who want to give them a hard time. I've got it all on film."

"You've got names as well?"

I picked out one particular shot taken on the steps of Davidson County Court House. "You ever hear of Ben West?"

"I know who Mayor West is, and as far as I'm concerned he's the one who encouraged the blacks to vote. But what about all these front-line agitators?" he said. "These troublemakers need weeding out like barnyard grass or pigweed. It's sedition, and if Sollie Beech is fool enough to plaster their faces all over his rag then he's playing with fire. Does he even know who your pa is?"

"Of course he does. But he trusts me to keep an open mind. He says I have to remain professional." That was my second mistake.

Saul Beech had warned me to keep my powder dry. One Chicago Tribune crime reporter had been shot dead twenty years ago for double-crossing the Mob. And closer to home, there were rumours a freelance photographer for the Commercial Appeal was a known FBI informant.

But in my father's twisted world my new position as staff photographer was the most perfect irony - a newspaper owned by a white liberal who publicly announced his support of desegregation and racial integration paying the son of a racist bigot to spy on black activists and record the identities of those who sought to champion civil rights. Suddenly Parker Lee Hardy had a son he could be proud of.

I couldn't find a way to set him straight. Maybe if I had, things would have turned out different. Over the next few weeks Pa boasted to anyone who'd care to listen how his boy was doing the Good Lord's work under the very eyes of one of the most mendacious men he knew. I went along with the delusion up to a point. But deep down it was my pa and his cronies I had dreams of exposing.

We met up in various bars a couple of times a month, never the same bar twice. Pa and his friends. Joel Kennedy was there on most occasions along with a couple of other familiar faces I'd seen visiting Pa all hours when I'd been home convalescing. We'd sit in a corner booth and everybody got to study the latest batch of pictures. I made sure to hold back any photographs featuring the more fanatical activists even though most of their faces made it into the newspaper. I think Pa enjoyed the subterfuge, as if he and his troops were fighting their own private war.

Now and again I'd attach a name to a body or give my pa details of locations and dates. There were regulars from both sides of the fence who attended every downtown sit-in simply for the hell of it.

Howard and his old man might consider this sensitive information, but I saw no harm in letting Pa and his pals sift through a few pictures. In my defence I was protecting the ring-leaders and the more vulnerable by keeping their identities under wraps. Besides, I knew Pa would find it hard to act on any information I passed on since everything I showed him was already ancient history. He could have got the same news from any rag on sale at most news stands for five cents plus tax.

But by the fall of 1960 Pa began to demand more. Saul Beech had his finger on the pulse of the nation. Howard and I were often the only two reporters on the street when a demonstration or a show of solidarity was about to take place. He was already selling our stories to newspapers as far afield as San Francisco and Boston. It didn't take long for Pa to suspect the Courier was in collusion with the demonstrators, and he began to ask about my movements in advance. It took a heap of lies to put him off the scent.

Then one day we were told we'd be heading down to New Orleans to chase up a story about school desegregation. I still have the photograph I took of that poor child in her pretty white blouse and pinafore dress, carrying her satchel as if it held all that was precious to her, flanked on the steps of a white elementary school by a cordon of security officials.

Every morning demonstrators formed a crowd across the road, screaming abuse and waving placards. Some had packed lunches, and I lost count of the mothers who'd brought their babies along with them for the day.

'This is God's way.'

'God demands we segregate.'

'Cursed is the man who integrates' - Jeremiah 11:3-6.

I cursed my pa for sharing similar views and told Howard I'd maybe try and find what became of my ma while we were in town.

- 8 -

1960 - 1963

I had very little to go on. A first name. A date. Early April 1946. Other than that, the facts were hazy.

"What you hoping to find?"

I thought maybe an obituary. Or at least a suspicious death that might correspond with what Aunt Bertha had told me.

"Look for a white woman, in her twenties. Attacked maybe, or disappeared in suspicious circumstances. Round about the Spring of 1946. That's all I got."

Howard's pa had contacts in the State Times. They were sure to have archives the same as the Courier. Box-files in a dusty back room no doubt. But when we arrived at their offices we were met by one of the clerks who'd already been instructed to trawl through an entire year's collection of news stories on our behalf. A sheaf of papers awaiting us. Seventy-three deaths in total.

We retreated to one of the bars down by the river and I began to read. Shootings. Stabbings. Stranglings. I checked them all but most didn't seem to fit. There was a drowning, February 1946. A young woman's body found washed up on the West Bank of Bridge City. The authorities believed she jumped. Hair bleached white by the chemicals in the river, according to the coroner. That same month, a female torso had been left in a duffel bag in one of the storage lockers at the Union Passenger Terminal. A child's, as it turned out. But neither fitted by my reckoning. Then two months later, a fire in a townhouse in the French Quarter of the city appeared to have been started deliberately. The only casualties were two young prostitutes. One a new girl in town; an albino according to the neighbours.

"Could that be her, do you think?"

Ma a whore? What the hell did I know?

"Keep looking."

An automobile accident caused by a drunk driver who fled the scene on foot and was never caught. A shooting in Jackson Square. The police were calling it a crime of passion. But then another killing three nights later suggested both murders might have been connected to organised crime. By then, deep in my gut, I knew we'd already found her. I made a note of the date and searched for more details. The investigation had centred on Basin Street and a Cajun-speaking pimp who denied all knowledge of how the fire might have started. The alarm got raised sometime around midnight on April 20th. No one was ever apprehended, and only one body was ever recovered. A young woman buried in a pauper's grave in the Holt Cemetery. I tried to fit this in with what little I knew. Pa had been in New Orleans that time for sure, and he had a talent for starting fires.

I got Howard to drive me to the cemetery the morning

before we left town. It stood a block or so south of Lake Pontchartrain and looked like the kind of spooky graveyard you might come across in Dogpatch, Kentucky or in any other of them back page, Halloween cartoons. There were few if any marble headstones with angels and crosses and sentimental engravings. Here and there we came across sprays of dried flowers and desicated wreaths, but most of the graves were unmarked. The entire place looked abandoned and left me feeling more desperate than ever.

"How you gonna know which one's hers, even if she's in here?" Howard asked.

"She might still be alive and moved to Alaska for all we know," I said eventually.

I couldn't wait to get home. I even passed up the opportunity of calling in on my aunt as we approached Jackson and saw the signs for Vicksburg and Cary and Greenville.

Back in Olive Branch we'd taken to sleeping in separate rooms - 'in case Pa comes calling on a hunch,' was Howard's excuse. But I began to wonder whether our situation was always meant be temporary. Howard would leave me one day and find himself a good woman. Fine breeding stock to keep the Beech line alive regardless of the lie.

I no longer cared what anyone thought, including my pa or his associates. It had always been my bed Howard and I shared for lovemaking, and once he returned to his own room I felt his absence like a cold draught on my skin. Even when Donna Mae had put on a show, I'd never paid much attention to her hidden parts. It was more to do with her facial expression: the mean look in her eye, the sly grin, an involuntary bow of the head as soon as she knew she'd caught my attention.

In the same way, Howard presented an overwhelming feast for the senses. The soft drawl of his voice whenever he told me how much he loved me gave me goosebumps. The scent of his skin somehow always transferred itself to mine and I'd be reluctant to shower until later in the day. The touch of his cold fingers tracing the rise and fall of my rib cage was enough to get me hard. His clipped nails and fingertips stained by nicotine. The same fingertips smoothing the hairs on my belly. The taste of cigarette on his breath as he leaned in for a kiss. The heat and weight of a leg splayed across one of mine.

I'll never forget the feel and texture of his lips the first time he took me inside his mouth. The way his teeth closed ever so gently on the tip then the flick of his tongue, growing faster and faster. I wanted Pa to catch us - to watch all this with his own eyes and dare to condemn our passion for each other. He'd chosen my name and I intended living up to it.

- 9 -

1964 - 1968

They say you should be careful what you wish for in case it comes true. I often look back at this ghastly period of my life and wonder whether I pushed Pa too far in the end. He'd told me often enough how he felt betrayed by the country of his birth, by the woman who bore his one and only child, and by his own flesh and blood. I took that to mean my grandpa, Abraham Lee Hardy, who had willed my pa's birthright to Aunt Bertha.

"My blessed sister's welcome to the twenty acres of Mississippi bottomland she likes to call a farm. And I'm not saying Old Man Hardy had anything approaching what you or I might call a fortune. But disowning your own son, there ain't no greater sin than that in my book."

Yet, I knew he'd disown me without skipping a heartbeat if he found out the truth about me and Howard. Maybe that's what I wanted to happen. To be cut free from his small-minded bigotry once and for all. I'd heard the revulsion in his voice many a time when he spoke about the goings on in California. He'd read about the Castro neighbourhood of San Francisco. "No better than the sewer streets of New Orleans. There ain't no sense why decent people don't burn the place to the ground."

"Welcome to the 60's, Pa. The whole world has changed since when you were a teenager. Even folk down Mississippi are beginnng to move with the times, in case you ain't heard. There's a revolution takin' place."

"More like an abomination, Truman. And if we turn our back on the teachings of the Good Lord we'd better prepare for eternal damnation."

That's maybe why I never felt at ease with the lies and deception that bubbled under the surface. Howard and I had convinced ourselves we were doing no harm. He kept reminding me, as long as no one else knew, there'd be no hurt feelings. Besides, we were both American citizens so could plead the Fourteenth Amendment if anyone accused us of placing public morals and decency at risk. The fact that we were free white men who had never been black slaves was a mere formality according to Howard.

But I knew his ma, Emilene Beech, intended for her son to marry into Memphis high society one day and produce her a grandchild. And he never had the courage to set her straight. Whenever Howard brought home a new lady friend, his ma'd begin making wedding plans. I knew exactly what he was going through. I'd done my own share of play acting whenever Aunt Bertha brought up the topic of Miss Donna Mae Cobham, even though we'd both of us known it was an act. But Howard seemed more than happy to play along with the deception. That's how I knew he would be gone from my life sooner or later.

I suddenly began to wonder how Donna Mae felt to be

fooled so. I still have her photograph - stood on Aunt Bertha's porch in just a shift. Bare feet, a ribbon band to keep the hair out of her eyes, one arm across her midriff and the other folded so her chin is cupped in her hand, a broom leaning against the door post, our wash tub on the deck and a pile of kindling drying in the sun. That's the one I treasure the most.

I cherish a heap of other photographs as well, maybe more so now I'm free of Memphis. One features Howard Beech posed alongside his Silver Hawk parked outside a billiard hall on Beale Street, with a grin on his chops wide enough to swallow you whole. That was taken the day we treated Morgan from the print shop to a drive through the neighbourhood he grew up in. A neighbourhood he spoke about fondly many a time.

We stopped outside the Orpheum and he accused of us of behaving like a pair of schoolgirls when we asked him to point out the pickpockets who used to hang around, or the medicine shows and the wandering bluesmen. Of course, all were long gone and we already knew that.

There are other photographs. Ones I made certain to keep from my pa. Sheriff Jim Clark with a bull-whip in his hands laying into a young black man on Broad Street in Selma. A bunch of black housemaids and other cleaning staff, out there in front of a motel with their mops and their pushing carts. Mouths open in wonder as they watch a Civil Rights march go by while their white managers stand behind them keeping control. Blacks with their faces running with blood following an unprovoked attack by a bunch of white hoodlums. And that poor schoolgirl on the steps of a New Orleans school, as slight as a fluff of cotton candy.

I also keep a copy of the photograph I never got to take. One that appeared on every front page from Memphis to Milwaukee. Every time I look at it, I pray for forgiveness. I know things would have been different if I'd behaved more professionally; the way Saul Beech instructed me to behave. The way the Good Lord would have wanted it.

I'd been invited to attend the Lorraine Motel in Memphis with the King entourage and take a number of candid shots for posterity. It would be an undoubted honour. Saul Beech himself told me I'd finally made it. And I can remember telephoning Pa and telling him the news on the Sunday morning - five days before the event. All he did was make some sarcastic comments about my skin changing colour.

"They touched you up with a tar brush since I seen you last?" That's the last time we ever spoke.

It didn't register when the car pulled up outside our bungalow in the early hours on the day of the tragedy. Neither of us heard the snick of the latch as the street door opened at the front of the building. Whoever it was presumably saw Howard's car parked on the road and no doubt recognised my shoes in the hallway and my silk scarf and overcoat hanging on the peg. Yet they let us sleep.

Instead we discovered later that someone had also tampered with the fuel tank of Howard's Studebaker. By the time I figured out who had paid us a visit, it was too late.

Pa claimed to have contacts everywhere and it's likely he'd been told I was a faggot long before now. For a wonder he never chose to comment on that minor detail. But that didn't mean he was prepared to accept the notion. He cursed the hippies with flowers in their hair and free love. He cursed the bath houses and men openly co-habiting and walking the streets arm in arm. He cursed longhairs and Commies and queers with the same fervour reserved for niggers, and all I ever did was stoke the fire by speaking up on their behalf and letting my own hair grow down over my collar.

The night things finally came to a head had been weighed down by an unseasonal sultriness and Howard and I spent most of the time stretched out naked on top of my bed. The two rooms at the back of the house were always in shade, but there was no escaping the heat. I guess if our visitor had found us like that I wouldn't be here to tell my tale.

We'd shared a drink or two before bedtime and it was past midday when Howard and I finally got up. We showered together then I went through to the kitchen while he finished dressing. Howard had other plans for the evening. A fund-raising dinner at some golf club with a date his mother had arranged. We'd made a joke about it over supper the previous night.

"Miss Itchy Snatch, Nebraska."

When I went through to the hallway to pick up the morning newspaper, I found the screen door wide open and a framed photograph lay smashed on the outside step, as if someone had taken it out into the sunlight for a closer look before deliberately stamping on it. It showed two smiling faces in the sunshine on Beale Street. I picked up the broken frame and pieces of glass, salvaged the photo and went back into the kitchen. That's when I figured out who it was who'd paid us a visit in the dead of night - and why.

This is where it ended.

ODE TO PARKER LEE HARDY

- 1 -

1945

When it ended.

Pa didn't hold with hopin' and dreamin'. He belonged to the church of head down and hard graft. 'You don't reap right after you sow,' he'd tell me often enough. 'You reap after you plough deep. You sow and hoe and weed and then, if the Good Lord blesses your hard work, you reap.' I guess his harsh philosophy on life is what drove me away from the farm. That and the dreams of the balmy days ahead I'd get share with Angel, my buttermilk girl. Except the buttermilk curdled within less than a year.

By the time we reached Memphis, I had more contacts in

the Tennessee Klan than Harry Truman had voters on his side. Our lives were on the up. We had a three-room apartment and I got to wear a suit for work. I was finally somebody. But that didn't stop Angel taking my child away from me as soon as she got tired of acting the part of decent, God-fearing housewife.

Mort Sweeney reckoned she left home because she didn't hold with my politics. Never had. He'd seen the look on her face when I held meetings in our kitchen. But Jesus Christ, we were brothers doing what brothers are meant to do. Looking out for each other. A brotherhood that spanned the entire continent from the Rockies to Atlantic City, from the Great Lakes to the Mississippi delta. When I say the Great Lakes, I mean Chicago specifically. That's the place I last heard word about that bitching whore.

When Fin Harleson showed me them photographs I near enough threw up my breakfast right there on the kitchen table. Fin had picked up an old issue of the '*Chic-a-go-go Magazine*' inside the lobby of Honeysuckle Hall, one of several nigger brothels up in St Louis. He'd been visiting on Klan business, putting out word that the day of reckoning was coming to any American establishment promoting or profiteering from miscegenation.

The cover had turned yellow with age, but I recognised that Whore of Babylon as soon as I set eyes on her face. My snow white bride with her snow white skin, naked as the day she was born and wrapped around some two-bit nigger whore fresh from the gutter. The two of them, shaved bare with everything they had on show: arms, legs, feet, breasts, lips and their most private parts exposed to the world. Like a pair of swamp snakes, one body entwined around the other to form a single obscenity. A slur on the work of the

Creator.

The screed that accompanied the pictures told how two children, innocent as the day they were born, had been rescued from the street and raised like sisters in some two-bit bordello called the Lavender Garden. It was seen as some kind of miracle how the colour of their skin made no difference. They shared a bed in their own private salon, and paying visitors could watch them, oiled and perfumed, as they paraded their nakedness and squirmed against each other for anyone to watch and glory at the abomination.

Even worse was the knowledge that I'd sowed my precious seed inside her womb. Then I thought back to the other things we'd done in the back of that truck - the tricks she'd been taught back in Chicago - and my stomach twisted at the memory. I'd known back then she'd been raised in a cathouse. Angel had the mouth and claws to prove it. But part of me chose to disbelieve her tale, even though her tongue could spew lies as easy as spend kisses.

I'd also chosen to disbelieve her when she told me I wasn't the first, and that she was no more a gift from the Good Lord above than Betty Boop. It took time before I realised she'd been spreading her legs for a buck a trick since she was old enough to bleed. And here was the proof in black and white. The irony.

I got Fin to make further enquiries, starting at the Lavender Garden. He told me, sure enough, the brothel was still there on the South Side of the city. "One of them rundown neighbourhoods where niggers walk the sidewalk as if they rule the streets."

Then he mentioned the name of the owner. "Some small time hood called Mint Drago."

I left the boy in the care of Miss Du Pree. Our neighbour considered herself 'Old Memphis', with enough of her own money set aside to live comfortably without a need to foster the airs and graces of those who merely posessed pretentions of grandeur. The ones who she claimed were too poor to paint but too proud to whitewash.

Miss Du Pree was accustomed to sitting in with Truman whenever I was away overnight on business. I explained this particular business might take a day or two more, but I trusted her with my son and they got on well together. Truman was only six years old and good as gold - maybe too good. I told him I'd bring him home an extra special Christmas present from the Windy City. Then I jumped in my car, picked up Fin and we crossed the Mississippi River by way of Mound City, Missouri before heading north.

Fin had got his hands on a Luger Pistole 08, bought it off a guy fresh back from overseas who claimed it was the exact same gun Adolf Hitler owned and the one he blew his brains out with. I didn't have the heart to tell Fin he'd been hoodwinked out of thirty bucks. I drove most of the way - more than five hundred miles of black top. I made a point of always carrying spare cans of gas in the trunk and we only had to fill up twice en route: first outside of Arnold where the sidewalks were thick with frozen slush and hail, and again outside Channahon, Illinois where the attendant advised us to follow the signs for Joliet unless we aimed on ending up in Indiana or Iowa.

The closer we got to Chicago, the more it seemed a heavenly light was guiding me through the darkness; the same light that directed Paul along the road to Damascus. I'd aimed to arrive early evening when the cathouse would be relatively quiet. But it was nearer midnight when we finally pulled up across the road and I got to see the place for the first time. The sidewalk lay under six inches of snow, but the steps leading up to the canopied doorway had been swept clean like you'd expect outside of a five-star hotel. But this wasn't the Stevens. Lights and music from inside left no doubt what kind of establishment we'd found, and that it was doing fine for business.

Fin pointed out the two shadows lurking beneath the canopy. "Them guard dogs on the doors?"

One came across to us, and invited Fin to hand over his Luger before passing inside. I could tell by the way the city boy was twitching he was desperate for us to cause a ruckus, but that wouldn't get me any closer to finding Angel. I'd already warned Fin to act dumb if they asked us how we ended up picking out this particular establishment. "It don't matter none what reasons we give," I said. "Show them a five dollar bill or two and far as they know, we're just two farm boys lookin' to get laid. Right?"

Once we passed through the lobby, I pulled off my driving gloves and my hat as if I was planning on makin' myself at home. The bright lights cast a welcome glow I'd not been expecting, but when I asked the weedy looking spic at the desk if Mr Drago was on the premises I swear the temperature dropped a couple of degrees. He clammed up until I explained how Mint and I went way back. I put on my po' boy face and told how him and Angel had spent time on my pappy's farm down in Mississippi long before the War, and how Mint had told me to call in on him if I was ever in the neighbourhood.

"The name's Hardy. Pike Hardy. I don't suppose he talked about me much, but I know he'd be mighty pleased to see me again if you could tell me where I might find him."

"Mr Drago left town Fall time last year," he said. "He's not expected to return."

"Where'd he go, if you'll pardon my asking?"

"They took the Pullman to New Orleans, that's what I heard."

"He got company with him?" I said.

"I've already told you all I know, Mr. . ?"

"It's Hardy. Mr Hardy." Then I reached in my wallet and pulled out a twenty dollar bill. "And this here's Mr Jackson. President Andrew Jackson to be exact. Maybe you'd like to tell him what else you know."

- 2 -

1946

The journey south from Memphis took less than three hours, and the roads were easier on my car than they had been on Mint's truck seven years earlier. Truman sat up front for the first hour or so, but when the mud-brown Mississippi landscape began to look the same for mile after mile, he asked to lie on the back seat. That's where I left him, sound asleep, when I finally turned up at my pa's.

I didn't expect to see so much change. Everything looked run down and neglected, as if Pa had given up tending to the small stuff once I left. The gatepost at the edge of our property now slanted another twenty degrees from the vertical. The ditches either side of the track into our yard were clogged with bindweed and speargrass, and potholes deep enough to swallow a pack mule pock-marked its surface. I could see some of the shingles on the roof of the cabin had worked loose as well, and Pa's rocking chair sat empty on the open porch.

Then Bertha walked out the door. She must have heard the car pull up. I could detect a mixture of regret and anger in her voice as she called out to me. "Well look what the cat dragged in."

"Hey, sis. I see you've filled out some since I last saw you. Wide enough to fill a barn doorway."

"I growed some balls, if that's what you mean."

I followed her inside, and while she prepared a bite of food she told me of our parents' passing and how Pa had willed the farm to her soon after me and Angel left. As far as I was concerned, she was welcome to it.

Then, finally I let her carry Truman inside and set him down on the old couch next to the cooking range. I got down to business while she fussed over him. I swear, she couldn't pull her gaze away from the boy. "You in some kind of trouble in Memphis?" she asked when I told her I was heading south.

I gave her arm a gentle squeeze. "No, sister. I got a personal matter to deal with in New Orleans, that's all. Maybe a week - maybe more. I can't tell until I get there. He's yours while I'm gone, if that suits. But I'll be back for the boy. And if things work out, he might get to spend more time with his Aunt Bertha."

"What d'you mean?" Her face lit up, but I quickly made it clear I wasn't inviting her to move to Memphis to look ater Truman. I explained how I wanted him to experience the kind of upbringing I had. Summers hoeing the yard, cutting back dockweeds or fishing the shallows of the Tallahatchie for darters and bullheads instead of kicking his heels at home with his head stuck inside a damn book.

"I take it there's no man staying here, judging by the state of the property."

"I do my best, Pike." I could see her eyes filling with emotion.

"I don't doubt that for a minute. I'm just saying, I'd rather there was no Mississippi redneck sharing your bed while the boy stays here with you. I don't want no one puttin' any unsavoury notions in his head, you understand what I'm saying?"

1946

We'd been told at the Lavender Garden how they'd both left town together - the hobo drunkard and his white-haired, daughter-whore. I figured out they'd be easy enough to locate once I got to New Orleans. Mint had often boasted how he intended making a fortune from the roll of a dice or the run of the cards once he got his truck back on the road. Uncle Box would be able to give me some likely addresses if I pressed him.

Almost ten years had passed since our paths last crossed, but I well recall how my ma's brother liked to play roulette and keno. I figured he'd know most of the gambling dens in the Big Easy. Metairie was en route, and I planned on getting there before dark. Pa had always wondered how New Orleans ever got to prosper, based on what little he'd seen of it when we visited with my ma and little sister more than fifteen years ago. No one seemed inclined to put in an honest day's work. Instead people were happy to sit out in the street, getting drunk or high and listening to nigger music.

Pa reckoned there was no finer example of this incongruity than Robert O'Sullivan - Box O'Sullivan as the family called him on account of his having been offered a trade by an undertaker in Baton Rouge when he left school. Uncle Box was the shortest critter I ever met outside of a carney. But his larger than life personality made up for any physical deficiency, along with a wealth of questionable anecdotes. Box claimed to have come across more dead bodies, swollen by drowning or discoloured by all manner of diseases, during his apprenticeship, than most decent people ever get to see in a lifetime.

I'd seen my fair share of hobos and panhandlers laid out at the side of the road, more than enough to turn my stomach. But Box had elected to make a living out of death and destruction, praising the Lord each time He sent a flood or praying for an outbreak of yellow fever or typhoid when times got hard.

My uncle put me up for the night and as we shared a Kentucky nightcap - a glass of Old Charter Straight Bourbon - I told him about Pa and Ma.

He hadn't heard the news of their passing. "You look like you doin' mighty fine for yourself, and I'm sure your ma would have been proud of the way you turned out. But the Lord giveth, and the Lord taketh away, Parker. And there are times He asks us to pay back twice over for His munificence."

When he took a drink, Uncle Box spoke like he'd swallowed a dictionary. He'd always claimed undertakers were merely servants of the Lord, paving the way for the dearly departed to meet their Maker. But he admitted on occasion his Master worked in mysterious ways. For instance, undertakers five miles away in New Orleans were expected to bear the cost of reinterment out of their own purse whenever a casket popped up out of its grave following a flood.

"That's why I've always sworn by lead caskets, son. But lately the damn war put an end to all that. So you down these parts on business or pleasure?"

I spun a lie about meeting some associates and having a little spare cash and time to spend. "I might take a river cruise on one of them steamboats. I'm told you can get a game of poker or blackjack while sailing the Misissippi and drink all hours of day or night."

"There ain't no boats licensed for gambling anymore, son. But I can give you an address or two over the Jackson line where you might find yourself a game. Tell them Box O'Sullivan sent you and you'll be treated like family."

Next day I drove down River Road with a list of gambling joints in my waistcoat pocket. I'd allowed myself a week at most. Seven days to trawl from one back street to the next. Watching. Listening out for signs of a new big spender in town. A Chicago spiv with maybe an albino bitch dog in tow. But as it happened, all it took was forty-eight hours.

Towards the end of my second day in New Orleans I was seated in my car outside a roadside grill opposite the Southport Club finishing my late lunch when I caught sight of a familiar face. Mint had gained weight in the last seven years, and the stoop in his shoulders and his unsteady walk attested to the burden those few extra pounds had placed on his body. He wore a white, linen suit and a black fedora, and carried a cane that added an air of refinement to his appearance.

But despite his superficial similarity to the dozen or so southern grandees who entered the same premises, I knew it was Mint Drago. There was no sign of Angel, but I'm a patient man by nature. It got dark soon after nine o'clock and I'd almost given up hope of Mint emerging much before sunrise when he came out and wandered across to one of the trolleybus stops on Monticello Avenue. I managed to follow in my car, and eventually he got off outside a swanky hotel close to one of the parks bordering the waterfront. I watched him go inside as the bus pulled away and decided I'd be wisest waiting in the street in case he planned on heading back out again with Angel on his arm.

After an hour of sitting and watching the hotel entrance, it was clear Mint intended staying in for the remainder of the night. I had close on seventy bucks in my wallet and a fifty dollar bill sewn inside my belt for emergencies. The chances were I wouldn't need that. I'd book in, get an hour or two's sleep and catch Mint at breakfast time when we could have a friendly chat over a cup of coffee and some Eggs Benedict. Failing that, I'd sneak a look at the register when I checked in and take it from there.

M Drago : Suite 6D

Check-in date : Thursday 22nd November 1945

- 4 -

1946

There was no mention of Angel, but it was clear Mint had money and wasn't afraid to spend it on the finer things in life. I took the cheapest room available - nine bucks including breakfast. But they happily charged between twenty and thirty bucks a night for a suite that advertised full housekeepng and laundry services.

Mint had checked in almost four months ago, so it didn't take long to figure out he must have spent more money on a bed for the night than I'd paid for my Lincoln Zephyr, brand new out of the showroom. I saw little to justify the extra expense. On the sixth floor where the richer clientele squandered their cash, the corridors smelt no sweeter than the lobby of the Lavender. Stale cigar smoke, Jeyes fluid to keep the mosquitoes away maybe, and cheap perfume that reminded me of one or two women who'd shared my bed since Angel left.

What would I do if I found her right here in Mint's hotel suite? I'd fantasised the whole drive down how I would humiliate her and leave her less than worthless. I'd brought along Fin's Luger, but I wanted more than the satisfaction of placing a bullet behind her ear. I'd read how slaves were marked before being shipped over from Africa and how unfaithful wives got branded for committing adultery. There were other forms of disfigurement such as scalping or having the ears cropped off. But in my mind hamstringing seemed the most fitting punishment. That would put an end to her days of running away.

Eight doors. Each one far enough apart to suggest the suites on the sixth floor were larger than your average town apartment. I guessed there'd be a sitting room, a private bathroom and a bedroom - maybe two. Mint living like some two-bit Al Capone on his summer vacation made me laugh. I could walk in and kill him while he slept - easy as gutting a fish.

The door to 6D was locked, but Chester and I had forced our way into many a neighbour's hooch store after dark. Yet I decided a more gentlemanly approach might be in order. If there was to be a scene, better in the privacy of his suite than at the crowded breakfast bar or out in the street. I tapped the door. Twice. The second time loud enough to raise the dead.

"Room service. Telegram for Mr Drago."

The door opened a crack and the first thing I saw was Mint's linen jacket on the floor next to an upholstered chair, like a pool of moonlight that had somehow gotten overlooked when the maid closed the drapes. Then I took a step back to allow him to open the door a little wider, the better to see the gun in my hand.

"Christ, Jesus, d'you even know how to shoot that thing?"

"No need to find out if you invite me inside," I said.

"What? So's you can rob me again?"

"I just need a word or two, that's all. And no offence, but I could have robbed you any time I wanted when I followed you home from the Southport."

He shuffled aside and opened the door wider. I could see two travel trunks stacked in one corner, cloaked in semi-darkness like the rest of the room. A silver tray on a side table held a decanter of brandy by the look of it, and a single dirty glass suggested Mint had taken a nightcap before retiring to bed alone.

There was no sign of Angel. No silk stocking draped on the chaise lounge, no lipsticked impression on the brandy glass, no trace of talcum powder or expensive perfume lingering inside the closed room. I could see two doors, both shut tight. One presumably led to the bedroom and the other to a bathroom.

I settled into one of the vacant chairs, rested the hand holding the gun in my lap, and rehearsed my script inside my head. It was close enough to dawn to rouse the birds that sat in the trees along the street outside, and strangely I was reminded of the bluebirds that sometimes nested in the eaves of our cabin when I was a boy.

Mint came and sat in the chair next to me and I pointed the barrel of the gun vaguely in his direction without bothering to raise my head to look at his face. "I ain't come to cause you no trouble."

"If you ain't brought trouble, boy, then what in tarnation d'you mean by waking a man in the dead of night?"

"I need information."

He got to his feet again and pulled the bathrobe tighter around his midriff. "I gotta pee first. But you'd better have a damn good reason for disturbin' my sleep or I'll have the Law on you."

"Be my guest. I ain't in no hurry."

He kept the bathroom door ajar and I heard the stream of piss spurt then falter then splash and sputter once or twice again until he figured he was done. Then he yanked the chain and I settled back in my chair.

"When I first saw you outside my door, I thought it was that soldier boy come chasing after his piece of white trash. Last person I expected to see was you."

"Soldier boy?" I said. This was the first I'd heard of any soldier boy.

He cleared his throat, pulled out a handkerchief from the pocket of the robe and spat out a wad of something resembling coal tar. "Take it easy. He'll not show his face if he knows what's good for him, so you can put that pop-gun away."

"That so?"

"My boys sent him packing before we quit Chicago. And there ain't no cause for you to send me on my way to Heaven any sooner than the Lord intended. The doctors give me six months at best, but I aim on seeing out a few more days before my time is up."

"I ain't planning on killing anyone right now, but you can die any time you feel like it once you tell me where she is."

He laughed. "So you still pining for Angel after all these years, Christ Almighty."

I pulled out a pack of cigars and offered him one. "I done pining for that bitch long ago. Far as I'm concerned, she died the day she walked out on me and the boy."

"I had heard," he said.

"About her walking out?" I struck a match and steadied my hand as he tried to light his cigar.

"About the boy. Told me she couldn't bear to have him raised under the same roof as you anymore."

"Ain't just the boy we're talking about here. And she's a fine one deciding what's right and what's wrong," I said. "I provided her with a home any decent woman would be grateful for, but instead she chose to go back to that cathouse in Chicago to start whoring again."

I pulled out the crumpled magazine from inside my waistcoat and passed it him. But he waved it aside. "Angel was just a child - got caught up in something she didn't understand. The poor kid didn't know any better. Did she ever tell you how her father took up with a showgirl soon after she was born, and her own ma walked out one winter's morning and never came back? Left her in filth, a mess of skin and bone wrapped in a threadbare shift without enough sense to even feed herself properly."

"I lost count of the lies that bitch told me."

"Maybe so. But she got led astray, one way or another. And I'm the one who saved that child from a life in the gutter."

"My heart bleeds for her. But sometimes a person's not

for saving, no matter how hard you try."

"So I guess you ain't come all the way down here on account of her soul."

"No. I'll start by explaining to her the difference between what's right and what's wrong."

"Boy, I don't see it's your place to be sermonising anybody." He laughed.

"Maybe not," I said. "You read the Good Book, so you know how Eve gave into temptation, took the apple and brought sin into this world."

"Is that how it goes?"

"The way I read it, yeah. And you know you can't unbite the apple, so what's done is done. Angel was born a whore and likely as not she'll die a whore. If not in your bed, then as sure as damnit in somebody else's."

"Well, in case you're wondering, she ain't keeping my bed warm. Check out for yourself if you don't believe me." He waved his arm in the direction of the bedroom but I took him at his word for once.

"Didn't you two leave Chicago in a mad rush, like you were off on honeymoon together? Or were you running away from the Mob?"

"Where'd you hear that?"

"I got my contacts."

Mint blew out a cloud of cigar smoke then took another draw. "Well, for your information we weren't running away. And if you drove all the way from Chicago just to teach Angel the difference between what's right and what's wrong, you're wasting your time. I already saved you the trouble."

"So you say, but I don't believe a damn thing that comes out of your mouth. 'Cause if I remember rightly, when you turned up in Greenwood with her on your arm all you did was sell us a mess of lies from the start."

"I had my reasons," Mint said. "And I never meant to hurt anyone."

"More excuses," I said.

"When you took off with my truck and the girl, your ma reckoned Angel had turned your head and you'd both run away to get married. But your pa soon figured you were running away to save your skin. He found out what you'd been up to with the Macarthy boy and decided he'd be better finding hisself a lawyer."

"To change his will."

"He never let on. Offered me a ride part of the way, and that's how I ended up in New Orleans. That was seven years ago."

"How come you never stayed?"

"I intended to. I boarded a steamer at Natchez with high hopes of making my fortune at the card table. But there was unfinished business to attend to back in Chicago and I had to take my leave of this place."

"What kind of business?"

"That don't matter now, but I promised myself I'd come back when the time was right."

"Fine. So you gonna quit giving me your life story and tell

me where she is or are you still gonna hold out on me 'til I pay you back what's owing?"

"There ain't nothing owing. Angel's settled her account, so far as I'm concerned we're quits."

"How d'you mean she settled her account?"

"I mean we're square. I don't hold no grudge against you or that damn girl no more. I took back what I was owed from her then we split."

The vision of Angel being made to pay for her sins right before my eyes was beginning to fade. "That may be so, but there's still the boy to think of," I said. "I can't run the risk of having that whore turn up on our door step claiming back a part of her life she already threw away."

"So you come down here to kill her. Now I get the picture."

I stood up, walked across to the window and pulled back the drapes. There were already people parading along the gravel paths than cut across the park in the direction of the river. I could hear traffic, and in the distance the deep, bass notes of a steamboat docking at one of the wharves that ran alongside the walkways. "Is she still in New Orleans?" I said, expecting to catch sight of her maybe as she sat on one of the park benches, folding up her parasol and lifting her face to the morning sun.

He nodded as he stubbed out his cigar. "Take a stroll along Basin Street once it gets dark, you might come across her on one of the corners. And if she doesn't show, you'll find Blind Billy leaning against the bar at Lafitte's down on Bourbon Street."

"Blind who?"

"Billy - the guy I sold her to. He's got her book." He flicked the stub of his cigar into the ashtray and rubbed both hands together as if our business was over and done with. "Angel cheated on me one time too many. So if she's still drawing breath, she'll be with the other street girls earning her keep. Do whatever it is you want to do to her, but keep my name out of it."

- 5 -

1946

Once I got back to my room, I knelt down and prayed. I prayed for strength and courage and guidance. And He answered the way He always does. The edge of my switchblade drew blood as I ran it across the ball of my thumb. I knew what I had to do.

I stayed in bed until early afternoon, the feel of cool, silk sheets a reminder of the way her skin sometimes felt. Her fingers touching me the way she knew best. I took out that magazine, uncreased the folds and leafed through the pages once more, picture after picture, revelling in their sin. But I felt no shame as I spilled my seed into my own hand. God made us in His image, every one of us the same.

Then as the heat of the day abated, I settled my account, drove to the French Quarter, parked my automobile outside one of the restaurants on the corner of Royal Street and ate dinner while the sky faded from red to pink to grey. I took a glass of wine then I headed one block north on foot.

Jigaboo music came out of almost every window and doorway. Wrought iron ballustrades supported verandas strung with lights along one side of the street. On the opposite side, Lafitte's. A ramshackled, grey building that barely stood out from the other properties, its windows barricaded with steel bars and a half-open door spilling out the smell of stale beer and cigar smoke.

A solitary street light cast a faint glow across its entrance and as I stepped into the porch I sensed someone lurking in the shadows. Then an arm reached out to wrap around my waist.

"*Bonswa, chérie.*"

Close up, her perfume failed to mask the pungent mix of ripe sweat and dirty bed sheets. I could see acne scars clustered on her sallow cheeks and her short-cropped, blonde hair grew darker at the roots.

"Some other time, honey."

Then the grip on my waist tightened, and when I tried to turn my face away I felt her lips graze my cheek. A warm voice whispered in my ear, "*Sentez ma chatte, chérie.*"

I pushed her away and she spat out a single word. "*Foutre.*" The voice was harsh now, and that's when I realised this was a man dressed up to look like a woman.

Uncle Box had warned me. "You lookin' for a day trip to Sodom, boy, you only need to drive a few miles south of here. You'll come across all kinds of depravities."

I watched as he rearranged the short skirt hiked above his knees and pulled down the hem of the vest that barely covered his midriff. Then maybe he noticed Fin's Luger hooked into my belt because the next thing he screamed out. "*Connard! Les keufs! Les keufs!*"

I pushed him aside and continued through the open door into the bar. I could hear a buzz of voices and the clink of glasses. It seemed his distress call went unnoticed.

A Latino, old enough to be my pa, sat at one end of the bar. Despite the white cane propped against his stool, he appeared to be reading a copy of the New Orleans Tribune, holding it up to the light of a solitary hurricane lamp and scrutinising every word. Girls in various states of undress sat in a line of booths along the back wall but there was no sign of Angel. I caught their eyes fluttering as soon as I walked in, and one of them stood up and came over to join me at the bar. She looked junkie thin and her fishnet stockings were torn across one knee.

"Anything here take your fancy?" she said.

"I ain't buying," I said. "I'm looking for someone. A girl."

"*C'est toi, Cedrice?*" the blind man growled.

"I got it, Billy."

I continued. "I was told you might know the whereabouts of a particular girl. New in town, from Chicago."

Cedrice gestured to the booths behind us. "I guess a snappy dresser like you has the tastes to match. Take your time, honey. There's more than enough to go round."

"I was addressing the gentleman here," I said.

Blind Billy turned to face me and I could see the haemorrhages flooding each eye. "I know many girls." His voice was coarse as river gravel. "You look for *une fille de joie*, you come to the right place."

"This girl goes by the name of Angel."

"*Ki-ça?*"

"Angel Drago. She's an albino."

Billy let out a laugh and ordered Cedrice to bring a fresh shot glass. "*Byenvenu.* First we drink a toast to all the pretty girls in New Orleans. *Les poupées, les joupins, les souris.*"

Cedrice filled our glasses while Billy proceeded to tell me how he ended up in New Orleans more than twenty years ago. Born on the delta - he found work as a longshoreman once he was old enough to wipe his own ass.

"This was before they open up Panama," he said. "But once it happens I jump on ship to make my fortune."

Billy claimed to have travelled the Pacific coast of North America from California to Alaska and met more crib girls in BC than he cared to remember.

"They kept Chinese prostitutes in cages to entertain sailors on shore leave," Cedrice explained.

"*Bontem. Plézi.*" Billy raised his glass, clinked it against mine and we each tossed our drinks down our throats. Cheap tequila as smooth as kerosene.

"Billy turned up here between the wars in a battered old grocery truck and without a dime to his name," Cedrice said. "But he brought a half dozen girls with him. *Les Chinois.*"

"*Lapoud dòr.*" Billy motioned for Cedrice to refill our glasses.

"Good as gold dust," she continued as she poured another double measure in each. "He set up his own crib on Franklin Street, next door to Hilma Burt's. The girls preferred to do trade where the rivers didn't freeze over in winter."

"There is no woman a white man desires more than one who has coloured skin. *D'accord*?"

I couldn't answer. I slung back my shot and wiped the bitter taste off my lips.

"As many shades and flavours of woman as fish in the sea. *Arabe, Chinois, Indien Rouge, négroides*. Their flesh taste all different. But I never come upon the pure albino flesh until I meet your Angel."

I swallowed the bile in my throat. "So can I see her? It's family business."

He shook his head and spread open his hands. "*Mo tè donné twa mô konfyans*. It is not possible."

"She's holed up in the big house," Cedrice replied. "First off, we figured she'd brought a dose of syph with her all the way from the Lakes. Then it turns out she probably ate some bad shrimp so she's closed for business 'til further notice. But we got plenty other girls happy to suck you off for five bucks."

She called for one of the other girls in the neighbouring booths to come forward. "*Sinntya. Fé vit - un turlute*."

"I ain't come all the way from Chicago for a blow-job, honey. I got a message to deliver and it don't matter whether I do it right here or back in her sick room."

Cedrice patted my arm and shook her head. "*Énn fwa pli*. That don't matter none. She's in quarantine, boy. *Lamézon* 'til the doc says otherwise. But Cynthia here can show you a good time. *Di bonjou*."

- 6 -

1946

In the end I gave in and let Cynthia take me into a room behind the bar. The carpet stuck to the heels of my shoes with every step and she made me lie on a leather couch and watch while she took off all her clothes. But she got no further than unbuckling my belt before I offered her twenty bucks in return for an address.

I caught the dopey smile. The stupid bitch thought Angel and I were star-crossed lovers. "Ain't nothin' I like more than a real life romance."

It took less than fifteen minutes to drive to the corner of Iberville and Treme. I'd brought along a can of gasoline in the trunk of the car in case I needed to fill her up. Or in case I needed to burn down someone's house.

Once I pulled up outside the address I'd been given, I doused the headlights. There was a single light behind one of the windows on the first floor. A hurricane lamp that was eclipsed momentarily as someone crossed in front of it. Then I saw no further activity. But I sat and waited, sat and watched.

There's something about the smell of gasoline, and the sound it makes when it sloshes out of a can, the way the flame flares up when you light the touchpaper then runs across the ground like a living thing, consuming everything in its way. The sounds, a ripping, rasping hunger, and the sudden flash of heat. Wildfire that spreads like gossip. Like lies.

Back home we'd always used kerosene and lit torches and screamed and hollered to drive the vermin out of their hidey-holes before we burnt down their shacks. But this was different. I climbed the five steps leading off the sidewalk up to the front door of the house and emptied the can over the floor of the veranda. Then I set flame to that trashy, semen-stained pamphlet I'd been carrying folded up inside my jacket pocket the whole journey down here and watched as the evidence of what Angel and that nigger trash whore child had been up to crackled and burned to ashes.

Once I was sure the fire had taken proper hold, I climbed back inside my car and watched a while longer. I'd done my share of burning back in Greenwood. Heard the screams and watched as they ran outside, wreathed in flame. I'd thought those days were behind me but then it came to me as if in a vision how the Lord's work can never be carried out to completion until Judgement Day. Then the fires of righteousness will burn bright, and no sin will survive the flames of purity and forgiveness. Heaven or Hell, Angel was about to meet her Creator.

- 7 -

1946 - 1956

I spent the night at Uncle Box's and slept better than I had in weeks, as if a great weight had been lifted from my shoulders. And next morning, my hand remained as steady as always when I razored my face. I'd been tempted to call on Mint again and threaten him to keep his mouth shut tight if the police came asking questions. But I figured he knew enough to play dumb.

Soon after ten I was headed back up Route 51. I planned on following it as far as Jackson which would put me at Bertha's in time for tea. I let slip how I'd called on Angel down in New Orleans, but she never asked me how I found her or whether I'd managed to pass on my message. Instead we sat over supper and discussed the arrangements for the coming summer. Truman remained quiet on the drive back to Memphis next morning, but I could tell he was looking forward to spending more time with his aunt. I'd warned her she was not to spoil the boy and Bertha claimed there was no greater privilege than to be entrusted with my boy's life.

More by good fortune than by design, the weeks spent at Bertha's each summer did Truman a power of good. He'd always been a dreamer; happier with his head stuck inside a book than out in the street playing hot dog with the neighbourhood children. He'd always been too close to his mother when a child, but now I saw changes in him that became more noticeable each time he climbed off that train.

By the end of the third summer he'd lost that look of innocence. There was a sullen cast to his face, a look that spelled trouble ahead. Maybe he'd displeased my sister some way and she'd given him a seeing to, though God knows he'd always been an easy-going, mannerly boy according to Miss Du Pree. But now he'd slam doors without provocation and more than once I heard him cuss under his breath when I asked him to lift his head high or quit slouching.

I ended up having a quiet word with my neighbour. I had more pressing matters to attend to than the whims and moods of a nine-year-old. The upshot was, we decided to provide Truman with a regular playmate. Miss Du Pree's nephew, Harold, was four years older than Truman but he had pedigree. Howard's pa was a newspaper owner, a kike. But I had no misgivings about my son associatin' with the Beeches. They had money, and Truman would find out soon enough that there's no room for intolerance in this world while you're tryin' to get along and make a name for yourself.

Years passed before I discovered my sister had planted the seed of duplicity in Truman's heart when he was still a child. Allowing him to consort and conspire with all kinds of free-thinking, pinko trash while living on her farm. And by the time I learnt that Beech boy had also managed to poison my son's mind with his perverted ways, it was too late.

During Truman's last summer down south, there'd been a drowning in Leflore County - a nigger boy found floating face down in the shallows beneath the Tallahatchie Bridge. Chester and I had spent many an afternoon sitting in its shade fishing for minnows or cooling our heels. We'd share a bottle or two of beer stolen from his pa's cocktail cabinet. That was nothing more fancy than an old, abandoned chicken box nailed to the wall of Ross Macarthy's barn.

Word followed closely how Truman had somehow been involved with the dead boy and my heart filled up at the thought he'd somehow taken it upon hisself to kill a nigger. I tried to put his mind at ease as soon as he walked in the door, but his face gave him away. My son still didn't have the stomach to do what his pa did naturally.

And as those precious few weeks of late summer stretched out to nothing, it became clear my boy wasn't going to end up in Lovelace's yard either, despite my plans. Instead there came a time in my life when I was sorely tested. I was reminded of the story of Abraham and Isaac - how the father was instructed by the Lord to sacrifice his son to prove his loyalty. Pa taught me how God was an intolerant god, who could destroy a season's crops by flood or drought one year and provide bounty beyond calculation the next. A vengeful god who lost His own son and now seemed intent on taking mine. I never saw a body burn up with fever so. And there were nights alone in my room when I pictured Angel burning in that cathouse and I prayed. Not for my own forgiveness but for Truman's.

It seemed my prayers were answered when Truman

recovered following a long period of convalescence. Then the day Howard Beech took Truman to his pa's newspaper office, it was as if the scales were lifted from his eyes. I should have known better than to allow my own flesh and blood to turn his back on his birthright.

- 8 -

1968

I've been on this Earth forty-five years and I tremble to think how much America has changed during that time, and how much it will change by the time Truman reaches my age. I hope I'll be dead and buried long before then. But in the meantime I have a dream to shape this nation's destiny. Each one of us has a duty to defend our country's future.

Better men who passed this way before me have died without seeing the Promised Land. But I hope and pray before I die I'll get to breathe in the pure, clean air of a new America where the white man can reclaim his superiority. Goddamn it, we built this country and we created all that is good about it. The times they may be changin' but that don't give them no-good, in-bred intellectuals in Washington the right to throw that all away just to relieve their consciences; liberal pinkos who never done an honest day's work in their entire lives.

Truman knew how to hurt me more than any other living soul who ever crossed my path. There were days when I looked at him and I was ashamed my blood ran through his veins. It wasn't just the way he let his hair grow down to his shoulders and the way he'd talk about my friends. He called us dinosaurs more than once. Kept telling me it was time to 'get with it'. I took that all in my stride. The boy was still young enough to learn from his mistakes. But then he telephoned one morning and I swear he could barely get the words out of his mouth fast enough.

"You heard all about Dr Martin Luther King."

I knew that son of a bitch and how he was planning on fighting for equal rights for blacks. I knew all about Resurrection City as well and it made my blood curdle.

"He's in town, and I'm the only press photographer allowed to meet with him before he addresses a crowd of workers later in the week."

If I'd been able to put him straight, I'd have done it right there and then. A punch to the jaw. A bullet in the head. It didn't matter to me which.

"How come they chose you?"

"It's all down to Mr Beech, I reckon. He says I've finally made it."

"So where's this special meeting meant to take place?"

"Thursday - the Lorraine on Mulberry Street."

"You sharing the honeymoon suite?" I couldn't help myself.

"Second floor is all they told me. The Abernathy Suite. There's a meal laid on for 6.00 pm but I'm not invited to that."

"You sure your skin ain't turning colour under all that

hippy hair, Truman? 'Cause it seems to me someone touched you up with a tar brush."

"I'm just doing my job, Pa. How many times do I have to tell you?"

There was so much he hadn't told me. Things I found out from the letters my sister kept writing him. Letters I somehow forgot to forward, including lies she was anxious to pass on to him relating to events down in New Orleans.

The nigger boy Truman had been teaching to read. Gospel? There was something that didn't smell right; the way she kept referring to the tragedy and the loss, as if he was family. And the young woman she shared her home with now. Donna Mae. I'd never heard Truman mention her name. Yet Bertha was desperate to let him know they were involved in a Freedom School to educate the poor blacks. She reckoned he would have been so proud.

It made my anger boil over until there was no control left to make me think twice about how I intended setting things right again.

Jim's Grill was close to the Lorraine Motel. I'd met with some of the boys there on more than one occasion. The motel was gaining a reputation for allowing blacks to rent rooms, and we'd sit around watching the comings and goings. Joel said he never felt comfortable in the neighbourhood.

"Too many nigger men in suits, if you ask me."

Maybe that's why I told no one what I had in mind. If I couldn't lynch Dr King, at least I could put a bullet in his brain. It didn't matter to me if I finished up getting sent to the chair. The Good Lord has already set aside a new chair for me right alongside His throne.

I'd leave my car on Talbot Street or in the shade of Bessie Brewer's on South Main Street. Less than a five minute stroll and I'd be in the lobby of the motel. But first I had to do something about Truman. I couldn't let my boy be seen associating with the likes of King and that so-called Reverend Jackson.

That's where fate stepped in, or maybe the Lord working in one of His manifold ways. I'd watched Howard Beech visit Miss Du Pree often enough in his Silver Hawk. The cissy way he'd stroll up to her front door, a bunch of flowers in his hand and a sway to his hips. He'd developed a routine of calling once or twice each month - mostly on Wednesday afternoons. I'd made arrangements to get my hands on a fake security pass next day. If need be, I'd talk my way into the motel and find a suitable hiding place. But in the back of my mind I knew there had to be an easier option.

Beech stayed at my neighbour's 'til after dark. That's what gave me the notion to follow him back to Olive Branch. I'd driven past their wooden fronted bungalow once or twice, never in my own car in case Truman was on watch. The roads were quiet and it took less than forty-five minutes to make the journey. I parked on the grass shoulder four doors down and waited. The lights went out at the front of the house soon after eleven by which time I'd figured a way to finish things. I had a can of gas in the boot of the car.

- 9 -

1968

The hallway stank of their perfume. Faggy hair gel or aftershave. I neither knew nor cared which. I ran my fingers along the length of Truman's silk scarf hanging on one of the coat pegs. I could maybe use it to strangle the Beech boy before dragging Truman out of his bed and setting fire to the house.

But when I found them both stretched out naked on one of the beds at the back of the house, curled up close with their arms and legs wrapped around each other like ivy clings to a tree, I could feel the bile rise in my throat. The boy had transformed into the exact same image as his mother. Her flawless white body pressed tight against that street trash, nigger whore child. I felt for the butt of my pistol and I swear I'd have killed them both if Truman hadn't spoke out in his sleep.

Something about Nebraska. Maybe they planned on leaving Tennessee. That would be a blessing. I looked around the room for clues. A packed trunk, maybe, or a train ticket. But instead I saw the framed photograph on the bedside table. Howard Beech and my boy looking as if they hadn't a care in the world. It was too late to do anything else. The fire pits of Hell awaited them both.

I retraced my steps to the front of the house and saw the kitchen door was wide open. Truman's Graflex Speed Graphic camera sat on the dining table along with his fedora, his Press pass and a pair of driving gloves. Out of nowhere, the Good Lord showed me how I could retrieve the situation without sacrificing my one and only son. It came as a vision, clear as day. I'd take Truman's Press pass and camera and pose as a newspaper photographer. Without the tools of his trade, it's unlikely Truman would ever be allowed to enter the motel and join in the party.

Just to make sure, I searched the kitchen cupboards for a bag of sugar, then pulled the outside door shut behind me and cursed as the picture frame slipped out of my grip and fell onto the door step. Nothing stirred. But there was no time to sweep up the broken glass or retrieve the photograph. I crossed the street to Howard's car, unscrewed the fuel cap and emptied the sugar into his tank. Then I drove home to Davis Street.

All the following day I expected Truman to telephone and curse me to Hell and back. But that call never came. Maybe he hadn't figured out I was the one who'd paid him and his fancy man a visit. Maybe he assumed if it had been me I'd have shot them both dead where they lay.

On the stroke of five I arrived at Mulberry Street and parked across the road from the motel. I had Truman's camera case slung around my shoulder and his Press card tucked into the band of my hat. There were two other vehicles parked on the sidewalk outside the motel's main entrance. Two black men sat inside both cars, but they didn't give me more than a cursory glance at first.

Then one of the pair inside the white Cadillac seemed to be watching closely as I stepped out of the car, slammed the door shut and pulled my camera case tight against my chest. He got out and started walking in my direction as I crossed the street. Then I heard a sound like a car backfiring.

This is when it ended.

ODE TO KATIE JO COBHAM

- 1 -

1966

How it ended.

The telegram came the day of Katie Jo's eighth birthday. Some of my friends from the Freedom School had got Miss Bertha to lay on a party, and when the envelope arrived, delivered by hand, we thought it might be word from someone special wishing my darling daughter many happy returns. But when Miss Bertha passed me the telegram I didn't need to read the stark message it contained. I already knew in my blood the moment Bo got shot.

First, there had been the smell of slime at water's edge that I couldn't get out of my nostrils; the stench of rotting greenery and the swill of human waste. Then I heard a shrill cry in a voice more animal than human. It woke me in the night, and I swear I dreamed how Bo turned up for his daughter's special day, all spruced in an Army uniform with a look of such pride on his face that I didn't have the heart to tell him I hated the very idea of him fighting in this war. He sat with me by the stove awhile, and after we tumbled in the sheets I held him close and asked him what I should do if the worst ever happened. "How you expectin' us all to survive if you get yourself killed?"

"It won't come to that," he said. But his voice was far from convincing.

"I guessed you'd go off one day to somehwere like Jackson, get drunk and beat up a couple of rednecks. I can live with that side of your character. But why would you want to go to some jungle far overseas and kill a bunch of Reds you never even met?"

That's when he told me. "Maybe I got a death wish, Donna Mae. It's what comes of growin' up in a place as desperate as this. Pickin' cotton for somebody else is a sure fire guarantee you die young and you die poor. But you're gonna cope without me the way you always have, so don't go frettin'. Whether I'm here or not, you're gonna do just fine."

America was fighting a just war, and everyone told me what a brave soldier Bo Dean had been. But the truth is, he'd never fired a single round in anger as far as I know. He'd always saved his bloodshot rages for me, and now here I was, a widow woman at twenty-six years old even though we were never man and wife. The authorities only got in touch with me because he'd given them Miss Bertha's name and address as next of kin.

They'd covered the coffin in the Stars and Stripes flag, and my pa and Miss Hardy stood at my side as they lowered Bo into his grave. Somewhere a bugle played the Last Post, but all I could focus on was the heap of soil, like brown sugar and honey combined. Then the ground beneath my feet turned into river-bed silt and I felt myself sinking.

- 2 -

1968

The time of grieving for Bo Dean passed. Then came a time of fresh grieving - for the loss of a brave new nation's dream, the loss of a new dawn. Miss Bertha and I spent many a night sat next to her stove sipping black coffee and asking ourselves how this country was turning out so bad. There had been talk of changes in Washington. The likes of Bo's brother and his poisoning ways would become a thing of the past in this lifetime. And even though a Republican sat in the White House, Nixon seemed like an honest, clean-living politician.

His promise to bring our troops home one day and restore the nation's pride seemed genuine and put a smile on Miss Bertha's face. But I swear I never saw her smile so much as she did on the September morning Truman walked into her yard again like a ghost from the past - or as Katie Jo said later, like a soldier returning home from war.

We'd been sittin' round on the porch. Miss Bertha lay in her hammock sippin' juice while Katie Jo and I shelled beans for tea. We never heard a sound until this voice called out.

"Anybody home?"

It had an unfamiliar Tennessee twang so I kept cautious. There were hobos passing by all the time, begging a cup of water or a crust of bread. Looking for somewhere to hole up overnight. And Miss Bertha was always big on charity. Many's the time she'd let some poor soul squat in her old cabin across the yard. But, give them their dues, they were always gone by daybreak and seldom left any sign they'd been here.

Tad Brooks swore travellers placed a mark on every fencepost or tree, identifying properties where there'd be a welcome. Or places you'd do well to avoid, where maybe a hot-tempered share-cropper owned a shotgun and a ferocious dog looking to guard his territory.

But one look showed me this was no hobo. Despite his lank, greasy hair and unshaven face, he wore a smart suit, a proper shirt with a collar and tie, and a fancy white hat with a brown band. He carried a battered leather suitcase so I tagged him as a door-to-door salesman or an evangelist spreadin' the gospel.

"Whatever you're sellin', whether it's carpet sweepers or the Good Word, we ain't buyin'," I called out.

"Bless ma soul, is dat Miss Donna Mae Cobham?"

The lapse into a Mississippi drawl didn't sound genuine and I stood up and squinted for all of three seconds. Then I let my basket and paring knife fall to the ground and leapt to my feet. "Truman? Is that really you, Truman Hardy?"

"Last time I checked," he said. He grabbed me by the arms and pulled me up close.

"Lord above, I can't believe my eyes,"

Miss Bertha and I had spoke of Truman often enough, whenever she was writing him a letter to send off in the post. I'd often wondered why his aunt went to such trouble since there'd been no reply for eight years or more by my reckoning. For all we knew Truman was dead and buried. The chances were he'd got himself drafted overseas to fight the gooks at least. Yet, there he stood on our yard. A ghost from the past made flesh and blood. I couldn't decide whether to plant a kiss on his lips or curse him all the way to New Orleans and back.

"Why didn't you send word?" Miss Bertha said. "You've got me all of a flummox."

He took off his hat and looked crestfallen as he aproached the house. "I never heard from you all in such a long time, I didn't know what to expect."

"But we wrote. Regular as clockwork, every fall and spring. Donna here even sent you a Christmas card."

"To Davis Street? 'Cause I done left home a while back."

"Your pa never let on," she said. "But why in tarnation are we stood out here. Come inside. I got some ham hock stewing on the stove and you look like you ain't eaten a decent meal in weeks."

We ushered him inside and something scuttled out of the shadows. "Oh, my. I'm forgetting my manners. This here's Katie Jo." I pushed my daughter in front of him as if seeking his approval.

"My pleasure," he said. He leant forward and put a hand underneath her chin. "My God, you're as cute as your momma was first time I ever set eyes on her."

"Can you see she's got her pa's smile as well?" I said.

He studied my daughter's face a while longer and nodded. "Is Bo about?"

I sent my little girl out to play while the three of us sat around the table and slowly caught up on each other's news.

"How old was Bo when he got killed?" Truman asked eventually.

"Twenty-six years old. Katie Jo was only eight when she lost her pa, can you believe? And her grand pappy died two months later. His heart stopped beating just like that. We put that all in our letters, but when you never got back in touch we just thought. . ."

"Pa had a habit of opening my mail, but what the hell? I'm home now and it's like I never left this place." Truman had already let his gaze cover every inch of the kitchen as if desperate to take in every detail. "You'll never believe the number of times I dreamed about being back here. The times I longed to jump back on that Greenwood train and come back."

"This'll always be your home, Truman."

He took his aunt's hand in his and squeezed tight. Then he took hold of mine in his other hand and it was like we were in a prayer meeting. "You're all the family I got now, I reckon."

"Pike still alive?" Miss Bertha finally asked.

"Last I heard," Truman replied. "Though how the Good

Lord can spare the likes of him and let a good man like Bo Dean Macarthy perish, I just don't know."

"He ain't changed his ways, I guess."

Truman let his head drop a fraction. "Never will. And I gotta tell you this. There was a time, not so long ago, when I thought he did something so dreadful I wouldn't want to admit his blood ran through my veins. And I was the one who put him up to it - telling him where to go and when. By the time I called the police and got him picked up it was too late. They found a gun, but there ain't no law against carrying. Pa always knew his rights."

"Ain't no need to burden yourself with his guilt any longer, son. We're all family here, and I reckon whatever you think your Pa did is best kept buried."

"I know. Besides, I got it all wrong as it happens. That James Earl Ray got arrested three months ago, as you probaby heard, so whatever my pa was really doing on Mulberry Street, he wasn't the one who shot Dr King."

I couldn't believe what Truman was suggesting, but the look on his face and the tone of his voice proved he'd thought it the truth for long enough.

"It's why I left Memphis," he said.

"But what about your work? I thought you said you was a newspaper reporter in your last letter," Miss Bertha said.

"I was a photographer, but I quit. And as far as I'm concerned, I won't ever return to that damn city."

"You leave anyone else back there?" I asked, dreading to hear the truth.

"I had a friend. Howard Beech. A good friend, but I wasn't straight with him and in the end I betrayed him the same way I betrayed everybody else. He knows about my pa now and how I was feeding him information just to continue the lie that I was just like him. Maybe I am." He squeezed my hand harder and I could feel something soften inside my broken heart.

"Don't be so hard on yourself, sugar. You and Gospel. . ." I didn't get to finish the sentence.

"I was ashamed of myself. Not on account of the colour of his skin but on account of my feelings towards him. I could never tell him, and I ain't ever told anybody else until now."

"You think we didn't notice any of that, Truman?" I said.

"It don't matter," he replied. "I don't plan on returning to Memphis. There ain't no close kin that'll miss me being around."

Then Miss Bertha spoke up again and broke the spell. "I take it that means you ain't heard from your ma."

- 3 -

1969

Some say the deluge of '69 did good. Some say different. The crops along the bottomlands, not yet ready for picking, were lost for another season. Most of Miss Bertha's ditches were breached. But like it always does, the Tallahatchie laid down a whole new bounty of alluvium and the Sumpters almost doubled their cotton yield the following year. That was the balance of nature that had always tempered life in these parts. The rich got richer and the poor got whatever was left.

Many of the characters in this story died before their time, but their ghosts still haunt the Flats. The lies we attached to their stories got carried downstream like silt and got laid down someplace else. But as long as that river keeps flowing, the truth will always find its way to the surface.

I guess I should leave it to my daughter to write what's left of this story, sometime when I'm dead and buried maybe. Eleven years old and she's already set her heart on becoming a journalist. I blame Truman. He's seen a lot more of life than me, the good and the bad. And despite all the bad, the wounds of the past are healing. Scarring over, you might say.

Truman eventually got a publishing deal in New York for a book of photographs he'd taken during the early days of the Civil Rights movement. Some of them still turn my stomach, but he always says the camera don't lie. And now he's taking pictures on a regular basis for a local Mississippi newspaper, we decided we'd set up home and see how things work out. Truman found us a small cabin on Choctaw Ridge close enough to Greenwood for us to visit Miss Bertha and Lucille whenever we like.

We'd taken a trip downriver that first summer after Truman returned home - the three of us masquerading as a real family. Miss Hardy had a New Orleans address. A place where blind people were offered as normal a life as possible. "It's called the Lighthouse. On State Street in Lafayette. That's all they told me when they wrote on behalf of your ma asking to be put in touch with you."

We were met in the craft room by a young woman, spindly as a hay rake, helping a group of people assemble a selection of reed baskets. Truman had been told his ma was the same age as Miss Bertha, but Angel looked just like a child. Yet there was no mistaking who she was. Her hair shone like silver and she and Truman shared the same jawline.

One of the women at reception told us how Angel had been found wandering the city's streets some years earlier, in a confused state of mind following a fire. "Went by the name of Lucille Trenton and claimed she was no more than fifteen years old. Kept asking us to help find her ma."

Whatever the reason for Angel's current situation, I swear I caught a spark of hope behind her vacant eyes as soon as Truman introduced himself. By then it was clear he'd made up his mind. He told me later how it was less hurtful to tell one big lie than keep living inside a heap of smaller deceptions.

"This here's Donna Mae, and our little girl Katie Jo. Here. Give your grand-daughter a hug if you want to."

There's been many times since that day when I have to pinch myself. Our life is so blessed I'm scared to look too close. Truman and I respect and cherish each other, and we don't care what other folk say about us anymore. The truth is, I've received more tenderness from Truman than I ever thought possible. And as Miss Bertha said, there are times when a lie is the only way to deal with the truth.

Miss Bertha said a lot of things that put our lives in perspective. "You ain't doing no one any harm, Donna Mae, and it's clear Katie Jo adores her new pa. So shame on those who would deny you this one blessing. The world will keep on spinning long after we're dead and buried so I don't see no sense in trying to make it stop or turn it around the other way."

So be it.

This is how it ended.

AUTHOR'S NOTE

Writing can be a solitary activity at the best of times, so extra special thanks to Karen, Lewis, Eryn and Matt and Adam and Phim for allowing me more than my fair share of family distractions to make the exercise more bearable. Also huge thanks to Corky and Maggie for some much-needed feline and canine therapy.

Huge thanks are also due to Nigel Sibbett for another careful proof reading, and to fellow-writer Christy Guenther Okie for casting an American eye over the final draft. Many of the enhancements are down to them. Any retained flaws are entirely my own fault.

Finally thanks to you for reading.

If you enjoyed TALLAHATCHIE LIES please consider leaving a short review on Amazon. It would be greatly appreciated.

Feel free to contact me at

cyanbrodie@gmail.com

Other books by the same author:

THE LOCHINVER TRILOGY
(Tartan Noir for a New Generation)

1   DARK SKY

When schoolgirl Caddy Neilson is found strangled in a remote Scottish village, the police are quick to establish both murderer and motive.

But those closest to Caddy suspect they've got it wrong.

Best friend Amy and part-time student/small-time drugs dealer, Matt, uncover evidence linking the young girl to a major crime.

But the search for the truth not only jeopardises their growing relationship. It also places their lives in peril.

2   WHITE SHORE

When seventeen-year-old Amy Metcalf's best friend is murdered Amy's world changes overnight. The tiny fishing village of Lochinver is no longer the safe haven of their childhood.

While her on-off boyfriend, Matt Neilson, is in prison Amy is forced to rebuild her life. Matt has adapted well to his new surroundings, falling in with a bad crowd. Amy finds herself increasingly isolated.

When a face from their past declares war, Amy is forced to accept an offer of support from an unlikely source. But when this new relationship develops into something more than friendship, events escalate into an uncontrollable explosion of misplaced jealousy and revenge.

3   BLACK ICE

Eighteen-year-old Amy Metcalf has made a new start. Life in Aberdeen is good. But when a Polish girl is found dead in one of the city's hotels, secrets from Amy's past return to haunt her.

The one-man war waged in WHITE SHORE has intensified as three characters return to Lochinver from overseas. Each of them has an agenda. Each is set on revenge.

Amy and her troubled ex-boyfriend, Matt Neilson, are caught up in the maelstrom - their lives and their turbulent relationship once more put at risk. But this time they discover friends can often come disguised as enemies. And giving up on friendship is never an option.

DREAMGIRL

16-year-old diabetic, Ruby MacGregor, is probably the most conscientious, considerate and level-headed teenager in Edinburgh. Not the kind of girl you would expect to experiment with illegal substances, start an on-line relationship with a guy 8 years her senior and steal her best friend's boyfriend.

Ruby's cyber-friend is certainly a shady character; not only does he convince her to pose for him on her webcam, there's the distinct possibility he might also be a serial killer who targets teenaged girls.

How does Ruby know this? Because of the dreams she keeps experiencing: nightmares that so far have featured two young girls, Levi and Cody, who both appear to have been abducted then murdered.

Who are they? Where are they from? And more to the point, when her own sister's life is in peril, how much will Ruby risk to save her?

DreamGirl was joint winner of the Red Telephone Young Adult novel 2014.

TOAD IN THE HOLE AND TOLEY BAGS

When 13-year-old Katie MacCallum's best friend, Nadia, goes missing everyone assumes she's run away from home.

Only Katie and her light-fingered brother seem interested in investigating Nadia's disappearance.

Katie is convinced her friend has been abducted by aliens. But the school photographer is also behaving very weirdly.

Katie discovers a vital piece of evidence proving his involvement, but by then it could be too late.

All available in paperback and on Kindle

and writing as Phil Jones:

80 POEMS (poetry collection)

SUMMERTIME BLUES (short stories)

20 PIECES (short stories)

THE OUTLANDER (for younger readers)

All available on Kindle and in paperback.

and

80 HILLS IN NORTH-WESTERN SNOWDONIA

(published by Gwasg Garreg Gwalch)

Available only in paperback (including free CD with more than 1400 photographs).

Printed in Poland
by Amazon Fulfillment
Poland Sp. z o.o., Wrocław